IN CASE WE DIE

IN CASE

DANNY

FANTAGRAPHICS BOOKS

WE DIE

BLAND

SEATTLE, WASHINGTON

FANTAGRAPHICS BOOKS, INC.
Seattle, Washington, USA

Editor and Associate Publisher: Eric Reynolds
Book Design: Emory Liu
Interior Photographs: Lance Mercer
Production: Paul Baresh
Copy Editor: Janice Lee
Carrie Finch's handwriting: Jen Vaughn
Additional proofreading: Tom Graham and Jack McKean
Consulting Editors: Rachel Flotard & Diane Porter
Publishers: Gary Groth & Kim Thompson

In Case We Die is also available as an audiobook on Local
638 Records featuring Steve Earle, Dave Alvin, Duff
McKagan, John Doe, Damien Echols, Marc Maron,
Mark Lanegan, Greg Dulli, Lew Temple, Dana Gould,
Blag Dalhia, Rob Delaney, Jacob Pitts, Lou Beach, Donal
Logue, John Sinclair, Aimee Mann and many more.

ISBN 978-1-60699-675-1
First hardcover printing: July, 2013

www.fantagraphics.com
local638records.com
dannybland.com

CONTENTS

**I WROTE THIS BOOK
FOR AMY FARRIS.**

ours is a story
written on hotel room walls
with fifty cent words

1. SLIP INSIDE THIS HOUSE

Had you not spent five nights a week in there like I did, upon entering the Champ Arcade, your senses might have been overwhelmed by the prurient cacophony of it all. Tits and asses; cocks and snatches; eyes come-hither, eyes rolled back. Blinking lights everywhere — beckoning you to phallic monstrosities too gruesome to imagine handling, much less inserting; directing you to unguents and salves, lotions and greases; assaulting your higher mind to abandon ship, to leave and trust your dirty little lizard brain to call the shots.

You might have tried to subdue this onslaught by limiting your gaze to the glass enclosures immediately to your left. Here, coach whips, blindfolds and handcuffs — articles of confusion when discovered in a well-hidden shoebox in your mother's closet — were nostalgic, romantic even. But this was no place for sweetness. A closer inspection would reveal so many other trinkets and tchotchkes that you would be overwhelmed all over again. Single-serve packets of flavored lube, canisters of amyl nitrite, Spanish fly, French ticklers, cock rings, enema kits, latex gloves, medical face masks, ball gags, dental dams, paddles, rectal thermometers, forceps, nose clamps, an assortment of stainless steel speculums and a box of X-Acto blades. Utensils for the truly depraved.

You might have sought shelter in the uniform predictability of more than 10,000 VHS tapes on racks, their covers of deep reds and soft focus promising blonde Scandinavian maidens, erotic courtesans of the Orient, black chicks.

Maybe you were like me. Maybe you'd never forgotten your hairier and greasier first loves — *The Devil in Miss Jones, Talk Dirty to Me, Taboo II* — and found some perverse feeling of home just looking at these boxes. You might browse the new releases purely for shits and giggles — no, scratch that. Careful what you wish for here. Best to say you might browse the new releases *on a whim.* You might even find yourself engaged by these excessively fit stars and starlets with lives built around salons and tanning beds, pills and enemas. You might appreciate the perfectly retouched droplets glistening on perfectly retouched skin, a touch of marketing class belying the jabbing and squirting waiting within.

But then maybe you weren't like me. Maybe you were a dilettante stopping by only because you drew the short straw and were assigned to fetch the entertainment for your co-worker's bachelor party. You would probably gravitate to the light-hearted fare of the novelty section, selecting a copy of *Edward Penishands* or *All That Jizz* or the midget porn classic, *Naughty Napoleon.* This would show your workmates that you didn't take your smut too seriously, that this was foreign terrain for you.

Hopefully, you weren't interested in our bargain bin, that haphazard graveyard for skin flicks at their worst. Most of these videos had been brought back by UPS after attempted returns to producers no longer in business. In the fly-by-night world of adult film, today's queen could be tomorrow's victim of a business manager with a coke habit and access to the production company's bank account. While we'd rather not have had these taking up valuable floor space, a sidewalk sale on the tourist-laden corner of 1st and Pike would have been frowned upon. Dropping off volumes 1–50 of the *Lick My Butthole* series at the Salvation Army was likewise out of the question. Marking down merchandise to move and throwing it into a crudely constructed bin wasn't necessarily fantastically inventive, but it was our best option.

Many among us, after completing our first visit, have craved the confessional, a hot rape shower, 15 minutes of keening, or some combination of all three. Yet, if you, like me, were somehow to find yourself employed there — slogging the midnight to eight shift, no less — you'd have gradually found the place and the work challenging, complete with moments to up-sell when feeling ambitious. "Do you want butt-plugs with that?" "This version costs a little more, but if you're serious about watching Filipino women eat food out of each other..." We ran our own line of the thirty-one fucking flavors of Baskin-Robbins. The implements of semi-torture were our Pralines 'n Cream; the latest issue of *Blowjob Bonanza* our Daiquiri Ice. We would serve up either without rolling our eyes because we knew full well that the cock's heart wants what the cock's heart wants. If a sick freak felt the urge to consult with me about what they wanted to do with another consenting sick freak, it only made the evening go faster. We might even find ourselves downright sick-freak-helpful.

"You're gonna want to pick up some of these absorbent pads to put under your sheets if you're gonna buy that, mister," we might suggest.

Of course, to be fair, there were also the other times.

"Do I look like the kind of fuckwit who scours *Consumer Reports* researching products you'd enjoy sticking up your ass?" This to a perfectly polite couple who asked for an opinion regarding my preference on the two most popular models of butt plug. It all depended on the mood, and the mood depended on a simple equation: a high Charlie equaled a happy Charlie.

I might meander in a skoche drunk at a quarter to midnight. Job security? Not an issue, as the responsibilities of the position were somewhere near "slight." Bob and Randy, the swing shift guys, would be packing up their belongings and counting out the register and would tend to overlook any whiskey on my breath. Many a previous employee had left them hanging with a last-minute sick call or a plain old no-show. They considered me, if not a model employee, someone they could at least count on to be corporeally present.

"You know, Charlie, your one-year anniversary is coming up," Randy might inform me. Both Randy and Bob were proud of their 20-plus years of shop employment, Randy a little more so.

"Yeah, they're gonna buy you a fucking gold watch," Bob would bleat, cigar to one side of a squalid mouth.

In truth I was hired as temporary Christmas help a couple of months shy of a year past today. You might be questioning the increase in porno store traffic around the holidays, as I was at the time, but let me assure you, it is extraordinary. Also remarkable were the customers' assumptions.

"Sorry sir, you're going to have to wrap that vibrator yourself when you get home," you might have said to the nervous junior bank teller. You might have informed the pomaded cook from the corner breakfast place about the gift-wrapping booth at Macy's that the Girl Scouts were running for charity this year.

Randy and Bob took me under their broad and experienced wings and showed me the ropes of the adult retail industry. Randy, a 60-something confirmed bachelor with a precisely trimmed mustache and high, womanish voice, was very hands-on. He very much enjoyed quizzing the clientele about their likes and dislikes, making recommendations in his god-awfully cloying and spooky way. Bob, on the other hand, was the perfect bulldog-human hybrid. With a constantly unlit cigar stuck between fleshy gills, and what I assumed were two bags of bloodshot behind permanently affixed Ray-Bans, Bob's approach to the mercantile was more subdued. His speech consisted of a variety of mutt grunts. He was there to sell "stag films," not make friends. The one time I did hear him laugh aloud was the night I arrived for my shift with a freshly blackened eye and several bleeding claw marks on my face after being ferociously assaulted by a Jagermeister-fueled ex. He bent at the waist, hands on his knees, howling till he up-coughed half a lung.

"Are you dating a fuckin' werewolf, Hyatt?" he cried between hacks.

We would supervise the entire operation from a perch behind the retail counter, a good foot higher than the clientele, as they perused rows and rows of magazines, blow-up dolls and Mephistophelian toys. It was here where we could truly survey our domain. If you, like me, were somehow preternaturally able to ignore the TV monitors with the giant genitalia smashing into each other and the cigarette smog, the retail section was as well-lit and organized as any other corner shop. Dreggy content aside, the place was aseptic and impeccably managed. But if you were in the market for debasement or aberration or debauchery, then the front of the store was a mere appetizer, a simple finger food, a quick way to wet your whistle. It was the back of the house where things got enchanting. The Champ Arcade in the very back was more of a scabrous wonderland than a dirty bookstore. A heavy red velvet curtain separated the pros from the amateurs, the wheat from the chaff, the men from the boys.

If you were to purchase two dollars' worth of tokens, like I on occasion did, and walk through that red curtain, past the sign that read "Private Dances/Video Booths," you would have been abused by the smell of Lysol as you paused to allow your eyes to adjust to the near darkness. Then, with music louder than need be, you might have made your way past the first row of booths. The moans and lascivious screams of dozens of videos playing simultaneously could have given you the impression that you had just buckled in for a ride through a carnival's haunted house. You might not have been scared, exactly, but a nausea of unease would not be far off. What might jump out from the murk to try and forcibly mate with you would be a thought hard to dismiss.

You might then have thankfully noticed Wayne Newton — a 6½-foot-tall redheaded monster whose mother had an unnatural love of the Vegas entertainer — unleashing his flashlight for his hourly walk-through. His wasn't the worst job in the joint. The twelve inches between the floor and the bottom of each video booth's door offered plenty of room to detect any attempts at partnering up inside or any attempted defilement of the working

5

ladies. One person per booth was pretty much the only rule strictly enforced here. Anything else was Masturbator's Choice.

A dozen red booths lined the walls on either side as you would make your way through the maze, unsure of just what your cock's heart was desiring. One booth might contain a single video monitor with 20 channels of filth to whack to. Another might open directly onto the main stage where one token opened a window for 30 seconds of live nude girl. Along one wall were the fish tanks: 4 x 4 foot glass enclosures containing dancers waiting their turn to hit the main stage. Each tank contained a fetish, a taste, from Catholic schoolgirl to leather dominatrix to girl-next-door-freshly-home-from-drill-team — all forms of fantasy on the fluffer buffet, available back of house.

Go in, drop a token. A curtain is pulled and negotiations begin. Up close and personal, dirty talk and adult toys are all available, as long as you have a generous amount of folding cash, the dexterity to slip that cash through the slot and the capacity to suspend your disbelief that the glass wall impedes anything from bobbing on your fractured libido. Crumpled tissues decorate the floor as if the jackoff Hansel had left a trail of cum rags to find his way out after releasing on the Plexiglas of his cubicle sex doll Gretel.

My shift began at midnight, but it was after two in the morning when the place would become a whirlwind of activity, with dancers leaving after a hard night of shaking it on the main stage or giving it up in private booths for the reprobate. Some might wait for their drug dealer or soon to be next big thing, rock-star boyfriend, others might load into their regular cab driver's back seat or, on some nights, into an awaiting police cruiser.

"Good night, Lexi."

"G'night, Angel."

The girls would tease me on the way out, mock-begging me to come home with them, knowing damn well I was stuck in paradise until morning.

"One of these days, ladies, I'm gonna disappoint you sexually like no one quite has before."

You might have sized them up as they paraded by, the ghostly spawn of missing fathers and wayward moms. Junkie, mentally disturbed, cutter, molested as a child, molested, molested.

A is for Angel, touched as a child
B is for Betty, burned, scarred and defiled
C is for Cassandra, angry with Dad
D is for Dixie, born just plain bad
E is for Eva whose self-worth is low
F is for Felicity who does too much blow
G is for Ginger, kids taken away
H is for Honey, secretly gay
I is for Izzy, she fucks married men
J is for Jasmine who nips at sloe gin
K is for Kat, the Queen of them all
L is for Lexi who turns tricks at the mall
M is for Madison who never does smile
N is for Nadine, locked away for a while
O is for Olivia who cuts herself deep
P is for Precious who married a creep
Q is for Quinn who fucked her babysitter
R is for Roxy whose dad used to hit her
S is for Sasha with nothing to lose
T is for Trixie who can't handle booze
U is for Ursula, addicted to meth
V is for Violet, her mom beat to death
W is for Willa who wasted her life
X is for Xenia who carries a knife
Y is for Yolanda who's just not that bright
Z is for Zoe who won't make it home tonight.

2. DON'T SLANDER ME

It wasn't the pounding headache or the all-too-familiar taste of blood in my mouth that woke me that morning, but the stink of cat piss. They all have cats. Cats and bad tattoos and mops of dyed black hair that reek of cigarettes and watermelon Bubblicious. They all have ripped fishnets and dark red lips and daddy issues. What starts out as a seemingly innocent walk home from the bar turns into a seemingly innocent kiss in her foyer and quickly degenerates into a whirling dervish of teeth and hips and torn shirts and pulled hair.

But you couldn't just let a young lady wander the mean streets of Capitol Hill unescorted, now could you?

I surveyed my front teeth with the tip of my tongue to assess the damage. I got lucky this time. I tried to calculate the odds of sunlight before opening my eyes, but it was useless. As I lay in the darkness a couple of questions came to mind: Where the fuck was I? How the fuck did I get here? The wretched idea of raising my head at that moment was overruled by the depth of my curiosity. I was on a mattress on the floor with my clothes and most of hers lying next to me. A single strand of blue Christmas lights lined the ceiling and several defaced prayer candles were strategically placed around the bed. On her milk-crate nightstand was a half-empty bottle of Bushmills whiskey, a spoon, two syringes, my wallet and a Radio Shack alarm clock that read 5:30. Two more questions came to mind: a.m.? p.m.?

The spoon and syringes told me nothing further — heroin was my steadfast accomplice now — but the bottle told me this was Tuesday, Wednesday at the latest. My boss, you see, is ex-military. His men get paid every Monday. That way, be it Vietnam or the dirty bookstore, his grunts were always so broke by the weekend we could never put together enough cash to buy a plane ticket back to Indiana or Cleveland or wherever the fuck we came from. Furthermore, it curtailed many a barroom brawl and all but quashed impulsive AWOL episodes. I, Charlie Hyatt, was his midnight-to-eight man, a soldier on the front lines of filth.

While I knew well enough that there is no such thing as leftover drugs, I did a quiet recon of the area while my hostess lay face down in her pillow. I rifled through her purse and pocketed a wad of dollar bills. Experience told me she was either a cocktail waitress or a dancer, one or the other or both. Under black hair, over pale skin and just above the sheet, I could make out a tattoo of an inverted cross between her shoulder blades. This may have revealed Satanic alliances, it may have explained the defaced prayer-candle configuration, it may have indicated she was the type of woman who could get so fucked up she'd get tattooed upside down. No matter, this was my kind of girl.

I lifted the arm that had been draped over me all night; it fell limp to the mattress. Her wrist was wrapped in a bandage and my inquisitive nature could not resist the temptation. I carefully peeled back the medical tape; the bloody gauze stuck to her skin but still she lay undisturbed. One last quick tear exposed the words "HELP ME" carved deeply into her flesh. It might as well have just said "YOUR TYPE." I was aroused. Wistfully, now, I do recall the days when irony could give me an erection. I leaned in closer to examine the wound. I wanted to taste it but stopped myself. Still, I saw no reason why a little medicinal hangover sex would be out of order.

"Hey," I whispered.

I nudged her hard. Nothing.

"Honey?"

I saw a stack of mail on the small kitchen table, so I decided to try and put a name to this shapely mess inert on the mattress before me. There were a half-dozen bills, a wedding invitation and a Victoria's Secret catalog all addressed to my maladjusted bachelorette #1.

Returning to her side I said sternly, "Nicole!"

Then, softly and still to no avail, "Nicky?"

I slipped on my jeans and negotiated my way through the bedlam, a strange landscape of empty bottles and full ashtrays, and located the bathroom. I was startled when I switched on the bare bulb that hung above the grimy, littered sink. The fluorescent glare, bright white walls and the explosion of girly smells sucker-punched the throb in my skull. Looking into the mirror, I pushed back greasy dark hair and focused on the mess I had become. Now, I couldn't be called classically good-looking — unless Alice Cooper was your idea of a classic — but I could muster a killer smile when the situation called for it, and if you were in the market for a creepy someone to bring home to scare the shit out of your parents, I was your man. This morning I had none of that charm, more closely resembling the aftermath of a car accident.

I fingered my nostrils, which were thickly encrusted with dried blood, as were the corners of my mouth, my chin, neck and collarbone. My heartbeat quickened. I could see the prone reflection of Nicole in the mirror. She hadn't moved. I listened for her to stir, snore, anything.

I filled the sink with warm water and dunked my head in, holding my breath for as long as possible. Already formulating an escape plan, I stood up dripping wet and took the longest piss of my life. Oh, that was interesting:

my pubic hair was matted with dried blood as well. I frantically searched my torso and scalp for lacerations or cuts. Nothing. I squeezed the bridge of my nose to check for trauma. Nada. An idea I'd later consider desperate took hold. I looked up at the mirror and slowly opened the palms of my hands. Goddammit. No stigmata. Murderer it was, then.

Mosquitoes flitted around my empty stomach and my feet were frozen on the cold linoleum floor. Errant drops of pee flecked my toes as I stood there hoping for a generous meteor to fall from the sky and end this miserable course once and for all. I couldn't remember anything about last night or this woman — not her name nor her occupation, where she lived or what kinds of bands she hated (which was, of course, always so much more important than which ones she liked). I briefly wondered how many other men right this second were standing half-naked in front of a mirror considering the survival of their evening's companion. I wondered if they, like me, put their hands behind their backs and crossed them at the wrists to see what they would look like being escorted to a squad car in handcuffs.

Desperately, I scanned the bathroom for that small window through which the good guy always escapes. No dice. My mind fast-forwarded through the arrest, the headlines, her bereaved parents on a local TV news show and straight to the dank 6 x 8 foot cell in which I would spend the rest of my days, praying for a visitor with a nail file baked into a cake to set me free.

Perhaps they'd give me a corny nickname like "The Capitol Hill Cannibal," and I would appear next to "The Campus Killer," Ted Bundy, and Richard Ramirez, "The Night Stalker," in criminology textbooks. Maybe the chief of police would seize the opportunity to blame a few unsolved murders on me. Maybe I would request sushi and a couple of Dick's Deluxe burgers for my last meal, guaranteeing a nightmare situation for whoever had to clean up the gurney they would strap me to.

I paced the five feet from the tub to the opposing wall and realized that being in a stranger's bathroom meant being near a stranger's medicine cabinet. Goddammit. On the one hand, her being dead made this a horrible time to rummage for prescription meds. On the other hand, her being dead made her not one to stand on ceremony. I licked my lips in anticipation. Cracking open a stranger's medicine cabinet had been a thrill I hadn't passed up since I was a youngster.

As a teenager in Phoenix, Arizona, I had organized a troop of Mexican ne'er-do-well kids from the block to break into neighborhood homes during summer break. Miguel was 12 years old; as the elder of the crew, he was the Artful Dodger to my Fagin. He followed my directions precisely: Do not destroy the place, do not disturb the "valuables," and get in and out quickly. I wasn't interested in their TVs and jewelry; it was their pharmaceuticals I coveted. Miguel would return to my place alone and empty his pockets, and with my handy 1978 Physician's Desk Reference I would sort out the good pills from the bad ones, pay him a fraction of what they were worth and send him on his merry way. In retrospect it seemed like a recipe for disaster, but after a couple of summers Miguel and company just stopped coming around. I imagine that they found someone who paid better or began to partake in their ill-gotten gains themselves.

The shelves were in disarray, a massive collection of her half-empty lipstick tubes, powders and potions. I found an empty prescription bottle. I squinted at the label: Percodan. Why would she keep an empty prescription bottle? And why was this giving me such a feeling of déjà vu? Had I already slept with this girl before? Had she already been robbed before I got there? I stuck my thumb in the coin pocket of my jeans. That explained it. Five yellow pills told me I had done my due diligence the night before. I popped the pills in my mouth and swallowed them with a handful of water from the sink.

Then, from the corner of my eye, I saw my salvation. A reprieve as if called in by the governor himself: a fresh, bloody tampon next to a couple of used, bloody condoms in the trashcan.

I wiped the sweat off my forehead with the pink, germ-infested towel hanging from the shower curtain rod and used it to muffle my mirthless laughter.

Clicking off the light, I tiptoed out of the bathroom and dressed quietly, never taking my eyes off my new young lady friend. The wailing siren of an ambulance startled me as it roared past the apartment building. I leaned down to gather my wallet and rigs from the impromptu nightstand, cleaned the burn marks from the spoon and made a clumsy attempt to wipe the fingerprints from the whiskey bottle with my t-shirt. I picked up a matchbook that had my name and phone number written on it and stuck it in my pocket.

Standing up to leave, I heard a mysterious gurgling sound from the far corner of the room behind me. The gurgle segued into tiny laughter. I moved slowly toward the sound and lit a match to get a better look.

First I saw the mobile with circus animals and clowns, then the crib below. I hovered in a place where the scent of baby oil overpowered the stale cigarette smoke from the rest of the room. The child lay on its back, opening and closing its tiny hands as if they were new discoveries. I couldn't tell you how old the kid was, for I had never even held a baby in my arms. I assumed it was a boy from the blue blanket and just stared at this sinless, otherworldly being.

For a minute I couldn't even imagine how he got there. I wanted to lean in closer, but I was sure I would appear a monstrous gargoyle to the infant, and a screaming baby was right at the top of my list of the last things in the world I needed right then. I remained in the shadows. Was I staring at history doomed to repeat itself, or just an unfortunate client of the worst babysitter in the world? I wasn't about to stick around and find out.

3. YOU AREN'T YOUR ONLY SIN

I stepped out the front door of her building onto the corner of Denny and Summit, the raindrops punching holes in my head. I lit a cigarette, yawned deeply and raised a middle finger to the sky, the way I started every waking morning.

My feet began to move, against my wishes. For the last two mornings I had made the trek to the King County Detox knowing damn well I would never get in. In order to be accepted to the facility you need to arrive as early in the morning as possible, first-come, first-served. Since most of the clients are homeless alcoholics and drug addicts, they set up camp on the front steps the night before, leaving us employed junkies and drunks with busy social schedules little or no chance to make the cut. Imagine my heartbreak.

There were — believe it or not — a good-sized throng of people interested in my well-being. Oh, not my family, they were thousands of miles away and oblivious to everything. And no, not my co-workers, they were just glad I showed up so they didn't have to deal with the cavalcade of scum that came though the shop while they were comfortably tucked away in their beds. No, it was my friends, my misguided and often fucked-up themselves friends. They worried about me. They loved me. I guess there's no accounting for taste.

My current situation could have been worse I suppose. I could easily have regained consciousness in Kent or Bellevue or some other hellish suburb that would require a humiliating trek back on public transportation, but instead I was afforded a leisurely escape on foot, having had the luck, dumb or otherwise, to have come back to life in my own neighborhood. In a few minutes I would be sitting in the waiting room of the detox center. After a couple of hours they would read off the names of the newly accepted patients, I would feign disappointment and be on my merry way.

We were in the middle of a month-long run of overcast days, the kind of days that made everyone else shudder but made me feel alive. This is the time of the year I walked out of the shop after an eight-hour shift of selling raunchy periodicals and masturbation accessories not to the sunny beginnings of a brand new day, but to a city still cloaked in darkness. The sun, if it decided to come out at all, was barely peeking over the horizon by the time I crawled into bed, and by the time my alarm went off at 4:30 in the afternoon it was all but gone. It was beautiful. I preferred the gloom. I suppose I could blame my lifelong obsession with horror movies or my fair skin or the fact that my pupils were pinned most of the time, but the truth is I'm from Arizona and I don't care if I ever see the sun again.

There's something about this weather that compels men to use Drop D tuning on their guitars, the ladies to wear overalls and the whole damn city to throw themselves off the tallest landmarks they can find. Apparently the same clouds that I adored for shielding me from god's prying eyes and the drizzle that rinsed my filth away had the opposite effect on other folks. The city personally greeted me with two hours of gridlocked traffic the day I arrived in my beat-up Chevy van with nothing but two trash bags full of clothes as some poor soul considered To Be or Not To Be from high atop the Aurora Bridge. Nowadays, the corporate home of a major software company is located underneath this same bridge, and while most jumpers hit the water, about a half dozen times a year the employees arrive in the morning to witness a truly gruesome display of human desperation in their parking lot.

As I walked my mind raced. I tried to piece together the night before. Pussy Galore played at the Vogue and the place was packed. I remembered avoiding the hateful gaze of an old girlfriend. I remembered standing next to my friend Chris Pugh as the band played. He was strategically standing where he could see the stage and peer into the ladies' room; he was a first-rate deviant. I remembered being clever and charming as I sweet-talked the girl I woke up with that morning. I remembered her cleavage and her lips as she spoke to me, but I would have had a hard time picking her out of a police line-up. I remembered stumbling into a convenience store with her to purchase condoms. With her draped over my shoulder, we stood in front of the tiny section of toiletries.

"Where's the goddamned rubbers!?" she called to the annoyed cashier.

In his thick East Indian accent he pointed to the shelf, "Can't you see? Straight in front of you."

Reaching for the box she fired back, "If I could see straight do ya think I'd be fuckin' him?"

My very cells protested as I neared my destination. They reminded me that in a couple of hours we'd be sick as fuckin' dogs. They called me weak and worthless. Let's go, man. We've got 30 or 40 bucks from that chick; wouldn't we rather go home and get loaded? We deserve it. They told me to face facts: I was a liar and fraud. Who did we think we were fooling? We weren't the slightest bit interested in getting clean. We were just tired of the abscesses on our arms and the judgmental looks from old ladies and our negative bank balance. We just didn't want to hear another exhausted sigh from our landlord because he had had it up to here with our erratic behavior. We just wanted our friends to stop accusing us of stealing their records, which of course we had done but would never admit to. We just wanted our girlfriend to stop threatening to move out even though she's no fuckin' angel herself. We just didn't like the monster we were becoming. We just wanted to get high.

I grabbed a place in line and exchanged good-morning nods with the new line-up of degenerate hopefuls. I squatted down and leaned against the brick wall to blend in with my fellow dirt, broken glass and grimy brethren.

I was about a dozen people deep in a line of thirty-five or so. The building was painted that awful beige color that all publicly financed buildings that don't need to be inviting or picturesque are painted. I imagined there was a government warehouse with cans of it stacked to the ceiling just waiting for the next time the DMV or some low-income childcare facility needed another coat. I watched a couple of crows peck away at the smashed corpse of an unlucky squirrel that didn't quite make it across the street. I thought about how this sight should've made me ill but only reminded me of the frozen macaroni and cheese I had waiting for me at home.

As we were corralled into the waiting room, we were each handed a clipboard with a tiny, eraserless pencil attached by string.

"Have a seat and fill out the questionnaire," the attractive black woman with the blue lab coat instructed us.

I had spent the last couple of mornings ogling her over the pages of the same 3-year-old *People* magazine I stashed under what I considered to be *my* seat, the one in the farthest corner from the desk. She recognized me and we exchanged pleasant good mornings.

As culturally diverse as my neighborhood was, you couldn't exactly call it ethnically so. Unless, of course, you were sitting in the waiting room of the King County Detox Center; only here was I a minority. As a group we were Native American, African American and Latino with a sprinkling of Whitey. We were all ages and both sexes but mostly male, with several of questionable orientation. We had two things in common: We were poor and we were fucked up.

Patient name: *CHARLES M. HYATT*

Date: *OCT. 21, 1990*

Age: *29*

Address: *906 E. JOHN ST., APT. 311, SEATTLE*

Occupation: *BOOKSTORE MANAGER*

Marital status: *SINGLE*

Ethnicity: *WHITE*

Substance: *HEROIN*

Level of recent use: *HEAVY*

Treatment history: *NONE*

Main motivating force at time of admit: *NONE*

I filled out the rest just as I had in the days before, phone number, Social Security, then signed at the bottom underneath the ominous statement, "The below signed agrees to stay under the care of the King County Detox Center for a minimum of 72 hours."

As I approached the young lady's desk to drop off my paperwork I noticed a tattooed name peeking out from under her sleeve. There was something naughty and subversive that I could work with. All I needed to do now was strike up a conversation.

"So, why do you work here?" I asked.

"Oh, I dunno," her mind calculating, "about 7 months or so."

"No, no...*why* do you work here?"

"I suppose I started working in the field because I lost my sister to this disease." I paused for a moment to give her a chance to clarify. I must've looked puzzled because she went on to explain.

"You know, alcoholism."

"Oh, I'm sorry...I'm here for drugs."

"I see that," she said, eyeballing my clipboard.

"But the truth is I was just raised wrong," I said, trying to be cute.

"You better have a seat, Sugar, or the other patients will think I'm playing favorites."

4. TWO HEADED DOG
(RED TEMPLE PRAYER)

I managed to exit the car fairly smoothly, but two poorly chosen steps later I was lying face down in a bush. The girls laughed and quickly rescued me, each pulling on an arm until I was on my feet and as composed as could be expected. I was the kind of entertaining train wreck that girls loved to take care of, a way to bring the party home.

Because I weighed in at a scant 150 pounds, they had no trouble getting me up one flight of stairs, one on each side of me like wild, giggling crutches. All my movements consisted of lunges and falls, but my mind remained sharp and upright. They dropped me onto the couch and went to the kitchen for beer. Drunk and stranded in the suburbs, I somehow sat erect in spite of myself. Marcy set bottles of beer on the coffee table and put on a Hüsker Dü record. Kelly opened the door for other party guests, rolling her eyes as each group entered. I liked her. She hated everybody.

Marcy Triggs was the northwest rep for a major record label. I had a hard time recognizing her enthusiasm for life, the ease with which she smiled and the furor with which she threw her arms around me whenever we met as anything other than a mental disorder. She had a bizarre hab-it — and probably several more I didn't know about — of screaming into the phone whenever I'd identify myself. It had gotten to the point where I would dial her number, then put the phone down until her volume had chosen whatever too-loud level it would be at on that day. She was sweet as pie and never had a bad word for anyone — a complete alien.

Kelly Thompson, on the other hand, was a hellion, feral, with a sharp tongue and a perfect ass. Her search for vitiation was so calculating and businesslike it was on the blade edge of frightening. She was a shark. I nursed a beer while Kelly leaned in close and talked shit about everyone at the party. She was a bloodthirsty riot, and I was eternally grateful to have any small talk asphyxiated by conversation with her.

When she had had enough of the living room, she took my arm and walked me to the spare bedroom, opened the door and put her index finger to her lips, the international sign for "shut the fuck up." I sat on the edge of the bed as she knelt on the floor, spreading out party favors. Her pouch contained cotton balls, rigs, a lighter, spoon and the all-important cellophane wrapper of dope. Everything my coal-black, Vicodin-sized heart could desire.

Some drunk asshole's voice palavered on outside the door as Kelly held the lighter under the spoon, the smell of burnt brown sugar and dope filling the air. She tied off with the belt of a bathrobe that hung from the closet door and fixed herself, paused for a moment and turned her attention to me. Although I was more than capable of hitting myself, she seemed to want to play nurse, so I lay back and waited for the familiar sting. I looked down at my arm as the needle popped through the scar tissue of my favorite vein and watched the syringe fill with blood before she slowly pushed down on the plunger.

The soothing warmth filled my lungs and brain. I felt as if I were sink-ing into the mattress when a hard, deep kiss brought me back to the room. Miss Thompson was straddling me, unbuttoning my shirt. What little light there was in the room was blocked out by her auburn curls and her fierce kisses. I fumbled about, trying to pull her shirt off over her head as she unbuttoned my jeans. She pushed herself off of me and stood at the foot of the bed. Grabbing hold of the bottom of each of my pant legs, she pulled them off in one fell swoop. She leaned forward and took hold of my hard dick, examining it closely.

Half-dressed, she escaped from the room as I lay there crippled by the ghosts of strong spirits and opiates. "I knew this was too good to be true," I thought to myself as I struggled to sit up and cover my ghoulish nudity.

I got one of my socks on before she reappeared, a silhouette in the doorway.

"Where do you think you're goin'?" she asked, putting the palm of her hand on my chest and pushing me back onto the bed. I saw the flash of stainless steel in her other hand. If there had been time I would have prayed, or at least impersonated someone praying. I was amazed that I couldn't scream for help and even more astonished that when she grabbed hold of my cock, I was still erect.

"Shit, I wish I had some smaller scissors," she said.

I had at least two problems with that sentence, both of them deal-breakers. In an instinctive "fuck-or-fight" mode, I hauled back and popped her in the face with my fist.

"What the fuck are you doing?" she snarled.

"What the fuck are *you* doing?" I shrieked, gesturing toward the scissors in her hand.

She looked at the scissors, then at me and back at the scissors before she started to giggle, a single drop of blood running out of her left nostril.

"I'm trimming your pubes, dipshit," she said. "I did it last time, too."

"Next time you decide to come at me aiming a sharp piece of metal at my crotch...don't!" I said, while marveling at how ill-mannered of me it was not to remember her doing that previously. She laughed harder, which prompted a gush of sanguine fluid from the other nostril. She wiped her face on her forearm and abandoned me again for the bathroom. I was stunned, bewildered, aghast, numb. If there is one thing in this world I can't stand, it's a woman-beater. I'm in no position to cast moral aspersions or assess the credibility of any other two-legged creature, but a chicken-shit abuser of the fairer sex is my one permanent line in the sand.

The bathroom door swung open when I knocked to apologize, sobered by the violence. She stood in front of the mirror in a black bra and panties, dabbing her nose and front teeth with Kleenex.

"Listen..." I said sheepishly.

"Babe, I'll be right back after I powder my nose."

I stepped in, closed the door behind me and watched her in the mirror. The room was littered with bottles and cigarette butts from the party. She stood in her bare feet on a floor sticky with beer and broken glass, applying her lipstick with surgical precision.

Watching a girl apply lipstick is one of those fervid freebies that I've relished since boyhood. My mind vaulted back to a hospital where I sat as an 8-year-old, watching a nurse behind glass apply gratifying amounts of bright red lipstick to her heavy, generous mouth. A new feeling had surged through me like electricity, distracting me, if only temporarily, from worrying about my mother, who sat across from me, pale and shaking.

Then to a stale classroom where I later sat, a confused 12-year-old completely giving up on the idea of excelling in the public education system as I watched Rochelle Collins roll on bubblegum lipgloss while cradling a compact in her palm. Then to a rapid-fire succession of puckered lips being decorated in reflective panes of glass, store windows, bus windows, all oblivious to my ardent stare. I lacked the sociopathic bravery required to be a real peeping tom, but stole glimpses whenever I could.

I was catapulted back to the present when Miss Thompson leaned forward and kissed her reflection in the mirror as I leered over her shoulder. I drew a quick breath as she pulled back to admire her work, a perfect reproduction of her mouth in dark red. I could see by her raised eyebrow that my physical reaction was not lost on her.

"Again?" she purred.

"Please," I whispered, placing the palm of my hand between her shoulder blades, guiding her back toward the mirror.

She touched the tip of her tongue to the looking glass before planting a deep, prolonged kiss. This time the result was a smear accented with blood from the reactivated wound for which I was responsible. I moved my hand from her shoulder blades to the back of her head as she went back to the mirror for more, trickling tiny droplets of blood into the sink and knocking a toothbrush and perfume bottle to the floor. My cock sprang back to life as I watched her sanguinary self-make-out session, both her hands on the wall as she grinded into the sink violently with her hips. She licked the gore and lipstick from the mirror, turned to me and lunged her tongue into my mouth, kisses so ungoverned they should have broken both our teeth.

She pushed me against the wall, tearing at the buttons of my jeans. With every move we made, something fell to the ground: a bottle of lotion, a portrait of our host's dog in a Halloween costume, a dish of fancy little soaps, Kelly to her knees. The whole damn room was imploding. I felt the shower-curtain rings snap, one, two, three, as I gripped the curtain for balance. I heard her gasping for air between bouts of viciously swallowing my cock. Spots of blood speckled the tiled floor. There was nothing loving, tender or pretty about this.

I grabbed a fistful of her hair and lifted her to her feet.

"Hit me again" she whispered.

"No fucking way."

We stood there staring at each other, panting.

She stood on her tiptoes and I felt her breath on my neck as she moved in close. "If you don't hit me again, I'll tell everyone that you did," she purred.

How could something so nasty turn out...so nasty?

The nurse called my mother over to her station. My little sister was asleep with her head in my lap. We had never been to the hospital off-base before. They spoke in hushed tones because of the strange notion that kids are naturally oblivious to their surroundings, but I overheard most of the conversation.

The nurse questioned her suspiciously. "I'm required by law to ask you this, Mrs. Hyatt. Who did this to you?"

"It was an accident, ma'am, I told you, I fell down the stairs," she replied.

"You know where I'm goin' with this, don't you?"

"Yes ma'am, my husband is on active duty overseas right now, I'm just a klutz."

I didn't want to get in trouble, but Dad was home and we didn't have any stairs.

I realized from the half-smile above Kelly's bloodstained chin that she was not bluffing.

"One," she said.

"Kelly, I'm not..."

"Two."

Jesus Fucking Christ!

"Three. MARCY!"

I put my hand around her throat and slammed her against the wall before she could say another word. Silently I mouthed the words "Shut the holy mother-of-fuck up," as I looked her in the eye. Her body shook with an orgasm as she grasped for breath.

"You okay, Honey?" Marcy inquired from the other side of the door.

I loosened my grip for a moment.

"I'm good, Sugar, just playin' around," she responded.

"Turn around and put your hands on the wall," I ordered. "Don't fucking move." I let go of her neck, put my hands on her hips and slid her panties to the ground.

I stood back. She arched her back and parted her legs, her panties still tangled around one ankle. With shaking hands I fished in my back pocket for my wallet. I pulled out a condom and fumbled with the wrapper.

"Fuck you, just fuck me!" she barked.

Your wish is my command.

5. I WALKED WITH A ZOMBIE

I sat on my bed and counted the other beds in the room: there were six. I counted the cigarettes left in my pack: twelve. My length of stay would be seven days, and it would be three days till I could use the phone. I had been told there would be no math.

My mattress was covered in plastic and my pillow was crunchy; just lying down created a soundscape of annoyance. Hanging on the walls were framed inspirational posters: "One Day At A Time," and "You Get Out Of It What You Put Into It," with supposedly breathtaking photos of the Grand Canyon and waves breaking over a reef. I sighed heavily and put on my institutional slippers. They had taken my boots and my wallet, making escape impossible.

Upon leaving the waiting room, we were divided by gender then taken into a large room and searched. We were handed more clipboards with more tiny, eraserless pencils to answer the same questions over and over again. We were given hospital gowns, slippers and a garbage bag to put our clothes in for storage until graduation.

I heard my name blast over the P.A. system, ordering me to visit the nurse's office. At once I was happy to be alive again. The thought of a sexy, top-heavy nurse pouring me a couple handfuls of interesting pills put a skip in my step as I headed down the hallway toward the counseling center. The publicly funded linoleum floors and the horrid canary-yellow walls I recognized from grade school, libraries and the food stamp office, except that the walls here were dingy from Librium-drenched alcoholics leaning as they strolled, killing time between bouts of DTs. I weaved my way through the other zombies and skipped over a fresh puddle of puke while kicking around a few smooth lines in my head.

First, I'd check out her name tag.

"Well hello, Nurse Candy, Charles M. Hyatt reporting as ordered," followed by a charming little salute.

"Have a seat, Mr. Hyatt."

"And might I add, I've always had a thing for a woman in uniform."

"Right arm, please."

She would then gently apply the cuff of the sphygmomanometer to my arm, making occasional eye contact and being sure to warm up the stethoscope on her lab coat before she took my blood pressure.

"Blah, blah over blah, blah. Very nice," she would purr.

"Thanks, I try to take care of myself."

"We'll need to get you tested for hepatitis and HIV."

"Aren't you sweet!"

After numerous tests, pokes and prods, she would finally take out that tight ponytail and shake out her long blond hair, sighing, "Oh, that's much better," and continuing to make notes among her assorted charts and graphs.

Next, she would remove her thick-framed glasses as she began to fill up a grocery bag with bottles of prescription pills, some I recognized, some I didn't. She'd toss them in haphazardly: Percodan, Vicodin, Percocet, codeine, methadone, some kind of patches and even a morphine suppository for good measure.

"There you go, Mr. Hyatt. That should get you through your stay with us."

"Please, call me Charlie."

Then she would stick a folded slip of paper into the front pocket of my hospital gown. "That's my home phone number — in case you need anything, you know, like a ride home or a place to stay after your little ordeal here," she would say, following up with a tiny kiss on my forehead.

I turned the corner and saw the actual medical office waiting room. A few things didn't match up with my fantasy. For instance, instead of Nurse Candy and me alone in a room with pristine white leather furniture and Muzak versions of The Damned's first album, there were a lot of shaky and sweaty guys leaning and squatting and moaning everywhere. There were no bowls of mints, no complimentary bottles of water, and no VIP line. Worse still, Nurse Candy was apparently on break. I decided to go have a smoke.

The freshly mopped TV room was the only place you could smoke except in the late afternoon. At that time you were allowed to meander down to the fenced concrete yard for a little recreation time. I plopped down in a hard plastic chair, lit up and watched a few minutes of *Alf* at high volume. This room doubled as an AA meeting room between the hours of 8 and 10 p.m. before converting back to TV lounge for an hour before lights-out. I wanted to wander over to the open window to escape the lemony stench and get a glimpse of the real world, but I was too tired to move. Too tired to get up and get the entertainment section of the newspaper sitting by the huge industrial dispenser of grape Kool-Aid. Too tired to do anything but stare at the wall.

I was fortunate to have easy access to drugs on an almost daily basis, but I was familiar with the first disquieting feelings of withdrawal. My foot tapped nervously and my skin began to crawl. This is the body's first friendly reminder. These are common experiences in a junkie's life, just like past-due phone bills and forgotten birthdays.

1   WE ADMITTED WE WERE PUSSIES AND COULDN'T HANDLE OUR ALCOHOL.

2   WE CAME TO BELIEVE IN GOD BECAUSE WE COULDN'T HANDLE REAL LIFE ON OUR OWN, AND SO WE DESPERATELY TURNED TO THAT BEARDED FAIRY-TALE DICTATOR IN THE SKY.

3   WE WENT TOTALLY INSANE AND TURNED OUR WILL AND OUR LIVES OVER TO THE CARE OF GOD, AS WE WERE BROWBEATEN INTO BELIEVING SINCE INFANCY.

4   WE MADE A SEARCHING AND FEARLESS MORAL INVENTORY OF OUR PIECE-OF-SHIT SELVES.

5   WE ADMITTED TO GOD, TO OURSELVES — AND TO THE POLICE — THE EXACT NATURE OF OUR WRONGS.

6   WE WERE ENTIRELY READY TO HAVE GOD REMOVE ALL THESE DETECTIVE CHARACTERS.

7   WE HUMBLY ASKED HIM TO NOT MAKE US CUM TOO SOON.

8   WE MADE A LIST OF ALL PERSONS WE HAD HARMED AND BECAME WILLING TO AVOID THEM ALL.

9   WE MADE DIRECT AMENDS TO SUCH PEOPLE WHEREVER POSSIBLE, EXCEPT WHEN TO DO SO WOULD BE OF SOME INCONVENIENCE.

10 WE CONTINUED TO TAKE PERSONAL INVENTORY, AND WHEN WE WERE WRONG, PROMPTLY BLAMED OUR PARENTS.

11 WE SOUGHT THROUGH PRAYER AND MEDITATION TO IMPROVE OUR CONSCIOUS CONTACT WITH GOD AS WE UNDERSTOOD HIM, PRAYING ONLY FOR KNOWLEDGE OF "OH MY GOD, WHAT AM I DOIN' HERE?"

12 HAVING HAD A SPIRITUAL AWAKENING AS THE RESULT OF THESE STEPS, WE TRIED TO CARRY THIS MIND-NUMBINGLY ILL-CONCEIVED MESSAGE TO OTHER ALCOHOLICS AND TO PRACTICE THESE PRINCIPLES IN ALL OUR AFFAIRS.

I gave a cracked-out brother a cigarette in exchange for checking down the hall on the length of the line at the nurse's office. It was still a dozen addicts deep, he reported back. He introduced himself as Romeo and we made small talk. He was suspiciously friendly and went on and on about the blessing of a safe place to sleep and the good food and the hope and light this place had brought into his life. I nodded my head politely and considered how I might use my newfound friend to my advantage. Since he had been here for the better part of a week, he already had phone privileges, although he claimed he had no one to call. For the price of another Lucky Strike, he agreed to place a call to my girlfriend for me. If I was going to be stuck here, I was going to need supplies. Furthermore, I supposed it would only be polite to let her know that I was still alive, and where.

I jotted down the number and then paused as I tried to imagine what it was that the staff would actually allow me to have. One thing was for sure: If Romeo was going to continue to run errands for me, I was going to need more cigarettes.

"Just ask her to bring me a carton of smokes and, uh, tell her I miss her," I said, handing him my last quarter, feeling a rare jolt of remorse for my behavior of late.

Romeo headed toward the door, paused and turned around. "What she look like?"

I just looked at him, inquisitively.

"I mean, does she have big ol' titties?" he asked, demonstrating with hand gestures in case I had gone deaf in the last ten seconds.

"No, she's a petite girl, she doesn't have big ol' anything."

"Blonde?"

"I dunno, Romeo," I said, exhausted with the questioning. "It changes from week to week. Just make the fucking phone call."

An old episode of *The Addams Family* started, so I settled in to fondly relive my childhood crush on Morticia as my body slowly began to reject its own bones.

Romeo slithered back into the room about 15 minutes later. I handed him a smoke I had already pulled out of my pack in anticipation of his return and flipped open my Zippo to light him up. He gave me the bad news.

"No answer, I left a message."

Cunt! Maybe it was just the withdrawal talking, but I was pretty sure that if she wasn't answering her phone, the only possible alternative was that she was fucking that asswipe from the Razorbacks or that cocksucker from Crisis Party. On second thought, probably both.

Recreation time came and went and what little daylight there was had receded into darkness as I sat there. I was fully immersed in a plane hijacking story on the news when I noticed the room was empty and I was alone. Dinnertime, I imagined. Eating meals was mandatory, but since I was new they probably let me slide.

I bolted up and out of my chair when I realized that this would probably be my best chance at getting into Nurse Candy's office.

I had barely gotten through the door when the fundamentals of walking escaped me. Every joint in my body seized, pinning me to the wall. I fell to my hands and knees. As if on cue, a black giant appeared with a mop bucket and placed it on the ground in front of me.

"Here, you might need this," he said in a deep, resonating voice.

"No, no, I'll be fine, thank…" all of my internal organs suddenly liquefied and erupted out of my throat.

I coughed up lies, malice and spite.

I gagged on truculence, evil and sin.

I heaved Jesus fucking Christ.

When the deluge ended, he put his monstrous hand on my sweat-soaked forehead and pushed my hair back so he could look into my eyes.

"Goddamn son, we're gonna need another bucket."

"Forgive me, Father," I managed between wretches.

I looked up to see that I was a mere 25 feet from my salvation, with not a single patient to detour me from my sweet angel's sympathetic and, more importantly, pharmaceutical embrace.

The giant stepped over me, stuck one of those monstrous hands under each of my armpits, and lifted me up. "Let's get you to bed now."

"I'm good, I'm good. I've got an appointment with the nurse I really should be getting to." I tried to sound as stern and businesslike as possible.

"C'mon son, you'll feel better if you…" I cut him off by removing his paw from my shoulder.

"I," I wiped the puke from the corner of my mouth, "will be fine, thank you very much."

Between you and me, I was dying. That didn't change the fact that no crackhead, no wino, no pill-popping housewife, was going to get between me and my medication.

Somewhere in your Bible it says, "False pride cometh before the fall." In my case that fall was about two steps later. I came to slumped in a chair with some pudgy fucker sticking his fingers and a penlight in my eyeballs.

"What the shit?" There was that taste of blood again.

"That was quite a spill you took," he said, prodding my lymph nodes.

"Yeah, you fell right on your fuckin' face," Romeo chimed in, from his seat on a desk across the room.

"My name is Paul. I'll be running some tests on you."

My eyes adjusted to the office light. He was wearing a cheap dress shirt with an American flag-print tie under his stethoscope. Nurse Paul? Fuck.

In the background Rush Limbaugh was jerking off George Bush from a clock radio on a book shelf, and Romeo was contemplating the meaning of a framed picture of some footprints in the sand.

"How many fingers am I holding up?"

Fuck you. I held two fingers up.

"Many patients come in with malnutrition and dehydration," he continued in spite of my poor attitude. "Have you been drinking enough water?"

I honestly couldn't recall the last time I'd had water that wasn't run through coffee grounds or used to cook up dope.

"No sir, I don't suppose I have."

"Unprotected sex?" he asked, reaching for his clipboard.

"No thanks, I'm a little tired and I have puke breath." Not being the nurse of my dreams is one thing, but not laughing at that joke was just fucked up.

"Have you shared needles?"

Check.

"Daily use?"

"As close to a gram a day as I can afford."

"Ever overdose?"

"Knock on wood, sir."

"How long have you lived on the streets, Charles?"

"Doc, I'm not homeless; I just smell that way." Not even a smirk.

"Place of employment?"

I stared at him. Look at me, you fuck. I know your pudgy fingers. I put five dollars' worth of tokens into them every Monday, Wednesday and Friday night at the Champ Arcade. I waited. He looked. He saw another in an endless line of scraggly junkies. And then he saw me.

"I'd rather not say, Doc."

It was the *Citizen Kane* of uncomfortable silences.

6. CLICK YOUR FINGERS
APPLAUDING THE PLAY

I had stepped out of the store to get some fresh air — and by fresh air, I mean smoke a cigarette and leer at young ladies and drunks as they stumbled around 1ˢᵗ Avenue on a Friday night, and by Friday night I mean 1:30 on Saturday morning. It was almost time for the girls to punch out after their shift. The calm before the storm as a general rule. "Jimmy" followed me out and bummed a Lucky Strike and a light, of course. I could tell he wasn't a real smoker by the way he inhaled, the same way bad actors take a draw off a cigarette then blow it out quickly before the nicotine goodness gets a chance to hit their precious lungs.

Like the dancers, most of our regular customers preferred the anonymity of an alias. Nurse Paul's "Champ Arcade name" was Jimmy. Jimmy was the most annoying kind of regular, a loiterer. A man so twisted, so lost and lonely he turned to the employees of his neighborhood porno shop for mock companionship.

"You married?" he inquired.

"Nope." I kept my answer short and sweet to make sure he wasn't confusing this with a conversation.

"I bet you could fuck any girl working here, huh?"

"We have a strict 'no-fraternizing' policy here, Jimmy; besides, I'm a professional." I said with a wink.

"But they're all sluts, right?" he shot back.

I stepped toward him, exhaling smoke in his face as I spoke, "I'm not gonna let you talk about the girls that way." He winced as if I were going to hit him.

"Now, is there something you need? Is there something I can arrange for you, or are we finished here?" I turned to walk back in.

"I want to watch," he blurted out.

I turned around.

"I have money and I want to watch you fuck one of the girls."

I grabbed him by the arm and quickly walked him to the side of the building.

"I'm sorry. I'm sorry, I'm sorry," he repeated as I escorted him from the storefront.

"Shut up!" I slammed him against one of the cars. I took him by the shirt collar and pulled him close. "How much you got?"

Relief washed over him, "I'll give you four hundred dollars."

"Fuck you." I raised my fist.

"A thousand, I'll give you a thousand dollars."

"And where do you propose this happens, huh?" I let go of him.

"Ummm, how about the back seat of my car?" he stammered as he pointed to a black BMW with tinted windows parked behind me.

"You've thought this through, you sick fuck. Put five hundred bucks in my hand right now," I demanded.

He pulled five crisp hundred-dollar bills out of his wallet and folded them into my hand.

"Wait in your car, I'll be back."

They called her Mistress Kat. At 39, she was the oldest dancer in the place. A stunningly beautiful single mother of two teenage daughters, she was a money-making machine. In her younger days, she put herself through law school by stripping only to discover after a brief foray into the "real world" that she couldn't come close to making the same income as a public defender as she could peeling off her clothes and talking dirty in the private booths. She was a specialist, a leather-clad dominatrix with a tongue made for humiliating and belittling well-to-do businessmen. She had a following that would settle for no other dancer, each customer gleefully waiting his turn. She called her customers "pigs" right to their faces. She instructed them to send her flowers and presents to the shop. Almost every night when I arrived a few minutes before midnight there would be fresh flowers and unopened gift boxes in the trash can behind the counter. She was a wily veteran who had mastered the art of extracting cash from men. I liked her. We had an arrangement.

When she was feeling charitable and was approached with the proper amount of groveling by one of her regulars, she would instruct him to go out to the register and discreetly hand me one hundred and twenty dollars. I would pocket twenty and stick the rest in an envelope. The customer would then go out to his car, which he would describe to me and wait. When Miss Kat was good and ready, I would escort her out to the parking lot and stand guard while she delivered what I imagine to be the most brutal handjob of all time. The whole project usually took the time it takes to smoke a cigarette.

I knocked on the girls' dressing-room door. Most of them were already changed into their street clothes and counting the evening's take. Kat was sitting at a make-up mirror with a pile of cash neatly stacked in front of her. I beckoned her over to a secluded corner so we could chat.

"Maryanne," I addressed her by her real name so she knew I meant business. I slipped the five hundred dollars into her hand.

"I'm listening," she purred.

All of a sudden I was as nervous as a schoolboy. A minute earlier I was prepared to slap the shit out of a regular customer to get an extra few hundred bucks out of him, and now I was awkwardly proposing adolescent-style back-seat sex to a coworker to be well-financed by a voyeur gawking in the foreground. Eh. It wasn't the worst job I ever had.

"Hmmm," she paused, as she looked me up and down.

"Knock it off," I shot back.

"Let's do it," she said, lifting up her denim skirt, sliding her panties off and sticking them in her purse.

Performance anxiety washed over me, and it must've shown on my face.

"Don't worry baby, you'll do just fine," she said while brushing her hand across the front of my jeans. "You're halfway there already."

We locked eyes. "At least I hope that's only half of it."

The rest of the girls eyeballed us suspiciously.

Kat's version of post-work casual attire was hot pink Converse high-tops, a hot pink tube top, the aforementioned short denim skirt topped off with a black leather motorcycle jacket (which she was stuffing with cash), a canister of Mace and a small bottle of lube.

"Who's got a condom?" she announced to the room. A half dozen were produced, as if a hot chick at the bar were looking for a light.

"What's your brand, killer?" she asked as the whole room snickered and catcalled.

If I had the capacity to blush, I would have. I pointed to the familiar blue Trojan wrapper.

"What? Is it your birthday, Charlie?" came a wisecrack from the corner. I ignored it, choosing instead to focus on the task at hand.

"C'mon, let's go," I practically begged, just to escape the barrage of stares in the henhouse.

"Ya gotta make 'em wait, Sugar. It's half the show," she said, looking into the mirror, pulling her long brown hair back into a ponytail. It was trans-formative. Without the leather bustier, riding crop and all the make-up she looked 10 years younger, almost innocent.

"Aright Charlie, let's go fuck for money."

With that, the innocent young thing grabbed me by the hand and marched me off to the fucking sock hop.

So much for all the discretion I had practiced.

"I don't want Wayne to know what's goin' on," I whispered out of the side of my mouth.

"Wayne!" she called out, "Charlie is going on break, and he'll be right back."

In the eternity since I'd left "Jimmy" sitting in his car, it had begun raining. This was a good thing, less foot traffic in the parking lot, fewer chances of police cruising by, fewer crackheads trying to peek in the windows.

"Who are we doin' a show for, Hon?" she inquired as we strolled out to the parking lot.

"Jimmy."

"Aww, he must be experiencing a shame spiral again."

Sigh. Doctor, Lawyer, Hooker. I was fast becoming smitten with her.

Being a gentleman, I opened the door for her when we got to the car.

"You first, baby. Scoot all the way over." She seemed to be giving direction, and since I had no plan, I was happy to oblige.

I slid all the way over to the opposite door and unzipped my jacket. She crawled in on all fours after me.

"Mistress Kat?!" Jimmy shrieked.

"At ease, pig!" she turned her head and shot back at him.

"Now get this through your thick little skull. I'm not Mistress Kat. You could never be so lucky as to have Mistress Kat in your car; I'm Charlie's prom date. My name is..." she looked at me with a raised eyebrow.

"My name is..." she cocked her head, looking at me for an answer.

"Darla, your name is Darla."

"My name is Darla and I'm gonna fuck his brains out."

With that declaration, it was on. She lunged at my crotch, tearing my jeans open. I was so desensitized and detached from working there that it was as if I watched the whole scene unfold on a TV screen, unaware of my surroundings, unaware of my luck.

She pulled my cock out of my boxers and inhaled it. I smelled rental car. "Jimmy" opened his briefcase. I heard him pop a cassette into the player. "Two Steps Forward" by Muddy Waters came out of the speakers, and he set a travel-size package of Kleenex on the dashboard. He reached into the breast pocket of his jacket and pulled out his penlight.

With all his prep work, I was surprised he hadn't lit fuckin' candles. How long had he been planning this? How many times did he approach me only to lose his nerve?

When he turned his head to watch, quite literally and figuratively in the driver's seat, I understood. I finally understood.

The truth was, for me the exciting part was over. The Prom Queen had already been stripped of her crown; the impossibly cute barmaid's jeans were already on the floor of my kitchen, and the emotionally distressed next-door neighbor was lifting that perfectly timed glass of wine to her lips. I enjoyed the puzzle. Which charming words and in what order shall they be strung? How hard could I make them laugh and when would they realize I *wasn't like the others*? What part of my supposed horrible upbringing or my cool-guy demeanor or which of my subtly revealed secrets would melt their hearts just right? What opened door or carefully placed hand would trigger that "you'll never believe what I did last night" call to their girlfriends in the morning? No, fucking was never my thing. Manipulation was my prize. Orgasm was a formality.

"Kiss me, I can't get wet unless you kiss me," Kat panted in my ear.

Again, with no plan of my own, I was happy to oblige.

I cradled her head in my hands and kissed her deeply. "Jimmy's" penlight was working its way up our torsos when Kat batted it away.

"This part is not for you," she hissed.

She was still kissing me when she reached into her tube top and fished out the Trojan. She tore the package, placed the condom between her lips and lowered her mouth onto my hard cock. Drum roll, spotlight and perfect application. One of many magic tricks in her arsenal, I'm sure.

She rolled over onto her back and pulled me on top of her.

He and I aren't so different, I thought. But he misconstrued what was a fair exchange of currency for goods and services as power. He was getting off on the illusion of being in charge of something, anything, in his life. He was small and insignificant in this world, at his horrid job, in the eyes of his emasculating wife. He was scared of every little thing that moved but tonight, if only for a little while, he was in charge.

I fucking knew better than that. This was just a multi-car pile up of damaged souls. She was a sociopath with two sets of braces and private school to finance, not to mention fuckin' Christmas. And as for me, was I just happy acting as agent and intermediary between them, or was I just seizing an opportunity to have the most unattainable girl behind the glass?

I saw the silhouette of his profile in the windshield. I noticed the beads of sweat on his forehead. If he was masturbating, he was doing it with all the gusto of a field mouse.

"Cum for me, baby" she pleaded.

I needed to concentrate. She had one leg draped over the front seat and the other over my shoulder as I hammered away. If not for the torrential downpour, this would have been a very volatile situation. His oscillating BMW would tip off any authority figures patrolling our wicked little neck of the woods. Legal issues were not my concern now; I had a job to do.

"Cum for me!" her plea had turned to an order, and she emphasized this by digging her fingernails into my arm. With that and a fairly authentic groan, I crumbled on top of her.

Kat's arm shot out toward the front seat, her palm open, and her index finger beckoning for the remainder of her compensation.

He was flustered but he peeled them off, one, two, three, four, five, hundred-dollar bills. Kat folded the cash into her tube top and with a downward pull on her skirt, she was ready to go. I was less prepared for a hasty exit.

"Be a dear and walk me to my car, Charlie."

As I was stuffing my hard, latex-encased dick back in my jeans, Jimmy handed me an umbrella and thanked us.

Her car was only a few yards away, so I assumed that the invite was only a kindness to spare me any further awkward interactions with our temporary employer.

We strolled arm in arm as I held the open umbrella over her.

"Sorry for leaving you...umm...unfinished," she said, almost bashfully.

"S'ok doll, I'll take care of that later."

She reached into her cleavage and pulled out the money when we got to her car.

"For your services, sir," she said, sticking three hundred bucks into the front pocket of my jeans.

She dropped her keys on the pavement. When I reached down to pick them up, I almost clumsily decapitated her with the umbrella. Smooth. I retrieved the wet keys, opened her door and held it for her as she got in.

"Thanks, Charlie. You're sweet."

Yeah, that's what I was just thinkin'.

As I walked past Jimmy's BMW, the automatic window went down. I closed the umbrella and tossed it in without saying a word. That was the last time I saw Nurse Paul. That was about three weeks ago, I thought.

I was soaked by the time I walked back into the store. Wayne was perched behind the cash register striking his best "I'm bored" pose.

"What the hell was that about?" he inquired.

I pulled a hundred out and flicked it on the counter.

"Why don't you stop asking questions and go buy us some fuckin' dope."

With that, he dutifully hopped off into the night, the stale buzzer as the door opened announcing the end of my little reverie.

"You'll be experiencing some sleeplessness, not much we can do about that, of course, but for the cramps and diarrhea, I can give you something."

When Nurse Paul turned around from his desk, he had two plastic shot glasses, one containing a pink liquid, the other two pills.

"What's this?" I said, obliviously irritated.

"Pepto-Bismol and Tylenol — that ought to get you through the night."

7. NIGHT OF THE VAMPIRE

I guess the first few hours weren't so bad. All my roommates were crackheads, so they were fast asleep; I didn't have to make idle conversation. That's the way it works, crack fiends sleep the night and day away. I'm sure it was no picnic when they awoke, but I was a little jealous anyway. A heroin addict's withdrawal is a little more Zen, in-the-moment. We were lucky to get five minutes' sleep a night. We were awake to experience every nuance: the sweats, the shivers, the nausea, the shame, the regret, the murderous rage and the suicidal introspection.

I lay on my bed and got acquainted with the ceiling. I was OK. I was antsy, bored and thirsty, but I was fine. I was listening to a choir of snores, but it was good. I was all right. I couldn't sleep or move or fucking stand and I was ready to kill everyone in sight, but I was good. I noticed one of the crackheads had a book. I quietly slid out of my bed and snuck over to his nightstand. I stuck the paperback in the waistband of my boxer shorts and crept out the door.

A creepy-lookin' ex-biker type was sorting papers behind the reception counter. He was wearing some secondhand-store slacks and a crumpled dress shirt that he probably balled up and kept under the front seat of his car. I'm sure he'd mastered the art of changing clothes in the front seat of his El Camino in the parking lot just minutes before work. He looked in my direction, trying to make out who it was walking toward him in the soft "after-hours" lighting the detox center had taken on at bedtime. As I approached, clearing my throat, he simply pointed across the hall: restroom and water fountain, perfect. I walked into the restroom and fiddled about with the doorknob, attempting to secure it for a little privacy.

"The doors don't have locks here, buddy," he called out.

Of course. I figured that traffic would be sparse this time of night, so I removed the freshly misappropriated reading material from the front of my pants. Stephen King. Fuck. I tossed it in the wastebasket and took a piss.

I washed my hands for appearance's sake and decided I'd hit up my crusty new pal behind the counter for the late-night smoking spot. I walked out the door, but hadn't even opened my mouth before he spoke.

"You a smoker, Charles?" he asked, looking up from what I assume was my file.

I nodded.

"Follow me."

We walked down the hall in silence and went out the emergency exit.

"I disable the alarm at night. Anyone else finds out about this, I'll know who told 'em," he said with a spurious glare.

We stepped outside, he handed me a cigarette, lit me up and then himself.

"My name is Martin, I'm the graveyard guy," he said as he stuck his hand out.

"I'm Charlie, I guess I'm a graveyard guy too."

"So," I asked after an extended lull, "what happens next?"

"Next?"

"Yeah, you seem to have all the answers to my questions before I even ask."

"Ha, knowing a junkie is gonna want to piss and smoke in the middle of the night hardly makes me fuckin' Nostradamus, Charlie."

"Hmmm," he said, carefully considering my question, "The next thing that'll happen is you'll mistake this minor infraction of the rules and label me a ne'er-do-well, then wrongfully assume I can be persuaded to sneak drugs or some other kind of contraband into the facility for you," he said with a smirk.

"Who? Me?" I feigned innocence.

"That's what we do, Charlie, that's just what we do."

"We?"

"Yeah, we addicts," he continued, "We lie, cheat, steal and manipulate, that's what we do. It's our nature."

My foot wouldn't stop tapping and my hand shook when I brought the cigarette to my lips. I couldn't tell if it was my withdrawal or because I was suddenly nervous around this man. I had never heard anyone talk like this before. The people I knew never talked about anything substantial. When we were loaded we discussed art and music, maybe some nonsensical spirituality of some kind, but when we were standing around smoking and bullshitting we did just that, bullshit and smoke. This made me uneasy.

"Do they know you're an addict?" I asked, gesturing with my thumb toward the building.

"Ha, ha, you're brand fucking new, aren't you?" he laughed.

"First day, yeah," I mumbled.

"No man, I mean, you don't know shit about recovery. You know, the reason you're here."

I had no fucking idea what he was talking about. Still, I acted indignant, if only momentarily. I wanted to punch old Martin in the neck. I wanted to slap that smirk off his shit-biker face. I wanted to shut his fucking mouth. I wanted somebody to explain what was happening to me. I wanted my skin to stop crawling. I wanted my dealer's pager number to stop going though my head. I wanted to admit he was right.

I wanted his cigarettes. I wanted someone to talk to. I wanted it to be over.

"When's the last time you slept, Charlie?"

"Well, does being dragged down the hall unconscious to the nurse's office count as sleep?"

"I suppose not," he chuckled.

"Then it's been a couple of days."

I surveyed the grounds: concrete, chain link, 8-foot walls, nothing promising.

"What's to stop me from just walkin' out of here?" I asked.

"Me, some locked doors, the police," he said matter-of-factly as he exhaled smoke.

He handed me a travel-size package of Kleenex that he fished out of his back pocket. I hadn't realized my nose was running like a faucet.

"Don't go tough-guy on me, Charlie, I'm your friend. I know you better than you think I do," he said, handing me another cigarette.

Who was I kidding? I was in no shape to wrestle any keys away from this ogre and run barefoot into the night. I could barely stand with the muscle spasms in my legs and the cramps in my guts. Besides, he was being kind to me, which I don't suppose was in his job description.

"Do you mind if we sit down, Martin?"

"You go right ahead, boss," he said, looking down the hall through the little window in the door, "I gotta keep an eye out in case someone gets up."

I sat down on the stairs with my back to him.

"All right, I'll bite, what do you know about me?" I asked, not really looking for an answer but a means to continue the small talk and, more importantly, the flow of non-filtered Camels.

He paused for a moment.

"I know you live with a crazy woman," he said.

"How?" I laughed. "I'm not sayin' it's not true, I'm just interested in your theory."

"Well, I noticed in your file you live in one of those apartment buildings on the Hill, probably a studio, but they still ain't exactly cheap. Since you're uninsured and not exactly Microsoft-employee material, I'd guess you have a shitty job that doesn't pay that well. That being the case, you'd need two shitty incomes to maintain that living situation *and* a drug habit for very long. Furthermore, and I'm gonna throw caution to the wind here, I'll assume you'd prefer to cohabitate with a female, and *if* you managed to con a young lady into living with you, she'd have to be crazy."

I clapped slowly and sarcastically.

"Ha, good work, Columbo, what else do you know?"

"I know you're in a lot of pain."

"Yeah, I feel like shit," I admitted.

"No man, I mean that's why you do drugs. That's why *we* do drugs."

"I do drugs because I like to get high."

"No, people who smoke a joint and drink a couple of beers on the weekend like to get high. Guys like you and me who stick needles in our arms are tryin' to kill some pain."

I sighed. Maybe the free cigarettes weren't worth having this conversation.

"I've got good news for you though," he continued.

Jesus Christ, here comes the fucking God talk, I thought.

"You only have to do this once."

"Do what?" I said, looking back at him, quite annoyed.

"Kick dope, dumbass. If you play your cards right and follow some pretty fuckin' simple suggestions, you won't have to do this shit again. It's all in the book."

"I'll wait for the movie," I said, regretting it almost immediately.

The cramping in my guts was unbearable.

"I'm sorry, Martin," I said. "I know you're just trying to help, but I thought you were gettin' ready to lay some kind of a Jesus trip on me."

"Fuck no," he laughed. "I'm an atheist, but there's room for us too."

I crossed my arms over my torso and leaned forward, hoping for some relief from the pain.

"I can see you're not really ready to hear all this, so I guess I'll just try and make your stay here as pleasant as possible. Maybe we'll have better luck next time," he said.

"Martin, there will be no 'next time,'" I said.

"Ya wanna know what else I know about you?" he asked. "I know you're scared."

"Look, this has been a big misunderstanding," I groaned.

"You didn't let me finish. And I'm also pretty sure you just shit your pants."

Fuck, he was right. I couldn't imagine how this could get any worse.

"My eyesight ain't what it used to be, but my sense of smell is intact, my friend," he said, helping me to my feet.

"I can't begin to tell you how embarrassed I am," I said.

"Your secrets are safe with me, Charlie. You wouldn't be the first patient to underestimate a fart."

"Let's get you some clean britches," he said, opening the door and gesturing down the hallway.

The sun would be rising in a couple of hours, and since I declined Martin's suggestion of adult diapers I figured the best course of action was to just sit on the toilet till breakfast. Sleep did not appear to be in my immediate future.

There was a knock at the door.

"Occupied," I grumbled.

"I know," Martin said, coming in anyway. "We need to get your ass happy, joyous and free," he said, tossing a blue hardcover book at me.

What an odd fucking thing to say, I thought, as I cracked open the well-worn edition. The book was covered with scribbles and yellow highlighter marker. These people have got to learn how to take care of their things. I stopped at a random page and read an underlined sentence. Obviously this passage meant a great deal to someone or he wouldn't have bothered.

"We have found much of heaven and we have been rocketed into a fourth dimension of existence of which we had not even dreamed."

I reached over and dropped the book in the wastebasket on top of Stephen King. Happy, joyous and free. Happy, joyous and free.

8. I AM A DEMON

I was sorting through the Low Points of My Life Rolodex to see where to file this. Flipping past abortions, broken hearts, car wrecks, evictions, flat tires, lies I told to my grandma and venereal diseases, I came upon those events that were a little more difficult to allocate. How do you even classify rifling through your own trash bags in the dumpster behind your apartment in search of a syringe that was in working order? I filed that under Unpleasant.

Then there was the rather complicated matter of the terminal cancer patient who lived across the hall from us. A couple times a week I'd go over in the afternoons when I woke up and do little chores for him like take out the trash, wash a few dishes or run down to the deli and pick up some milk and lunch meat. He'd sit there and listen to old jazz records while smoking cigarettes and talking about the old days. Occasionally when his medication would cloud his manners, he would mention how fine my girlfriend's ass was and how he would tear that little white girl up. I would stand in the kitchen drying a bowl with his dish towel and smile and nod, and then change the direction of the conversation by asking about what we were listening to. Sometimes I would pretend that I was working at a retirement home for Black Panthers and that he would read to me from Mao's *Little Red Book* as I cleaned his guns when his arthritis was acting up. It was all very heartwarming and fuzzy until he dozed off.

The first time I went over there, I was being a good citizen, honest. The first time I used his bathroom it was legitimate and coincidental. But then I have that thing about medicine cabinets. When I opened his, everything changed.

There they stood, like tiny glass soldiers fallen into rank, dozens of bottles of morphine. Maybe I heard a chorus of angels singing, maybe I didn't.

The next time I went over I had several syringes neatly tucked in my jacket, and when I heard him quietly snoring in time with Coltrane, I set down his broom and dustpan and went to work. I siphoned half the contents of four or five bottles and refilled them with tap water. This went on for as long as Mr. Lewis did, which — for reasons I'm sure legitimate and coincidental — was only a couple more weeks. Sure, it was stealing, but it was so much more than that. I filed that under Remorse.

When your mom comes in your room and catches you masturbating to a picture of your cousin: Poor Planning. When the doctor at the clinic has grown so weary of seeing you that she provides you with supplies and instructions on how to burn off your genital warts at home: Gross. Some misconduct just isn't easy to catalogue.

These are the kinds of things one thinks about while trapped in a detox center sitting on the toilet with your ass leaking like an old faucet at 6 in the morning. If I were lucky, this would be the most soul-crushing and demoralizing experience of my life. The Low Points of My Life Rolodex was meticulous in its upkeep. The joyous moments sat like a poorly organized photo album in the corner of a dusty closet next to a high school yearbook I'd never looked at. I would use this story to one-up some fool in a bar somewhere, someday, who thinks he's had it rough. I wrote the word "Ugly" at the top of the card in large red marker and slid it through the slot in the front of my skull. I cradled my head in the palms of my hands and found a couple of minutes of sleep.

"Mornin', Paul," a voice blared though the door. Like most of us grave-yard shifters, Martin was louder at dawn than normal people. Our lack of interaction with folks during the wee hours can make us seem abrasive to the newly risen.

I got up, wiped, pulled up my pajama pants as quickly as possible and burst out the bathroom door. The reception area was empty except for Martin grinning over a stack of paperwork. With his reading glasses on, he appeared more college professor-like than biker.

"Paul? As in Nurse Paul?" I asked, looking back and forth down the hallway.

"Yeah, kid. He's in his office but he doesn't open for business till 7 or so."

He asked me how I was feeling, but I was already marching down the hall, choosing to focus my energy on clenching my ass cheeks rather than making chitchat.

The door was ajar but hardly welcoming. I pushed it in a bit and stuck my head in. He was sitting at his desk with his back to me, sorting though last evening's urine samples. What a fucking way to start out your workday. He unscrewed the lid of his thermos, poured a cup, and then held a shot glass-sized plastic container of piss at arm's length so he could read the name on it. At least Martin could admit when his eyesight was going. Paul wrote some notes in a file, then repeated the process over and over till the samples on the tray had dwindled by half. Due to a faulty lid or fate's cruel sense of humor or just plain old bad luck, the next container he held up ex-ploded, covering his hand, desk calendar and coffee cup in crackhead urine.

"Goddammit!"

The only way the morning could have gotten any worse for him was if he had to deal with the likes of me.

"Hello, Jimmy," I said.

Utterly defeated, he hung his head and let out a deep sigh that segued into a whimper. Suddenly he smashed his fist into the filing cabinet. He tore a week's worth of pages out of his desk calendar, balled them up and dropped them in his waste bin. Just when I thought his little tantrum was done, he cleared all the pee samples, files and a stapler off his desk and onto the floor with one mighty swoop of his forearm. He put his head in hands and began to weep.

I went in and closed the door behind me, paused for dramatic effect, and then locked the door, making sure he heard it.

A picture of the wife was sitting on a bookshelf next to a box of tissue. I took them both over and sat on his desk so he would have to look at me. I pulled out a couple of tissues and offered them to the quivering, lugubrious wreck, but I kept the framed picture for closer examination.

"No kids?" I asked.

He looked up at me for the first time and shook his head.

"She's a lovely woman, Jimmy. What does she do?"

He cleared his throat. "She's a lawyer."

I wasn't just blowing smoke up his ass; she was attractive. She was a brunette with smoky brown eyes, probably quite stunning in her younger days. She was elegant and statuesque, way out of Jimmy's league.

"Let me guess," I continued, "you met in college, you were pre-med and she was pre-law?"

"Yeah," he said. He tried to look at me, with maybe a half a second's worth of hope that I was somehow speaking to him as any kind of equal.

"Then apparently you didn't quite live up to your potential now, did you?"

He dabbed his eyes with the tissue, blew his nose and tried to compose himself. I picked up the engraved nameplate on his desk and read it: "Paul Difranco R.N."

"But judging from the car you drive and the amount of money you have to throw around getting your twisted little kicks, she must've done very well for herself," I said.

He started blubbering again. I handed him more tissue.

"How long do you suppose it'll take me to hunt down a lady lawyer named Difranco in town? Ten minutes? Fifteen minutes?" I asked.

"Fuck!" he cried, banging his forehead on the desk and leaving it there. And then Nurse Paul did something I didn't think possible. He stunned me. Right then and there, that little fuck did something that stopped me right in my tracks and made me think how completely foreign are the worlds right around us. In a sort of whispered lament, Nurse Paul called me a butthole.

I didn't know what to do. Shit or go blind seemed to be the options. But then my eye snagged itself on an interesting-looking cabinet with a padlock on it across the room from the bookshelf. I slid off the desk, walked over to it and fingered the lock.

"As terrible as this is, and I'm talkin' about my situation, not yours, I'm pretty sure that I'll live through it," I said. "I am not so sure that you will fare as well."

"What do you want, Charlie?" he asked, not even bothering to lift his head from his desk.

"Drugs, Doc. I want drugs."

9. STARRY EYES

"Hyatt! Up!"

I had fallen on the cobblestone street trying to avoid trampling two tiny children. Their mother glared at me, scooped them up and ran with the panicked crowd. The rolling thunder of German bombers drowned out the screams of foreign tongues everywhere. I was paralyzed. Chunks of debris and human flesh fell all around me.

"Get your ass up and fall in line!"

An unfamiliar form stood in shadow in the doorway bellowing at the top of his lungs over the jarring alarm. I bolted upright, soaked in sweat. I tried to focus my eyes on the clock, but I was jerked out of bed by my collar. I was placed in a single-file line, and I moved toward the emergency exit with Frankenstein-like grace. Through my narcotic fog came incessant barks of direction, apparently from someone who had just learned the phrase "orderly fashion." They wanted no talking. They wanted no horseplay. They wanted us — in an orderly fashion — to remain calm.

I was so calm I could barely move.

A counselor stuck his clipboard in the small of my back and nudged me along.

To no one in particular, I tried to ask: "What's happening here?" I heard my voice gurgle through phlegm, "Wh'abba heah?"

"Fire alarm. Outside," grumbled a voice behind me, in what must have been coincidence.

I stood there with my chin on my chest, my eyes closed and a string of drool from my bottom lip to my hospital gown until I received a less-than-polite poke in the shoulder blade. I looked down at my feet and raised my eyebrows as if to say, "Well, what are you waiting for?"

My feet stared back at me with glassy eyes. They began to move one step at a time, slowly, steadily, being careful not to falter, lest I topple forward and reduce the entire line of my fellow patients to a pile of dominoes. Panic was not an issue with me. I could have been on fire myself and I wouldn't have lost what I considered a great deal of composure at the time.

Each patient was being handed a yellow plastic poncho to protect us from the ever-present downpour. Gripes and outrage sounded off all around me. I was just happy to be able to remain vertical. Whether this was a drill or an actual life-or-death situation, my anesthetized shuffle was slowing the pace of our exodus. When I finally arrived at what appeared to be a lunch lady passing out the inclement-weather gear, she shoved a folded poncho toward my chest, where it promptly fell to the ground. I looked at it on the floor but didn't dare attempt to bend over to retrieve it. She looked me in the eyes and then pulled a penlight out of her breast pocket for closer inspection. Not a lunch lady, I guess.

"Oh, Lordy," she said, crouching down to pick up the garment.

"OK, Honey, put your arms up in the air," she told me kindly, as if I was one of her grandchildren.

As hard as I tried, I could only muster a sigh and a deadpan stare. She stuck the poncho under my arm and pushed me in the direction of the door. So much for kindly. Time was apparently of the essence.

The alarm continued to blare as I carefully descended each level of the grated-metal stairway toward the paved ground below. "Descended" might be exaggerating. I actually stood there, tightly gripping the railing as every patient and most of the staff squeezed past me. I guessed they were in a real hurry to line up on the predetermined painted line on the concrete below, maybe to see the fire trucks and emergency vehicles I could hear arriving at the front of the building.

A handful of the female patients were laughing at me through the chain-link fence that separated our recreation area from theirs. I wanted to cuss them out, but I knew any distraction from my footing would have me tumbling ass-over-face down the stairs.

At first I was incensed. That pack of cunts! Each and every one of them was more repulsive than the last. I eyeballed them, one at a time, plotting my revenge. Ghetto-trash cocksuckers! The offenders were three large black women in their late teens or early twenties, pointing at and nudging each other. I could tell they had developed calluses over the years, thick shields of resentment that would deflect any vulgarities I might shout at them. Retaliation was useless. I suppose they needed to capitalize on any opportunity to mock one of the few people in the world worse off than them. At least they had each other.

Standing next to them, wincing with every screech that came from their obnoxious gaggle, was a woman about my mother's age. My heart fell down the stairs in front of me. She was holding her notebook, her AA Big Book and several pamphlets in her crossed arms under her poncho. It had never occurred to me or anyone else marching out of that place to save anything but our cigarettes. "This is my last chance" might as well have been written across her face in permanent marker.

Next to her, a Latino pre-op was having its hair braided by a speed-freak-thin train wreck. They didn't seem to care or notice the rain at all. It warmed my heart a little to think that the detox center was forward-thinking enough to put the tranny in with the female population. Unfortunately, experience then took a shit on my warm heart: They probably learned where to put the junkie tranny the hard way.

"Charlie!" shouted Romeo from the line of yellow ponchos in front of me, "Stop starin' at all the bitches! You holdin' up the proceedins'!"

I heard heavy steps bounding down the stairs behind me. Nurse Paul put his hands on my shoulders and helped me down the rest of the way.

"Try and keep it together, would ya?" he hissed in my ear. "People are going to start asking questions."

"What the fuck…did you give me?" I managed to spit out.

"Thorazine," he said. "It's not like we have a big selection. Try not to make a scene, for Christ's sake."

I was transfixed by the new faces, the chance to consume and digest some fresh bodies. My dormitory of crack-soaked miscreants had long since passed their expiration date. I drank these in, dissecting them all as fast as I could. All the way down the line, from the loud and boisterous to the prideful and stupid to the scared and frail to the confused, beaten and thrown away, and then, lastly, to a translucent, soaking-wet Raggedy Ann doll of a girl I knew all too well.

Holy shit.

She had to have recognized me. I was unshaven and drugged beyond belief, but it was nothing she hadn't seen before. No wonder she hadn't answered the phone.

Patient name: *Carrie Noelle Finch*
Date: *10/23/90*
Age: *21*
Address: *906 E. John Street #311, Sea WA*
Occupation: *musician*

Marital status: Single
Ethnicity: White
Substance: more please
Level of recent use: Too ~~fucking~~ much
Treatment history: I went to church once.
Main motivating force at time of admit:
I need help.

"You have to let me do it one day," she panted. A drop of sweat fell off the tip of her nose and landed on my chin.

"You have to promise me."

Most of our arguments ended this way. Discussion would turn into debate, debate to dispute, and on through shouting, screaming and combat, until the end, here in bed with her naked on top of me. It seemed like the most natural thing in the world.

Another drop of sweat landed on my lips.

"Will you help me, Charlie…someday?" she whispered, her face inches away from mine.

It was useless to recite my list of reasons why this was absurd. When I told her she was smart and beautiful and talented, she only heard AM static coming out of my mouth. When I told her she was just sick and there was help, therapy, people she could talk to, she just stared at the floor and shook her head. When I reminded her she had a record to make and tour dates and people who depended on her, she just sighed.

In preschool and kindergarten she had been Captain of the Kissergirls, a group of girls who ran around chasing the boys, threatening to kiss them — of course they never did, that would be gross — but she was the ringleader. At age 4 she had a revelation: She spontaneously entertained the clientele of a local pizza restaurant by can-can dancing on the "stage" where you could go watch the guys making the pizzas. She'd run back to her table between songs, grab a bite of pizza and a sip of Coke, and race back to dance more when the music started again.

There were ballet classes and violin lessons, at all of which she excelled. "Mary Had a Little Lambs" turned into classical pieces and into first chairs. There were the afternoons she locked herself in her room and practiced for hours and hours, taking only the occasional break for *Bewitched* or *I Dream of Jeannie*. Soon came private tutors and symphony camp and recitals for the Governor. Everyone loved the little redheaded pixie that played with the fire of a classically trained veteran.

In extravagant hotel ballrooms, her father beamed with pride to see his blossoming teenage daughter in the fancy dresses he bought for her, and her mother drank with gusto once she realized that for the first time, all eyes were not on her.

Carrie's pitch was perfect and her unbridled enthusiasm obvious, but it was her aggressive stance — her feet a little farther apart than her teachers would have liked — and the way she attacked a piece of music that turned heads.

She stood on her tiptoes as her bow carved the last perfect note out of the air. Then she exhaled, just before the room burst into applause. She smiled and curtsied.

Older gentlemen in black ties and their wives in ridiculously bejeweled dresses that hung on them like suits of armor lined up to shower her with praise. Gangly young men with thick glasses stumbled over each other for an opportunity to talk with her. Photographers from the local papers took her by the arm and placed her between the Commissioner of something-or-other and the Chairman of some-other-thing for a quick shot for their entertainment sections. The best parts were the smile on her dad's face and the stolen sips of champagne when the adults weren't looking.

Despite all this, despite all the attention, despite being the Belle of the Ball, if you caught a glimpse of her between polite conversations, you would see a reticent, faraway look in her eyes and an insincere smile on her lips. None of it really registered, none of it mattered to her. You see, all she had ever really wanted since she was a little girl was to die.

Maybe it was because "we" could only ever be temporary that I could tell her things I'd never told anyone in my life. There would be no fairytale ending to this story, she guaranteed me that. No wedding, no kids, no meandering through Sears shopping for cookery, those things were for other people. She was dreamy in so many ways, but the perfect dream for a guy who was rotting away with intimacy issues like me.

She knew after orgasm I'd be rendered docile and agreeable to suggestion. I nodded my head like I had dozens of times before, but this time it wasn't good enough for her. She loved to hear the words.

"Say it," she ordered.

I spoke slowly and deliberately.

"I promise I'll let you kill yourself someday…but not today."

"Not today, baby," she said, kissing me on the forehead.

She rolled off of me, reached for the nightstand and lit a cigarette.

"If I don't know that I can do it someday, I'll just go fucking crazy," she said, taking a drag and handing the cigarette to me.

"I understand," I lied.

"No, you don't. But it's sweet of you to try."

She called it "the distortion." When the white noise crept up her spine and surrounded her skull. When her lips couldn't even crack a smile and her aching body lay paralyzed on the couch. No cycles of the moon, no harsh words from a stranger, no sequence of events would set it off. It just snuck up on her unannounced, always. It grabbed her by the back of her neck and whispered sinister words in her ear. It put a sharp object to her throat to show her that it meant business. Sometimes when it got bad, she would walk into our room with her arms extended, and I would pop a Roky Erickson tape into the ghetto blaster, switch off the light and hold her. She would bury her head in my chest and sob uncontrollably. We would sway slowly to the music.

I call your name in the midnight

But you don't hear me at all

She would never let me see her cry, but my shirt would be soaked with tears.

I love you so dearly and nearly

But you don't love me at all

I felt dumb and helpless in its presence. If I told her I loved her and everything would be all right, she'd simply reach up and put her hand over my mouth. I'd uselessly comb her matted hair with my fingers and hum along with the songs, waiting for it to pass. Sometimes it took ten minutes, sometimes an hour.

From the bed I could see the enormous Ziploc bag of pills I had been shaking at her as I screamed accusations only a half-hour earlier. She had worked a dozen doctors for tranquilizers, sedatives and anti-psychotics, hoarding them for her "someday." Contrary to my nature, I didn't see the mouth-watering potential of getting loaded but instead saw only her cold, calculated passport out.

I stared at the ceiling. She turned on her side and took the cigarette from my lips.

"Darlin', if you knew what this was like you'd want this for me."

I couldn't argue with her anymore.

"…But if it makes you feel any better, I don't feel like killing myself when your dick is inside me."

I raised my arm to wave across the yard, but could only manage to open and close my hand like a 3-year-old. She just stood there, staring straight ahead. One of the attendants walked up to her and helped her put her hood up to keep the rain at bay.

She must have seen me.

10. PICTURES (LEAVE YOUR BODY BEHIND)

I sat in an office in front of a huge oak desk and waited for Ms. Monahan, and waited, and waited. I tried to keep my head up. I forced my eyes open comically wide, hoping they'd co-operate. What I needed was a cigarette and a bed, not to be lectured to by the walls, traditions, steps, promises, shut up.

The place stunk of dusty old Bibles and potpourri. I cursed the chair for offering me a hundred different slouches, not one of them sustainable in anything resembling comfort.

They had pulled me out of the line when we were cleared to come back into the building. Apparently, I was in time for one of their bi-monthly fire drills. Just my luck. The kindly gentlemen who dragged me down the hall — I guess I wasn't moving fast enough for them — tossed me into this pernicious chair and explained to me that I was to see the boss lady.

This boss lady waited to arrive until the very instant I found sleep. Desk, garbage can, armrest, seat. Foot, foot, head, back. These were the contact points I was using to approximate "vertical" when she arrived. Handsomely dressed, older, accompanied by my dear friend, Nurse Paul, at her heels. He was carrying an armful of file folders at her bidding. I wiped the drool from my chin, sat up straight and pulled myself together.

"Charles, you're using. I'm not going to bother to ask *if* you're using because you wouldn't benefit from another opportunity to lie."

"You can call me Charlie, Ms. Monahan."

"You remember Mr. Difranco. He did your intake," she said, suddenly remembering introductions were in order.

"Sure, Nurse Paul and I go way back."

"And my name is Tricia Monahan, I am the executive director here."

"Charmed, I'm sure." I was trying my best for some sort of camaraderie, but it was not working for me.

"The reason you are here today is that we take any violations of our rules very seriously. We need to maintain a safe environment for our patients and staff and we simply cannot have someone in your… condition wandering around upsetting everyone."

Nurse Paul and I nodded in unison.

"What have you taken, Charlie?" she asked point-blank.

I let my head fall to my chest for my confession. "Bongo. Wacky taffy. A little TNT."

She nodded her head as if I wasn't speaking complete gibberish and took careful notes. Nurse Paul sat there sweating like a pig.

"Where did you get the drugs?"

Again I gave her my best hangdog. "I keistered 'em. You might actually want to give everyone here a pretty good inspection. It's… pretty bad. Rampant."

She scribbled down a few more notes.

"Since you've been forthright and cooperative with me, I'm going to allow you to start the program over again. Nurse Paul will have to give you an evaluation, and you'll be segregated from the other patients until you're a little more presentable."

"Program?" I sputtered. Did she really think this counted as a *program*? "My apologies, Miss, uh…" She stared at me blankly. "Miss Lady, but all we do is drink Kool-Aid and watch *Alf*."

"No, all *you* do is drink Kool-Aid and watch *Alf.* The rest of the patients attend lectures, 12-step workshops and group therapy sessions. Your counselor says you don't participate in anything."

"I have a counselor?!?" I was genuinely shocked.

It was a familiar feeling, the feeling that everyone in life had received a user's manual and I had missed it. Not that I would have read it, but still, it would have been nice to get one.

Nurse Paul handed me a clipboard and yet another tiny, eraserless pencil to write my life story with. Do these things even exist outside of the treatment world?

"May I have a grown-up pencil, please?"

Ms. Monahan handed me a full-sized pencil from her desk and explained to me that this opportunity for do-overs was a privilege and not a right and that I should be grateful to her and Nurse Paul for seeing the inherent good in me and God bless America and drive a Chevy truck and stand up straight and don't cuss and be respectful of your elders and kiss butterflies and I'm sure a fuckload of other good stuff. I wasn't paying attention. I was filling out my names, addresses and Social Security numbers for the hundredth fuckin' time. Just before signing the bottom of the page I once again read the ironically sobering small print. "The below signed agrees to stay under the care of the King County Detox Center for a minimum of 72 hours." Wait a minute.

"Excuse me," I interrupted their discussion of my treatment plan, "What day is it?"

They both scurried after me as I beat a line up the hallway toward Reception. It was a pretty good pace for someone still polluted with whatever horse-tranquilizing chemicals Nurse Paul had put in me.

"You realize, of course, that you're leaving against medical advice," wheezed Nurse Paul, trying to keep up.

"Martin, my good man!" I called the second he was in earshot, "Be a dear and fetch my stuff would ya? I'm going home."

Ms. Monahan was doing her best to reason with one side of my skull while Nurse Paul pleaded with the other. I'm sure they both presented slick and professional arguments, but I only heard white noise.

"Please!" I pounded my fist on the counter. "Your work here is done!"

"Please see that Mr. Hyatt is escorted off the property after he signs for his personal effects," ordered Ms. Monahan.

OK, so I behaved poorly, I admit that. But in a way I was grateful for the break. The way a man who's been bitten by a werewolf appreciates being locked in a windowless room on the full moon. The way a child molester appreciates solitary confinement in prison. It was a gift, really, the gift of carefree days of recreational drug use again. You know, when it was fun. Needles? I was done with them. I was done with heroin. I was in control again, and it felt good. Is all this talk extravagant at 10 o'clock in the morning when you're completely loaded on Thorazine? We think not.

"I want to thank you, Martin, I really enjoyed our talks."

"Talk. We had one talk," he said.

"Well, thanks for the cigarettes then, I really appreciate it."

"You really should get to some meetings, you know," Martin offered as we neared the edge of the parking lot. "It's the only way you're gonna stay clean."

"I'll be fine. I just needed a break, you know. I'm not going back to it. I don't wanna be a slave anymore."

"I'll see you next time, Charlie."

"Fuck you, Martin."

"Have a nice day."

Dear Charlie,
Where are you? It feels like you've
been gone for days. I called your
work, I called the hospital.
I'm NOT calling the PIGS.
There's no one here to tell me no.
I've gone someplace safe.
XX

The note was stuck to the bathroom mirror with a piece of clear tape. It made me feel a new kind of terrible, something I hadn't known before. I ripped it off the mirror and threw it in the trash. Then I saw her fury when she would inevitably find it, and fished it out to start smoothing it. It drove her insane whenever I would throw away birthday cards and Christmas cards from my parents moments after reading. I placed her note on the kitchen counter face down, not before seeing the familiar double X at the bottom. She always signed the end of letters and notes with two Xs. A kiss goodbye, and one in case we die.

We didn't have a mentor or a shaman advisor or a life coach or a priest. We had no shining example of anything from which to seek wisdom or garner advice. There had been no fedora-wearing shady character that led us naively down an alley and into a downward spiral of loose morals and drug addiction. There wasn't even a charismatic cult leader to steal us from our cribs and ply us with hippie-love philosophy that would somehow manage to have us selling our bodies on the street to make his Rolls-Royce payments. Hell, we didn't even fall into the wrong crowd. We were starting our own wrong crowd.

There was only her and me.

"Me and her," as she would point out if she were standing behind me now.

We sat with the medical textbooks she had checked out of the library, a bag of 10cc syringes we picked up at a drive-thru drugstore window on Indian School Road and a half-gram of cocaine. We didn't know where to get heroin, but cocaine was everywhere. It was the '80s after all.

This was it. We had worked our way up the drug food chain and were ready for the big leagues. We had drunk, smoked, swallowed and snorted everything we could get our hands on and now we were hell-bent on actively participating in some truly destructive behavior.

We may not have been born bad, but we were exploring all of our options with reckless abandon.

This was one in a succession of dilapidated rental houses I lived in with various local punk rockers. My room wasn't really a room but a large storage closet off the den. I ran an extension cord from the kitchen for power. The lack of windows never bothered me, but the lack of air conditioning in the upcoming Phoenix summer would be unbearable. These living situations rarely lasted for more than a year before we'd get the boot and move on to devalue the next unsuspecting landlord's investment property.

She had purchased rubber tubing and alcohol swabs from a medical supply store. The ease with which we acquired all the ingredients was a little disturbing. We spread all the utensils between us on my bed and stared at them with equal parts nervousness and excitement. We were children on the first day of school. I brought the phone into my room and put it at the foot of the bed.

"I'll go first, that way if I have a seizure or keel over dead or something you can call 911," I said, hoping not to sound like a pussy.

"Hmmm," she said, biting her lip in contemplation, "having my boyfriend die in front of me will probably emotionally scar my young mind," she laughed, "I say we do it at the same time."

Fair enough. In moments like these, practicality goes out the window. As seemingly well-prepared as we were, there were still so many questions — almost all of which involved the amount to use and the odds of dying. There were a few things we had learned from movies, dog-eared paperbacks and urban legend. The rest we did straight out of the book.

I bent the spoon to avoid spillage. She filled the syringe full with room-temperature water. In retrospect, that was too much. The coke dissolved instantly, no cooking required. We learned that from Burroughs. We dropped a tiny piece of cotton ball into the solution. She saw that in an Al Pacino movie. I drew half the clear liquid into my needle and half into hers. We held the syringes up to the light, needle pointed up, and tapped them so that the air bubbles would rise to the top. We pushed the plungers to remove the excess air until the contents of the barrel were solid liquid. That we had seen in every made-for-TV hospital drama broadcast since the beginning of time.

She had done her research and written copious notes on the pages she had bookmarked. According to a chart in the anatomy section of ASU's Procedural Medicine Manual, the most obvious point of entry was called the median cubital vein. She began to read aloud from a textbook entitled Fundamentals of Nursing.

"Tie the tourniquet. It should be placed approximately 4 inches above the puncture site, with the ends pointing upwards, away from the site. Oftentimes a tourniquet must be applied before a person is able to determine the puncture site." I wrapped the rubber tubing around my bicep.

"Insert the needle with the bevel facing up. The needle should be at a 15- to 20-degree angle and be placed in the same direction as the vein," she read from page 105 — the "Taking a Blood Sample" chapter from the Practical Nurse's Guide.

There was a slight sting as she poked the needle into my virginal vein. She drew back the plunger and a plume of blood filled the chamber. I cradled the needle on my fingers as she repeated the procedure on herself. Her arms were thin and delicate; no bulging veins disrupted the smoothness of her skin. And although her skin was so translucent you could all but see her circulatory system beneath, finding a vein with the tip of a needle was still pretty much a guessing game.

"Shit!" No blood registered on her first attempt; she had missed.

A shimmer of light off the needle hanging out of my arm caught my eye as a droplet of blood ran down my elbow. She jabbed herself again.

"Shit, shit, shit." Again, nothing.

"Here, let me," I offered.

"No. I got it. I got it." She was bold and stubborn and it had been two weeks and a day since her 16th birthday and she was quite capable of sticking her own goddamn needle in her own goddamn vein, thank you very much.

She took a deep breath and dug the point into her arm. I heard the front door open and boots stomping around in the kitchen. Then, the blaring of piano, drums and saxophones; someone had dropped the needle on the turntable in the living room. Undaunted, Carrie probed under her skin. A single, frustrated teardrop ran down her cheek. Still balancing the syringe stuck in my vein, I checked the door to make sure it was locked; this was not something you wanted your roommates to walk in on. When I turned back around she proudly stuck out her arm to display the dark red cloud that had filled up her syringe.

"Ready?" she asked sweetly.

She leaned over and kissed me.

"Ready," I said, my heart pounding.

"Kiss me again," she whispered, "in case we die."

11. MINE MINE MIND

There was no rhyme or reason to what might disappear from her mind's retention. She could recall, in exquisite detail, the Saturday-afternoon drives with her father when she was 6, but couldn't remember if or what we had had for breakfast that morning.

They would drive up I-10 with the windows down, the wind blowing and classical music on the radio. She sat there, pretty as a picture, a metal Partridge Family lunch box containing costume jewelry, loose rhinestones and other shiny trinkets on her lap. It was her treasure chest, and she didn't go anywhere without it.

"Daddy, will you tell me the poems?"

He would smile and switch off the radio. She had gotten a poetry book every birthday and every Christmas for as far back as she could remember. Her favorite was Edward Gorey, but her father memorized all of them because he was the smartest and most handsome man in the world. This was their special time. He worked late into the night on weekdays, so on Saturdays he would swoop her up into his arms and they would escape the sarcastic tongue of her mother and the brutish ways of her brother to run errands.

"Which one first, kitten?" he would ask.

"Two Dead Boys!"

One bright morning in the middle of the night, two dead boys got up to fight.

Back to back they faced each other, drew their swords and shot one another.

A deaf policeman heard the noise and came and shot the two dead boys."

She laughed and laughed and kicked her tiny feet, which barely hung over the edge of the huge Impala passenger seat.

"Now do 'The Wuggly Ump!' Now do 'The Insect God!'" She would squeal, but her father would have to make her wait.

"Later, kitten," he'd say. "You have a fan to attend."

He'd pull into the liquor-store parking lot. Jack, behind the counter, had a new toy for her almost every week — a baseball with the Budweiser logo on it, a giant inflatable Seagram's bottle taller than she was.

"There's a princess," Jack said from behind the register.

She ran behind the counter and leapt into his arms. Jack's ever-present cigarette would come out only to kiss her on the forehead. Yeah, he smelt real bad, but that's the kind of thing you put up with for presents.

He'd put her back on the ground and tell her to close her eyes. She'd comply...kind of. She'd *mostly* close her eyes, squinting hard so that through the tiny slits between her eyelids she could see whatever he was pulling out from beneath the counter.

"Ta-da!" he announced with great fanfare.

Her eyes popped open and she was handed a big wooden shoe from Holland. It was painted with windmills, flowers and dancing Dutch girls in those blue-and-white dresses, windmills and lots of flowers. Across the top in sparkly red letters were the words "St. Pauli Girl."

"I love it!" she hollered, and she ran around the store waving it over her head as her father purchased his bottle of Scotch and several bottles of Blue Nun for his wife.

The doctors wanted Carrie to come in to discuss her options. Unbeknownst to her, I had called them. In spite of the new pharmaceutical regimen and her weekly counseling sessions, her darkness was a more frequent visitor than ever.

The manic ups with their sleepless days on end, hair-trigger mood swings and constant scribbling in journals I could handle; it was the downs that got to me. Sometimes, if I employed enough sweet words, she would sit up in bed so I could comb her hair or help her change from one ratty nightgown into another. On a good day I would walk down to the video store and rent copies of *The Burns and Allen Show* and *The Honeymooners* and she would smoke cigarettes and stare at the black and white. Mostly she would just roll over and stare at the wall.

"My grandmother called it the blues," she mumbled, shuffling to the bathroom. They were the first words she had spoken in three days. When the door closed behind her I looked up the doctor's number in her phone book and snuck down to the lobby of our building to use the pay phone.

They said the procedure was extremely invasive. They also said the benefits definitely outweighed the drawbacks. Although she would be the youngest person they had ever performed it on at the hospital, they all agreed she qualified as a candidate for a new Washington state program that would cover all the costs. There would be paperwork to fill out, of course.

They handed her a manila folder and a pen. She immediately opened it up and started signing her name at the bottom of each page.

"Hold up now," I said, trying to slow down the proceedings, "What exactly are these drawbacks you speak of?"

"Well," said the doctor who seemed to be the most enthusiastic about the newly proposed treatment, "Short-term and possible long-term memory loss does occur, there will be disorientation and general confusion, muscle aches, but like I said, the benefits for someone with Carrie's…umm, issues have been quite positive."

"Memories aren't so goddamn precious anyway," she muttered under her breath as she signed everything they put in front of her.

The doctors insisted I use the proper term, ECT, or Electroconvulsive Therapy, during the consultation. You could tell they were uncomfortable with the barbaric images of *One Flew Over The Cuckoo's Nest*-type torture that the words "shock treatment" conjured up. They corrected me many times. They gently explained that they would put her to sleep with a combination of barbiturates and muscle relaxers before electrically inducing seizures. It was these seizures that would cast the demons from her brain and make it all better. This would happen twice a week for three weeks, then monthly follow-ups depending on how she responded. I was playing the part of her concerned brother, since they preferred a relative to pick up the patients afterward.

She wasn't allowed to drink or eat anything after midnight the night before. Nor was she allowed to wear perfume or lotion of any kind. This, I assumed, was so the subject wouldn't burst into flames. She was also told to wear loose-fitting clothing and no makeup.

She never acted scared, but the first time we strolled into the waiting room she clung tightly to my arm with both hands. She dug her nails so deeply into my arm that they punctured the skin. She seemed excited. We spoke in hushed tones in the corner while we waited for the doctor to see her.

"What was the bride of Frankenstein's name?" she whispered.

"Ummm, I don't think she had a name."

"Well, that's sexist," she snickered, in mock dismay.

"The monster didn't have a name either," I said. "Besides, it was written by a woman."

"Are you trying to tell me that Mary Shelley wrote *Bride of Frankenstein* too?"

"There was a *Bride of Frankenstein II?* I never saw that one" I said, blank-faced.

"Shut up, I'm tryin' to come up with a cute nickname for me while I'm getting shocked — which is your fucking job, by the way."

"Look, these people think I'm your brother. I don't think having cutesy pet names for each other is such a great idea."

"These people think what I need is to have 400 volts of electricity jammed up my ass. I don't think me flirtin' with my brother is gonna surprise them at all."

"Actually, dear," I countered, "If you would have bothered to look at the brochures they sent home with us, you would know that they apply the electrodes to your forehead, not your butthole."

She smirked. "I thought I told you to shut up."

Just then the door from the office burst open.

"Carrie Finch?" announced a tall, handsome East Indian man in a white lab coat.

Her fingernails immediately found my arm again.

We both stood up at the same time and moved toward the door.

"Don't you fuckin' leave me alone in there," she said, pulling me close to her by the arm of my jean jacket.

I already knew from the consultation that I wouldn't be allowed to stay during the procedure, but I lied anyway.

"Never," I whispered back.

The doctor introduced himself as Dr. Kenneth Bhaskaran. He had a very kind manner and put us both as much at ease as one can be considering the circumstances. We walked into the room, over-lit and windowless, and Carrie hopped up on the gurney like a kid hopping onto Grandpa's lap. Three nurses immediately surrounded her, taking pulses and temperatures and blood pressures and such. A Muzak version of *Close To You* by the Carpenters was playing unusually loud. She smiled and made idle chitchat with the nurses as the doctor and a technician made adjustments to the ECT machine and I watched from the corner of the room. When the anesthesiologist approached, Carrie quickly rolled up the sleeve of her right arm, the arm with the least amount of evidence of self-inflicted intravenous drug use. As they lay her back on the gurney, she reached out her hand to me. I gave it a squeeze and mouthed the words "I love you," which she never saw because her eyes were focused on my fingers.

The doctor walked over to me and cleared his throat. I locked eyes with him.

"Not yet...please?" I said under my breath.

The doctor gave me a nod and stood back, tapping his pencil against his clipboard.

The room was abuzz with highly professional people speaking highly technical jargon, double-checking this, double-checking that. A nurse dabbed ointment to Carrie's temples. The doctor waited a few heartbeats for the drone to settle down.

"OK, Ms. Finch? Are you comfortable?"

"I make a nice living." It was an old joke that always made her laugh.

It was as simple as that. They inserted her mouth guard, released the sedative into her IV bag and in a matter of moments, she was out. The doctor checked a few more things on his paperwork, then pointed at me with his pencil, then pointed at the door.

The journals Carrie had kept since she was a young girl became a living, breathing, integral part of her day-to-day life now that her memory had turned to Swiss cheese. They were her constant companion. The current one was never out of arm's reach until each page was filled with her bold, black-inked lettering, after which it would join the stack in the corner next to our bed until the pile would topple under its own weight. Only then would they be moved to the closet, and the entire process would start all over again.

She had been scribbling lyrics, poems and upcoming show dates in them forever, but now she was jotting down brief descriptions of the neighbors' dogs and which were nice or which were little assholes. She would write down notes about the people she met and where, in hopes of avoiding an embarrassing blank face that would approach her. She had to rely more and more on me to help keep her life in order. I was to be considered unreliable at best.

I never snooped, not once. Out of respect, yes, but mostly out of fear of learning what she really thought of me. *She* would reveal to me what she wanted to; *these* contained her heart undressed. A sharp word or even a hint as to how I may have hurt her, I couldn't bear. I loved her madly. Unfortunately, I did everything madly.

On vinyl she was fearless, the records became her confessionals. She opened up and bled in the recording studio as if no one would ever hear her purge. She admitted it all, heartbreak, anger, insanity, with the voice of a freight-train engine. Outside the studio, she was all smirks, razor-sharp quips and snappy comebacks. Inside, when she stepped up to the microphone to sing — and maybe I was the only one who saw it — just before she took a breath, her smile would disappear, her eyes would roll back and she would invite the madness in. At that point the engineer in her headphones was just another voice amongst many in her head.

On stage she was dangerous. A hip-shakin', damned and defiant piece of candy inviting you to put your hands on her. Some fools even would, and they tasted steel-toed motorcycle boots, the headstock of her guitar, and the floor as a result. In tight black jeans and a torn T-shirt, smoking a cigarette, swallowing every drink passed up to her, taking every pill put in her hand, awash in feedback, while the kids waited, the press waited, her band waited for her to give the order to open fire. "One, two, three, four!"

She was an incorrigible brat acting out in a celebration of bad for a five-dollar cover charge. She was brains wrapped in sex. She was the conduit for your clenched fist and your throat screamed raw at your father, your boyfriend, your asshole boss. She was the amalgamation of every pot-smokin', Van Halen T-shirt-wearin' bitch in every parking lot of every high school who had cultivated that don't-you-dare-talk-to-me stare that had you frozen in your tracks. You loved her because you didn't have a choice in the matter.

She was the fulfillment of the direction her father had unwittingly dictated to her years ago as she sat on his lap in the La-Z-Boy recliner while he read aloud the words of Henry Wadsworth Longfellow. She was that little girl who had a little curl right in the middle of her forehead; and when she was good, she was very, very good, but when she was bad, she was horrid.

In the morning you would return to your job at Minnie's or hustling produce down at the market or miss your early class altogether. I would carry her up the stairs to our apartment, where we would fall down, spent and feeling no pain, at least for a little while.

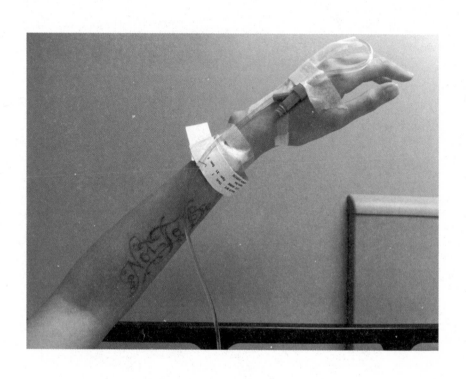

12. YOU DON'T LOVE ME YET

Dealers aren't exactly the most customer-service-oriented merchants. They take their sweet-ass time, because what are you going to do? Something besides stand there and wait for them?

For two hours, I had been trying to look as inconspicuous as possible while I waited at the usual place on 1st and Pike. The corner of 1st and Pike Streets in Seattle is the only place I can think of where you look suspicious if you're not enthralled by obnoxiously loud fish peddlers throwing huge chunks of salmon at one another. If you looked like me, it was worse. The fact that this was a hot spot for the local narcotic trade was not lost on anyone — not the police, not the merchants and certainly not, hardly the least of my worries, my boss. Although he seemed willing enough to overlook my showing up for my shift a little tipsy, he would definitely frown upon this type of endeavor. My most frequently used meeting place with José was located very conveniently, and most dangerously, kitty-corner to the Champ Arcade. But a downtown without drug activity is like a day without sunshine, right?

Forgetting about the two hours the second I saw the little fucker, I thanked him profusely when he finally showed up. After the traditional open-palmed handshake/cash transaction, we pretended to chat about sports or whatever the fuck people talk about. He casually scanned up and down the street for any authority figures, and then with a hearty farewell handshake he slipped me a small nugget of black tar heroin in a tiny red balloon and made his way into the market. I pretended to thumb through a magazine at the corner newspaper stand for a minute before I left, in case anyone was watching. When I was sure I looked completely calm and relaxed, I took off running at a dead heat for home. My lungs were on fire and my heart pounded in my throat as I rushed up the hill on Denny. I have *got* to quit smoking, I remember thinking. These things are going to kill me.

She was standing in front of the bathroom mirror putting on lipstick when I walked in the door. In the weeks since leaving the detox center, neither one of us could have been classified as a "success story," but the abuse part of our collective substance abuse had been tempered considerably.

"How do I look, babe?" she asked, smoothing the front of her dress with the palms of her hands, down her abdomen to the top of her thighs. It was a shimmery, tight red number with black fishnets.

"You look," I searched for the right words. "Fuck."

"I look fuck?" she asked, raising an eyebrow.

I had forgotten that we were going out that night. We were going to the Vogue to see Cat Butt and Swallow. I had no idea it would be a dressy affair. I quickly rummaged though the closet looking for my one good black Western shirt and my marry-'em-or-bury-'em suit jacket. I changed and went to the bathroom to brush my teeth and run my fingers through my hair, but not before quietly slipping a syringe and a spoon into my back pocket. This was — I knew at the time — me lying to her.

I had already made the promise that things would be different. There is a moment, early on in every junkie's using career, when a tiny ray of sanity shines into his psyche to tell him that he may, just may, have a problem here. I had had my moment, and after hours and hours of intense negotiations with myself, I had come to what seemed to be a perfectly acceptable compromise, an oh-so-grandiose and foolproof solution. I would only do dope "on the weekends."

I swear I wasn't lying when I said it. It's just that here we were.

I was not a stranger to being out of control. I actually enjoyed the indestructible feeling of it as it surged though my body. But this was different. My body acted of its own accord, calmly disinterested in my pleas for reason. I was genuinely touched by Carrie's gesture. She had gone out of her way to make this night special for some reason. But I didn't deserve it. I was simply going to do what I was doing to do and nobody could stop me.

I turned on the faucet to cover the sound. I dropped a small piece of dope and a few drops of water in the spoon. I held my lighter under the spoon and watched the heroin dissolve, all the while repeating to myself, I'm not going to do this, I'm not going to do this. I rolled up my sleeve; I'm not going to do this. I wrapped my belt around my bicep and tightened it; I'm not going to do this. I pushed down on the plunger of the needle with my thumb. I'm not going to do this. I was merely a spectator now, systematically destroying this life, that girl and whatever else came across my path. I no longer had a say in the matter.

The analgesic bliss coursed though my system, doing its best to dismantle what was left of shame and regret. As the toothbrush hit the sides of my molars and created its comforting locomotive cadence, I thought I heard the sound of a violin. I stopped and spit equal parts blood and toothpaste foam into the sink. The sound was too loud to be the television, too beautiful to be coming from our shitty ghetto blaster. I walked out to our room with the toothbrush still hanging out of my mouth.

She stood with her back to me. When she tossed her hair back to reach for some higher notes, I was mesmerized. Her dress so tight she stood pigeon-toed in those shiny black pumps, the reading lamp next to the bed producing a halo that outlined her entire body. I didn't dare move for fear of disrupting the picture. The slightest noise might bring her back to this awful apartment, this selfish boyfriend, this situation void of grace and beauty. It might send the instrument back into its case and back under the bed where it had been gathering dust since we moved in.

The last note vibrated into silence. I heard a car drive by our building. I heard her exhale though her nose.

"That was incredible. What was that called?" I quietly asked from the doorway.

"I dunno, just made it up," she said, setting the violin back in its case.

"Well, it was beautiful." I avoided eye contact.

"Thank you very much, dollface," she said, reaching for her purple faux fur coat. "Now let's get the fuck out of here. I need a drink."

We walked arm-in-arm into the darkened club to catcalls and whistles. The doorman waved Carrie through but I had to pay the cover, of course. He was not a fan of mine. He checked my ID every time I came into the place in hopes of one day being able to turn me away for forgetting it. Carrie waited for me as he gave my license the stink-eye. We made our way to the bar.

"The usual, darlin'," she called out to the bartender.

"One can of Rainier with a straw, so as to not fuck up your lipstick," he shouted over the crowd.

"Yes, please…and a shot of Bushmills for my handsome escort."

Monty and his lovely wife, Shawna, were the proprietors and bartenders at the Vogue, which was just a couple of blocks from my work. It was quite convenient, considering that at midnight I was going to turn into a smut-selling pumpkin.

They had live music on Tuesday nights, but most of the time it was a gothy dance club. The place was packed with scenesters and musicians.

Whether they were being supportive or they were just bored was anyone's guess. It was a nascent cavalcade of stars; a few years' time would bring a lot of them platinum records and world tours. For now, though, they were pooling their change to buy cheap pitchers of shitty beer.

Monty was lovely in his own right. Without a doubt he was wearing the shortest mini-skirt in the place and a matching brown leather halter-top as if he had just walked off the screen of a Russ Meyer film. He leaned over the bar on his massive bodybuilder arms and gave Carrie's dress the once-over.

"I could never pull that number off," he sighed. "My shoulders are just too broad."

He may have been the only cross-dresser in America who never got lip from anyone, ever. You wouldn't want to be seen getting your ass kicked by someone wearing a mini-skirt and go-go boots, now would you?

The first shot of whiskey was still burning in my throat when Cat Butt hit the stage. They looked like a gang of bikers had fucked a bunch of Dr. Seuss characters and forced their children to form a rock 'n' roll band. They sounded like the MC5 had never learned to tune their instruments. Christ, it was unbearable. I turned my shot glass upside down on the bar and Monty replaced it with a full one. I pulled a five-dollar bill out of my wallet and he waved it off. There were a few perks to having a girlfriend who was an up-and-coming underground rock phenom.

Carrie and I had a system worked out for shows and parties. She stuck close to me and I ran interference. She had confided in only her closest friends about her memory loss, and even then blamed the condition on her medication, not divulging anything about her shock treatments. That information was known to only her father and me. To avoid an awkward situation, if someone approached us whom she didn't recognize, she would lightly step on my toe.

"Jonathan Poneman, as I live and breathe," I announced with great fanfare.

She would throw her arms around the subject in question and another successful social interaction would be complete. Usually the music would be so loud that few words were necessary. Later, if circumstances and volume allowed, I would whisper a brief description in her ear so she could charm the unrecognized subject with her bawdy repartee.

"He's one of the guys who runs the record company. You like him," I told her when I got the chance.

I wondered if the day would ever come when she looked at *my* face with puzzlement, if I would ever have to roll over in bed some morning and reintroduce myself.

I leaned on the bar and watched her hold court in the back of the room, sipping beer through her straw and gesturing wildly with her hands. She spun around several times, showing off her dress and striking mock super-model poses for her cohorts.

My friend Lenny came up and handed me a shot of whiskey and yelled something made inaudible in the sonic stench of the band.

"What?!"

"I said, happy anniversary, asshole!"

I looked over at Carrie, who winked and raised her drink to me. Odds were that this was just a ploy to get free drinks and an excuse to get all dolled up, but we had broken up and gotten back together so many times you'd need an abacus to keep track, so I suppose it could have been. Either way, the drinks were flowing and she was smiling so I was pleased.

I closed my eyes and tossed back the whiskey. When I shook it off and opened them again, Kelly Thompson was standing in front of me with two shot glasses in her hands and a cigarette in her lips. Shit.

"You got a light, killer?" she asked, running her index finger down the lapel of my jacket.

I struck a match and lit her Marlboro.

"I understand we're celebrating," she shouted, handing me one of the shots.

89

"Yeah, something like that."

"Well, congratulations!" We touched glasses and knocked 'em back.

She kissed me on the lips and disappeared into the crowd.

That could've gone much, much worse, I thought to myself, wiping her lipstick from the corner of my mouth. I checked my watch — quarter to twelve. I walked over to Carrie's gang and interrupted her dissertation by kissing her goodbye and sticking a twenty-dollar bill in her bra strap.

"What's that for?" she asked.

"Cab fare, baby."

She pulled me in for another kiss and I strolled out the door, hammered and ready for another night's work.

13. DON'T SHAKE ME LUCIFER

Last call is a lot of things to a lot of people. Some will never hear it without being shocked that they had more than "just one" after-work beer. Some will greet it with a respectful nod to the impartial timekeeper who tells them their chasing of the night is over, and the night won again. And then there are those for whom last call is the final renunciation of an evening's worth of carnal invitations, when even the boldest of them slump into the street alone. Their glasses have been taken, their jukeboxes unplugged and buckets of grey water and mops have been rolled out onto their dance floors as the bouncers kindly instruct them to get the fuck out. Festivity devolves into failure quickly for these souls at this time of night, and not one of them is immune to its sting. It matters not your ethnicity, your sexual orientation or your economic standing. You are alone, again, and it is the witching hour.

Some fumble with their keys to get into cars they know they're in no condition to drive, some make their way to the Dog House and wallow in greasy diner food. The never-say-die types stick quarters into street-corner pay phones and place unsolicited calls to lady friends too smart to pick up.

When all these fail them, they head to the last place on earth that will have them, my place.

They shuffle in stinking of booze and cigarettes and misfortune, too defeated even to harass the dancers leaving at the end of their shifts. Fates sealed, they head straight for the backroom video booths that will serve as their partners for the evening. Gone is the teenage wonderment with masturbation. Gone are the piss-and-vinegar-filled, cum-filled bodies thumbing though the latest issue of *Circus* magazine trying to decide which one of the Wilson sisters of Heart to jerk off to. Gone is the hope that told you nothing was out of reach, emboldening you to choose both.

The luster of that once-divine act of self-love is gone now, as booze-thick fingers pull the last two dollars they have out of their wallets for a handful of sticky tokens. A sad anger — maybe it's an angry sadness — coats them like a second skin as they click through the video selections looking for that actress that resembles the girl they had a crush on in high school, or that dirty act their wives swore they liked before they were married, or that *ménage à trois* they never seemed to have the resources to pull off in real life. They lean inebriated against the wall and have at themselves, the Hail Mary of self-gratification.

Oh, but at that hour the Champ Arcade was so much more than just an unhappy masturbation emporium; it was also *the* late-night gay cruising spot. But not "gay" as in "young and fabulous" like they had on Capitol Hill. This was for the bad men, the ones who had no intention of giving up their self-loathing for fear of dampening their orgasms; trench-coated men with skin conditions and breath you'd have to send to a lab to determine which part of it made you hurl. They'd converge on the poorly lit maze with higher aspirations, in search of exotic innominate action. Needless to say, the blending of these two cultures — combined with the occasional mobilized and rambunctious bachelor party or a nosy tourist or two — could result in a highly volatile situation.

That night was an average one in our filthy little house of horrors. I was behind the counter settling up with the last of the dancers, a natural blonde beauty who went by the name Sam. She had no outward manifestations of what inner demons she possessed, but I'm sure they existed; she did, after all, work there. I had a crush on Sam. There were two things about her I found intriguing; while the other girls would sit in their private booths doing their nails or fixing their hair or giving come-hither looks to prospective customers, Sam would read, ignoring the approaching clientele until they knocked on her window. That, and her complete and utter disinterest in me, I found absolutely irresistible.

"'Night," she said, throwing her bag over her shoulder as her awaiting taxi honked outside. It was downright flirty.

I was watching the swing of her skirt as she walked out the door when Wayne called me over. He had been receiving a disturbing string of complaints from some of our regulars. Some clever little deviant had managed to sneak in some tools and had drilled a goddamned glory hole.

For anyone not familiar with this practice, a glory hole is a hole that has been cut into a wall or partition for the sole purpose of having your cock sucked anonymously. Contestant number one stands in one of the altered booths and waits for the neighboring booth to be occupied. Once a guest has entered the opposing booth, contestant number one slides his dick though the hole in hopes that contestant number two will suck him off. Afterwards, I assume there is some reciprocation and everyone is a winner.

Glory holes are found in public places frequented by homosexuals, perverts and, of course, truck drivers. Although I have always understood and even admired the daredevil aspect of this, I can't say our regular customers appreciated an uninvited penis intruding on their adult entertainment time.

Now, I sincerely didn't give a crap about how folks get their kicks and I was fortunate to work in the only business in the world where the customer is always wrong, but I wasn't about to spend my entire night listening to figurative pricks complain about being intruded upon by literal ones. As the graveyard manager, I was tasked with only two objectives: One, not to bother the boss, and two, that the building still be standing when he showed up in the morning, preferably not engulfed in flames. The boss sure as hell didn't like getting phone calls at two in the morning. So, while to me it was merely an inconvenience, to the guys getting ambushed by this rogue cock, it was an emergency and an outrage. It was time to take charge of the situation. Although I hate to act, think, or in any way imitate a police officer, it seemed our only option would be some sort of sting operation.

"An old-fashioned stake-out is what we need to do," I announced to my trusty staff that night. It was my best attempt at inviting everyone along for the fun, but although Wayne and I may have stared at each other for a brief moment in some Mexican standoff of wills, I knew this would be my mission. I did make a buck-fifty more an hour, after all, and with that came responsibility. I held out my hand and Wayne gave me a fistful of tokens and, with a snicker, wished me luck.

"If I'm not back in an hour, call the SWAT team," I mumbled.

As I pulled back the red velvet curtain, footsteps quickly scuttled off as customers scattered like cockroaches from my authority. As my eyes became accustomed to the blackness, I heard whispers and the closing of doors. Since we did regular rounds every hour to check for any drunken shenanigans, I did a deliberate lap around the backroom before quietly doubling back to search out the tarnished stall.

I crept along taking mental note of the occupied booths and various styles of footwear; this may come in handy later in capturing the offender, I thought. The crowd seemed to favor dress shoes, with work boots coming in a close second. Even on the muggiest of nights, no one dared wear flip-flops in here.

Since the ladies were gone for the night, the curtains were drawn on all the private booths except one. There was an empty pack of Camels, a purple vibrator, a small bottle of Astroglide and a well-worn edition of *Crime and Punishment.* Oh Sam, I could practically smell the vanilla and the stale cigarette smoke though the glass. I wondered briefly how I was gonna broach the subject of Russian literature with a girl who rarely strung together six words in a row.

I opened a few of the vacant booth doors until I found the one with the freshly drilled waist-high hole and settled in, trying not to think about the sticky floor. I jammed the tokens in the slot and the walls came alive, washed in blue television light. I lit a cigarette and switched through the channels looking for something that might attract the perpetrator. After much consideration I chose a nautical themed stud-fest titled "In The Navy 4" and waited.

Fortunately — or unfortunately — that wouldn't be long. The design of the booths offered easy confirmation of their occupancy from the hallway, but the partitions separating you from your neighbors were floor-to-ceiling barriers. The only way to ascertain inhabitancy was by listening. The grunting, moaning image on my screen was an overhead shot of a five-man circle jerk — pretty high production value for gay porn, now that I think of it — and was so loud I wasn't sure if I had heard the door to the next booth close. I reached for the volume knob, which immediately came off in my hand. Piece of shit! I leaned closer to the wall to hear better. Perhaps I should clear my throat or whistle, I thought. If I had known Morse code I would have tapped out "I WANT TO SUCK YOUR COCK" on the wall. Odds were pretty good he was a sailor. I heard the mystery man plug his tokens into the slot; he selected the same movie as me and played it at an even louder volume. Stereo hand jobs, incredible.

I was becoming anxious. An eternity had gone by. What if I wasn't his type? How would he know? Wasn't the whole point of this exercise to be nameless, faceless and above all, anonymous? Coincidentally, I was even wearing my snakeskin cowboy boots that night. They were the gayest article of clothing I owned, for cryin' out loud! Just as I was beginning to feel hostile and yes, a little bit hurt by the whole situation, the head of the culprit's hard cock started inching its way through the hole. Success!

My excitement at having caught him in the act quickly dimmed as I realized I had a new question: What now? In my fevered pursuit of justice, I hadn't really thought things out. If I were a cop perhaps I would have cuffed him, but without the authority to arrest — or the desire to grab hold of the evidence — I needed another plan fast.

Luckily, in the late-night porn business, having an effective way of defending yourself is essential. Taking on unruly drunks who are looking for a fight at 3 o'clock in the morning loses its allure quickly when you're getting paid $7.50 an hour and have no health insurance. The weapon of choice is the foot-long black metal Maglite, but that can be bloody; and if you happen to miss your foe's cranium, you then have to deal with an even angrier drunken asshole than you did in the first place. I preferred pepper spray or Mace. Nothing calms down an 8-foot, 400-pound ape man in the middle of a PCP-induced psychotic episode like a face full of tear gas. Makes 'em downright amiable.

I checked my pockets: Between the switchblade in the left and a small canister of pepper spray in the right, I assumed my gentleman caller would prefer the latter. Were there flaws in my plan? Possibly, but when one is staring into the eye of a loaded penis, one's decision-making skills may be a tad bit unreliable. For instance, I hadn't considered the size of the enclosure in which I was confined. I had really only thought about what would be the equivalent of getting your mouth washed out with soap. I took aim at the mystery dick with the canister and lightly tapped the button.

Apparently, it hurt a great deal. The cock disappeared instantly. An ungodly howl, a thud and some frantic thrashing came from the booth before the door swung open and the assailant galloped, as fast as a man can with his pants still around his ankles, for the front door, holding his crotch with one hand and pushing customers out of his way with the other.

Meanwhile, the booth I was in instantaneously turned into a gas chamber. "Fuck!" I coughed, and stumbled out to the front, blind and choking. Wayne led me to the restroom so I could wash the burning out of my eyes.

"Did you get a look at him?" I asked between hacks.

"Yeah, fortysomething white guy, balding, screaming," he laughed, describing about 90 percent of our customers.

When I got back to the counter, there was an expensive Italian loafer and a set of keys.

"What's this?"

"Your boyfriend dropped them on his way out the door," Wayne shot back from behind the register.

I twirled the keys around my index finger and imagined him coming back to ask for them. For the first time, I actually felt sorry for the poor bastard.

14. I AM HER HERO,
SHE IS MY HEROIN

"I used to work at one of those."

"Really?"

"Yep."

"You worked at a peep show? Um…"

It is at this point in a conversation when I can sense the gears in her head beginning to turn.

"So…did you have to…uh…" They work up, I guess, only half the gumption required to ask the question, because, with few exceptions, their voices trail off before they can ever quite complete their query.

"So…did you have to…you know…mop the ummm…you know?"

"Mop up the cum?!?" I respond indignantly and slightly louder than necessary. It's an old habit. Plus, I like the awkward pauses, nervous chuckles and the gathering and sequestering of children to a safer area of whatever barbecue or social gathering we might be attending.

"No, we had a janitor for that."

I couldn't tell you what his last name was. The boss didn't know it. Otis was a strictly cash-under-the-table type of character. A 71-year-old black gentleman unable to make it on his Social Security, he was spending his golden years pushing a mop at the Champ Arcade. He was a throwback to another time — the product of a small town, or perhaps of Seattle when Seattle itself was a small town. He was a widower with a handful of kids and an even bigger handful of grandkids living with him. Maybe all that family eased the loss of his wife, with her rose garden, her love of a sunny day and the oatmeal she made him every morning. He was dapper even in his work overalls. He had a smile, a tip of his hat and a "How do you do?" for anyone, shaking hands with everyone in the neighborhood on his way into work like he was running for mayor. He had my vote.

Otis, like so many countless, underpaid men and women of this world who mop up shit and blood from the floors of hospitals and slaughterhouses, did his unspeakable work with grace and dignity. It's interesting how what some Eastern religions consider the essence of life itself, upon hitting the floor of the back room, becomes a vile and untouchable deposit. And so it comes to pass that when someone these days asks me, "Who mopped up the cum?" my answer is a man who was my better in every way. Otis was who they had in mind when they came up with that whole "the meek shall inherit the earth" thing, so imagine my surprise to learn he was actually the only truly evil genius I had ever met.

At 5:30 a.m. there were two cars left, Wayne Newton's and the perpetrator's. I went out to the parking lot every hour or so after the "unpleasantness" to check on my unfortunate paramour's vehicle. It was a cream-colored late-model Volvo. I tried the key. Poor son of a bitch; I pictured him hobbling out to his car, realizing he left his key, then crawling off to a corner to die. Maybe he hopped in a cab. Maybe he was looking through the scope of a rifle at me right now from a downtown apartment or shitty hotel room. Maybe he was tipping a Jack Daniel's bottle to his lips trying to figure out if I was the one who maimed him. Maybe he was shifting the ice pack on his burned dick, still wearing the one shoe and a wet sock.

Was I getting soft? Wayne was *still* laughing his ass off. But he didn't hear the howls and shrieks up close and personal like I did. I didn't exactly want to apologize, but I at least wanted the guy to know I wasn't the kind of person who went around pepper spraying genitals willy-nilly. I didn't suppose a handshake and a promise not to do that again would suffice. The only comfort I could offer was to not have his car towed. Maybe he could take solace in knowing that the worst night of his life was behind him now and the rest of us only had ours to look forward to.

Otis always appeared promptly at 6 a.m., after stopping at the McDonald's around the corner for hash browns and coffee. One morning a couple of weeks before, an acquaintance of mine named Zach had stopped by to say hello after a particularly rough night out. Or so I thought. It wasn't unusual for this kind of thing to happen; after all, everyone knew I worked there, and it was an interesting place to drop by if you happened to be stumbling around wasted in the wee hours. I say "acquaintance" as opposed to "friend" because my only interaction with him was in matters of drugs. When I saw him enter, disheveled and weary, I smiled and waited for his half-hearted inquiry as to how my night was going. Instead, he asked if Otis was there.

"Otis? How do you know Otis?" I asked, puzzled.

"He's a friend of the family."

The words replayed in my head as he spotted Otis and darted over to the janitor's closet to talk with him. Now, I knew that Otis was a friend to everyone he met. And I knew that given the choice between talking with me and talking to Otis, most people would have had a more enjoyable time talking to Otis. However, the quickness with which Zach had answered, the immediate stare at nothing as the words fell out of his mouth, befuddled me. I watched them shake hands and have their quick conversation, scratching my head like mad. Why did Zach just give me a junkie's lie?

I cornered Otis as soon as Zach bolted out the door. "What was that all about?"

"Aww…whatcha talking about, Charlie?" he asked sheepishly.

"I know that guy, Otis. The two of you were not discussing your favorite window cleaners."

"No…no, sir." Uncomfortably for me, Otis seemed genuinely scared.

"It's not my intention to get you busted, my friend; I'm interested in what you have to sell."

Otis produced a handful of little colored balloons and we both smiled. I didn't suppose I'd be waiting for hours at 1ˢᵗ and Pike ever again.

His trade was fentanyl citrate, a synthetic painkiller prescribed to terminally ill patients or those with chronic pain. It was later discovered to cause spinal cord problems, but I didn't know that at the time and wouldn't have paid attention to a surgeon general's warning any fucking way.

Because it was in white powder form, it was easier to call it "China White" on the street. Most dope in Seattle — the entire West Coast for that matter — was black tar from Mexico. Since junkies aren't big on conversation when buying drugs on 1ˢᵗ and Pike, Otis simply let them believe they were getting a rare taste of the Far East. The effect was virtually the same, so no harm done.

In the Volvo, I smoked a cigarette and watched him conduct his early morning business. He took his post at the bus stop and was greeted by one client after another with hearty handshakes or hugs, followed by a quick and pleasant "Good Day" before the next customer stepped up to embrace their old friend. That was all he needed. There was never a mob scene to attract attention, just a steady stream of friends. And these were not just the tattooed, leather-clad hipsters I was accustomed to. Housewives and businessmen were thrown in, creating an oddly normal-looking cross-section of the community. Who knew there was a drug underground beneath the drug underground I knew so well?

It was the perfect cover. His work was so ghastly, so unpleasant, that most people would just as soon pretend he didn't exist than to put much thought into what purpose his vocation served. No cop would have wanted to follow him around while he did his repugnant duties and no one would ever drop a dime on him because he was the kindest man in the world; it would've been a goddamn crime against humanity. Here was a man the respectable people willfully ignored and the rabble strove to protect as if his goodness were the only holy thing left in the universe. This, friend, is a cover.

"Did I ever tell you about the time I shined Ray Charles' shoes outside the Black and Tan Club in 1947?" he would ask me, offering me a peppermint candy. I'd take the candy, never even suspecting he was commenting on my breath.

"He was a good man. He gave me a dollar for a shoeshine that cost a quarter, then he tipped me a dollar too! It was the craziest thing I ever saw. Tell the truth now, did I ever tell you that story?"

Dozens of times, Otis. But I always let you tell it.

"It's goddamned embarrassing," Wayne blurted out, pounding his fist on the bar. It was 8:15 in the morning and we were at the Turf.

The Turf was the shithole's shithole, packed every morning with hard-hats and fishmongers, assholes and dogfuckers, alcoholics one and all. It was offensive everywhere you turned, from its wretched fluorescent lighting to its modern country-music-ridden jukebox to the ancient foulness of a hundred thousand Marlboros that had been smoked there. But the drinks were cheap and it opened at 6:00, the only bar downtown that was open for a beer after work.

"Nickel-and-dime, penny-ante bullshit!" Wayne spat, crushing his Budweiser can. He was talking about our scam. We had thought we had a pretty good thing going until Otis revealed how bush league our criminality really was.

Our cash register stand was a good 12 inches above the retail floor. We towered over our customers, making them uncomfortable, making them feel unwelcome, inferior. When the average Joe walked into a porn store he was already nervous, and we made him feel even more so. Yes, we tended to have less shoplifting this way, but the unexpected and more important benefit was that customers were often in such a hurry to get the hell out of there they would leave their change behind.

It could have been just a random bit of change, but after discovering this phenomenon we learned to move slowly behind the register, to speak loudly, to make the buying experience all the more embarrassing. We never had to worry about nurturing return customers. As the out-of-town businessman raced for the door, leaving behind his $22.45 in change, we'd dutifully do our part by muttering "Hey buddy, don't forget your..." under our breath. They rarely came back for it. They would never use a credit card for fear of a paper trail the Mrs. could find. Add this up over the night and we were pocketing an extra $100 each. Tack onto that the occasional kickback from pointing a regular in the direction of a dancer who might be willing to give him a hand job in the parking lot, and we thought we were doing pretty well. Now, with an even conservative estimate putting over two grand in Otis's pocket every day before he took his morning coffee, we felt ambushed.

I watched Wayne drain another beer in silence, feeling a shit-ton of dread and responsibility for what he was thinking. I had to act quickly.

"Maybe we should go into business with him," I pretended to think out loud. Wayne's ears perked up and a slow smile crept across his thick face. I knew I had derailed his visions of extortion or strong-arm robbery, if only temporarily.

15. I AM (IN SATAN'S ALL PERFECT LOVE)

"I'm kidnapping you."

I looked up from the bus bench to see Kelly Thompson hanging out the passenger window of a midnight blue Mustang that had just screeched to a halt in front of me, her forefinger aimed at my head and her thumb cocked. I stood up and slowly put my hands in the air.

"Don't try anything stupid or I'll blow your dick off," she said, moving her sights from my skull to my crotch.

"You won't get much in ransom for me in that condition."

She stepped out of the car and pulled back the seat, motioning me in with her spurious weapon. I climbed in back. It had been a long, bizarre night already. Why not see what else it had in store?

A pretty brunette snuck a look at me in the rearview mirror from behind the steering wheel. I pushed a small mountain of clothes onto the seat next to me to make room. They were all inappropriately high-end blouses and slacks, all with the price tags still on them. My abductors were fashionable — don't get me wrong — but these ensembles didn't seem to be their style.

"You ladies been up to no good?" I asked, thumbing through their obviously ill-gotten plunder.

"If you must know, we're on a crime spree," Kelly said. They both broke into laughter.

"Who's your friend?" I asked, leaning over the seat to get a better look at the driver.

By way of introducing herself, I believe she said, "Shut up and give us your cigarettes or you'll be hogtied in the trunk."

I pulled out a smoke and tossed the rest of my pack between the front seats.

"There you go, ladies. I don't want any trouble."

They were evil bookends; green eyes made even more stunning by the overcast day and blood red lipstick, matching black leather jackets, freckled pale skin. Not twins, but a diabolical gang of two. Stereophonic heart-breaking, home-wrecking soul-crushers.

I put on my aviators as I sat back and watched the rest of the world go to work. I favored this life lived upside-down, it was true, and that's why I hated to think of something changing, not coming back. Day was my night, yes; bad was my good and wrong, my right. But upside-down has a continual need to perpetuate. Behind my shades, I was teetering on the edge of going further, off-balance and unsure, yet relaxing in the gray area between a bad situation and a good time as if it were the most natural thing in the world.

In the plus column, illicit drug use was more than likely going to happen. Also in the plus column was the very plausible chance of absurdly naughty sex with Kelly, and let us not dismiss the possibility that this absurd naughtiness might include sex with Kelly *and* her nameless accomplice. In the minus column was the risk of arrest. I needed to weigh my options. I could easily bolt out the door at the next red light and leave all that potential madness behind. I'd only be out a dozen cigarettes or so.

"Pull over here," Kelly ordered from the passenger seat, putting us half a block from a large department store in the middle of downtown.

"You get cash for the Nordstrom's stuff while I make out with our hostage." She handed me a container of breath mints and my fate was sealed.

As her minion rummaged through the trunk of the car gathering stolen merchandise to return, Kelly slid into the back seat with me. I put my arm around her waist and pulled her in close. It was exhilarating to kiss semistrange lips again, far less savage than our last encounter but exciting just the same. We groped like teenagers at a drive-in movie while dozens of downtown shoppers passed the car. When things got heated up pretty good, she took my hand out of her jeans and put it around her neck.

"Tighter," she ordered, but by then there was too much testosterone surging through me to be told what to do. I ignored her.

"Please," she whispered, and playful turned to ugly just like that.

I considered it. Maybe it was resentment at being told what to do, maybe I was just insulted by her giving me a breath mint first, but this time it was easy. Her whole body trembled as I clenched her throat. I felt her heart pounding in her esophagus. I thought of the bike cop who might happen by and see some creep choking a young lady with a car full of verboten women's wear. I held my face close to hers and heard a guttural moan escape from her chest. She shook violently and pushed me off her, red-faced and gasping.

She pulled a flask from her inside jacket pocket and took a swig before passing it to me. She kissed me on the cheek and said thank you. I wasn't up on the latest open-container laws but I pondered just how much more fucking illegal activity we could shove into the back seat of a late-'70s Mustang anyway. Just when I was sure this situation had reached the point of diminishing returns, the driver's-side door opened. Our comrade had returned.

Kelly hastily crawled between the front seats and they secretively counted their loot. I didn't care how much money they got, I was just happy it was over so I could get the hell out of there.

"OK, now I'll take back the Bon Marché stuff and *you* make out with the hostage." Maybe I heard a chorus of angels singing, maybe I didn't.

The brunette produced a matching flask from the inside pocket of her jacket and they toasted their as-yet successful criminal racket. They exited the car simultaneously; Kelly gathering the clothes from the back seat while the other one slid in next to me.

"So, do you have a name?" I asked.

"I'm not going to kiss you, dummy."

We sat staring straight ahead with our hands folded in our laps.

"So, what do I call you while you're not kissing me?"

"My name is Rose," she finally volunteered.

"What's a nice girl like you doin'..."

"Listen, jerk," she interrupted my cutesy small talk, "I'm not making out with you and when we get back to Kelly's place I'm gonna fake-pass-out on the couch so don't you fuckin' dare try anything. I don't care what that little psychopath has planned."

"Nice to meet you, darlin'."

A thousand awkward minutes later we saw Kelly a block away, walking quickly toward the car, and Rose threw her arms around my shoulders.

"Make it look good," she hissed.

I sunk my teeth into her neck; she punched me in the rib cage.

"I thought we were goin' for authenticity," I laughed.

She shoved her tongue in my mouth until Miss Thompson flung open the passenger door.

"Oh good, I was hoping you two would get along."

"Mmmm, he's delicious," Rose testified convincingly.

We strolled into the Nitelite and pulled up three stools at the bar. To refer to the place as a dive would have been generous. I ordered up three Budweisers and a pack of Camels from the barkeep. The girls supplemented their beers with tequila shots. We were waiting for a friend of Kelly's. I leaned with my back to the bar and watched the door for what I assumed would be a stealthy, mustachioed, russet-skinned man by the name Miguel or José. All the drug dealers in this part of town were named Miguel or José. They didn't even care which name you called 'em.

An hour had passed. The girls were dancing with all the old-man regulars to Sinatra songs on the jukebox and knocking back more free drinks than I bothered to count. I had six balloons of Otis's dope in my pocket, but if I could practice just a tiny bit more patience I would reap the rewards of the ladies' misdemeanors and save mine for myself. Besides, at this point I really was a hostage; I couldn't let either one of those girls drive in the shape they were in. Alcohol was no longer a thrill for me; it was something to do while waiting for drugs. I wondered if the cumulative hours I had waited for dealers in my life had added up to a year yet.

"Dance with us, Charlie," shouted a pleasantly intoxicated Rose from across the makeshift dance floor. It was without a doubt the most lively lunchtime crowd the bar had ever seen.

She thrust her hand forward in dainty ballroom fashion and approached me with grand poise and grace. I believe she was even smiling. As I reluctantly reached out my hand for hers, she tripped over the leg of a chair and fell face first on the floor. Bam!

"What did you do?" shouted the old man waltzing with Kelly.

I reached down to help her up.

"You motherfucker," spat the lady behind the bar.

Kelly shot me a wink before yanking open the collar of her shirt. "And he tried to choke me in his car!"

Just as the entire scene was about to deteriorate into chaos, a portly Mexican in a cowboy hat walked through the front door.

Ah, Kelly Thompson. You were a real hoot in retrospect.

In the rearview mirror I could see Rose tilting her head back and using a leftover stolen blouse to stop the bleeding. The cut on her forehead was minor, but that nose was gonna gush awhile. Kelly was riding shotgun next to me, pulling open the cellophane wrapper of the chunk of black tar heroin she had just purchased and smelling it like it was a fine cabernet.

My parallel parking job was less than stellar, but we were finally marching up the stairs to Kelly's apartment. Her place was nice, much nicer than I thought it would be. Maybe I was expecting more of a medieval torture chamber or an Old West brothel vibe, not tastefully painted chartreuse walls and oriental paper lanterns. The kitchenette was stocked with expensive glassware and smelled of dark coffee and sesame oil. It didn't turn out to be the case, but it's a testament to Kelly that I just assumed we had broken into someone else's place.

It was almost one in the afternoon, which meant it was way past my bedtime. I collapsed on the bed and decided to rest my eyes while the girls did whatever it is girls do from the time they get somewhere to the time they manage to get something accomplished.

I heard drawers opening and closing. I heard a needle drop on side 1 of a scratched-up copy of *Here Are the Sonics* on the stereo. I felt the full weight of Kelly as she sat on me, straddling my hips. I opened my eyes to see her in her panties and a Mudhoney T-shirt, her thighs squeezing my ribcage.

"Wake up, slave boy," she managed to say with a syringe between her teeth.

She was using my chest as her operating table, laying out the spoon, dope and Q-tips but wisely choosing to put the glass of water on the nightstand. Rose cozied up to us from the other side of the bed. She lay on her side in a white terrycloth robe with her head propped on her hand, watching the master at work. I watched Kelly's face, the tip of her tongue sticking out of the corner of her mouth as she held the lighter under the spoon. She put the spoon down on my shirt and giggled, knowing damn well it would burn me. I exhaled slowly though my nose and bit my lip so that I would neither spill the dope everywhere nor give her the satisfaction of seeing me react to the pain.

"Who's first?" she asked.

"Oh, me, me, me, me," Rose squealed, sitting up and sticking out her arm.

She laughed as she remembered that she still had a bloody piece of Kleenex in of one of her nostrils and pulled it out. She looped the sash of her robe around her arm several times and pulled it tight, then licked her lips, waiting for the stab from Nurse Thompson.

When the needle was extracted from her arm, Rose leaned forward and gave her a deep kiss. Kelly ground her crotch into my hips. Rose gripped Kelly's lower lip in her teeth for several heartbeats, then stretched out on the bed next to me and drifted off to heaven, fake or not.

I watched as Kelly held the needle up to the light and squeezed the air bubble out. She unraveled the sash from Rose's arm and wrapped it around her own, gripping it with her teeth to hold it tight as her fingers ran the length of her forearm to find a suitable vein. She tilted her head to one side and made a circular motion as the narcotic warmth encompassed her.

"Goddamn," she moaned.

Last, and I like to think not least, was me. She delicately removed the syringe from my arm and licked the single drop of blood from the puncture wound.

Goddamn, indeed.

She got up, peeled off her T-shirt and tossed it at my head before sauntering off to the kitchen. I closed my eyes and all of my deceit, deception and self-loathing faded into blackness. I was at home in this ugliness. I was comfortable with being wrong.

"You're gonna like this," she said, walking back in. She had her panties in one hand, a ginger ale in the other.

She sat on the edge of the bed and unbuttoned my jeans.

"It's a little trick I learned in junior high. I dunno why ginger ale works best, but it does," she explained to me while her cold fingers reached into my boxers.

I looked to my right and caught a split second of eye contact with Rose before her eyelids slammed shut.

16. YOU'RE GONNA MISS ME

There was a coaster from Ernie Steele's stuck to the refrigerator door when I came home from work that morning; she'd scrawled words across it in red marker:

starve myself today
then a tight green velvet dress
for master and slave
XX

I smiled to myself as I poured a glass half full of tap water and grabbed a spoon from the drawer. She had pre-programmed the coffee maker to start at 8:45 a.m. and the whole apartment smelled like heaven. I poured myself a cup.

I crept into the room quietly so as not to wake her. I moved a pile of clothes from the chair I got her on her last birthday. It was a hard plastic monstrosity in the shape of a giant black hand that was infinitely uncomfortable but she loved it. I put it on lay-away and chipped away at the payments $20 at a time. I picked it up only an hour before her surprise party at the Comet and carried it, much to the driver's chagrin, on the bus from Fremont to Capitol Hill. I had no wrapping paper or greeting card, of course. I lifted it over my head and carried it though the crowded bar and plopped it down next to her at our regular table. She almost burst into tears. I had never seen her so happy.

I took off my jacket, sat in the giant palm and pulled the needles and balloons of dope out of my inside pocket, the one we referred to as the shoplifting pocket. Carrie's eyes sprung open when I flicked open my Zippo and placed it under the spoon.

"Whatcha doin'?" she said in the sweet little girl voice that was strictly reserved for early mornings.

"Cooking breakfast, my dear."

Yes, I was curious about Otis's fentanyl, but there was also the fringe benefit of a diversion tactic. I had been missing in action for a couple of days, and I was rolling the dice on the potency of her recent shock treatments.

Over the past few months I had been granted immunity for more than a few nasty things I had said or done just because the events had simply disappeared. Her mind's own redacted inventory of my misdeeds and malevolence was working in my favor.

Most men brought home roses and candy as a peace offering. I brought narcotics.

Carrie gave a long, erotic stretch, then extended her arm in my direction.

I unbuckled my belt and knelt by the bed. I fashioned the belt into a noose, slipped it over her forearm and tightened it below her bicep. She squeezed her fist and the veins on her pale arm rose to the occasion. I bent

113

down and touched my target with the tip of my tongue and playfully kissed it.

I mustered my best doctoral bedside manner and whispered, "You might feel a little prick."

"OK, but can we do the drugs first?" she shot back in the same whisper.

I deserved that for throwing such a slow pitch to a wiseass of her caliber.

The brand-new needle slid easily into her favorite vein. I pulled back the plunger and a crimson cloud overpowered the clear liquid in the syringe, then I slowly pressed it back down, sending the solution into her system. She gave a little cough, closed her eyes and smiled her approval. Sweet Christ, she had me. What I really wanted most in this life was to scoop this dream up in my arms and protect her from the cold world outside. Her face was so angelic and innocent before the ever-present red lipstick and mascara was applied, the ghost of the little girl she once was, before she had forsaken the violin for a Les Paul junior, before she had met me.

Seven years earlier and another world away, I was lighting a cigarette behind a little rock 'n' roll dive called the Mason Jar in Phoenix, Arizona. I had kicked open the back door hoping to escape the sweltering heat of the bar, and had succeeded in stumbling into the sweltering heat of the parking lot. She was sitting on the hood of a car with her friends, drinking beers from paper bags. I was somewhere past eight dollars deep into the bar's nightly drink special, Franco's seventy-five-cent Kamikazes. Somewhere, muffled by the cinder-block walls of the Mason Jar, Tex & the Horseheads were falling apart on stage, scoring our fateful meeting.

We had been exchanging glances the entire show. Full of vodka gallantry and lacking anything that resembled a smooth opening line, I simply walked up, leaned into her and kissed her deeply. She didn't seem to object, and her friends scurried away. She grabbed my shirt, held me at arm's length long enough to take a long pull on her beer can, tossed it over her shoulder and pulled me back in for more.

I fell into her groping hands, her piranha kisses, her gravelly purr and powder white skin. She was a mad, fire engine red-dyed mess shooting in every direction, a hurricane of youthful indiscretion on the hood of an enormous and dusty Oldsmobile, a car I assumed was hers until a patron from the neighboring bar ventured out long enough to offer a suggestion:

"You faggots wanna get the fuck off of my car?"

I grabbed her by the waist, tossed her over my shoulder and carried her though the back door of the Mason Jar. Her friends were waiting patiently at a table. My friends had ditched me. Big spender that I was, I bought a round of specials for the table and thus gained acceptance into their tribe.

The six of us piled into a Pinto. A Big Gulp cup full of Jack Daniel's and just enough Coke to call it a Jack and Coke was passed around. *Wild Gift* blasted out of the one working speaker. With the window rolled down and all 90 pounds of Miss Finch sitting in my lap, I drifted off into oblivion.

"Get up!" a woman's voice shrieked.

For a split second I thought I was in my own room. The walls were covered with the same Xeroxed mementos of Social Distortion, X and JFA shows; the air was filled with the same novena-candle wax and dirty-sock smell; the floor was piled with the same masses of records and books.

"Get your ass up!" There was a sudden sharp pain in my ribs.

I sat up. I was on a futon on the floor with Carrie lying next to me and a hysterical middle-aged women standing over us, kicking me for a second time square in the back.

"Motherfuck!" I screamed, trying to get a look at my attacker and my situation.

Carrie sat up next to me, startled, and covered herself with the sheet. Beautiful. Even more so when she leaned forward and defiantly kissed me.

"Good morning, monster," she said sweetly.

I was still drunk, but mainly I was in shock. The screaming woman

115

standing over me was reacting as if I were a demon who had fallen from the sky to terrorize a toddler, instead of just a guy her daughter brought home from a bar. I needed her shrill screech to cease. I needed her to relax. I needed her to take a breath. But mostly I need her to realize that I was just another red-blooded, alcohol-fueled 21-year-old dumbass and her *precious* angel was…

"She's 14 years old!" the woman screamed.

Shit.

"Lady, please," I begged, "in spite of appearances I am a gentleman, but if you kick me one more time I swear to God I will…"

Her shoe landed viciously in my ribs again. She had called my bluff.

I turned to Carrie and mouthed the words, "I'm sorry."

"Kiss me again," she said, putting her head on my shoulder.

At the risk of getting this harpy's sensible shoe jammed up my ass, I obliged her.

I *was* fully dressed, after all. "No harm, no foul" should have been the call. But Mom didn't quite see it that way. I was escorted unceremoniously to the front door by the ear.

"Don't you ever show your goddamn face around here again!" she spat at me.

I sat on the curb and put my socks and boots on. It was already 100 degrees out. I had no shades, no money, and no idea where I was. It looked like an upscale neighborhood, which meant I was far from home. I put my head between my knees and dry-heaved. An old pick-up truck with several lawn mowers in the back drove by slowly; one of the cowboys inside yelled "Devo!" and pitched a full Coors can at me. Luckily he was a poor marksman, because I wouldn't have had the wherewithal to duck.

As I was getting up to leave I heard the screen door slam behind me. Carrie ran out and handed me a folded scrap of paper. Then, without a word, she turned and darted back inside.

I looked down both sides of the street. It couldn't have mattered less. "Fuck it," I mumbled, and started walking. When I was out of eyeshot of the house I opened the note. In blue ink on lined notebook paper she wrote, "I have a crush on you." I folded the piece of paper and stuck it in my wallet, where it remains to this day.

I turned my attention back to the spoon and sucked the remaining dope into the needle, taking it with me to the bathroom to shower off another lovely evening at the porn shop. I kicked off my boots and stripped off my jacket and shirt while the water warmed up. I stood over the sink and hit a vein in my wrist. I stretched and waited for the blissful cloud of dope to cover me.

Carrie's alarm clock began to buzz.

BRAAP, BRAAP, BRAAP, BRAAP

I exhaled as the warmth hit my lungs.

BRAAP, BRAAP, BRAAP

I watched in the mirror as my pupils all but disappeared.

BRAAP BRAAP

I gripped the sink to steady myself. This was strong shit, much stronger than I usually got.

BRAAP, BRAAP, BRAAP

My legs turned to jelly beneath me. My vision went dark. Panic set in.

"Carrie? You ok?" I called though the door.

BRAAP, BRAAP, BRAAP

I tore open the door. Her skin was blue. Not "blue," as in some medical parlance for "pale." It was blue like a fucking blue thing. Like a crayon or a can of paint. She hadn't moved, her eyes were closed, her mouth agape. Carrie! I pulled the sheet back. She was cold. Fuck! Fuck!

She had finally gotten her wish.

BRAAP, BRAAP, BRAAP

117

Baby, say something. Please, please, please say something.

I looked at the phone on the desk. No. I promised, I promised, I promised.

BRAAP, BRAAP, BRAAP

Above the desk was a framed photo that had appeared in *Melody Maker* magazine the year before. In it, she was topless, holding her breasts with her hands, the words "do not resuscitate" written across her chest in marker.

BRAAP, BRAAP, BRAAP

I threw the alarm clock against the wall.

I dropped to my knees by the bed and took her in my arms. I felt her wrist for a pulse, but my own heart was thumping so hard I couldn't tell if it was hers or mine. Now that the clock was silenced, my staccato breathing drowned out any other sound in the room.

She would want me to hold her till it was too late. She would want me to hold her till it was too late. I sat on the bed rocking her in my arms. She would want me to hold her till it was too late. I fucking promised.

I sat on the steps outside and tried to light a cigarette but my hands were shaking too much to strike a match. I thought about how I didn't know the difference between right and wrong anymore, or whether I ever did at all. I thought about when I came home from work last year on Christmas morning to find her in bed with a plastic bag over her head. I took off my boots and crawled into bed with her even though the mattress was soaked with piss. I untied the string she had used to secure the bag around her neck and pulled it off her.

"Not today, my dear," I whispered.

She rolled over facing the wall, and sobbed. I held her in my arms until we both fell asleep. The next day we pooled the Christmas money our parents had sent us and bought a new bed.

I watched two police cars pull in behind the fire truck and the ambulance. They'd certainly want to speak with me. The female EMT asked me to clear out; there wasn't enough room in our tiny studio apartment for all of them plus their oxygen tanks, defibrillator and the stretcher. I had used all my junior lifeguard training — tilt the head back, pinch the nose, blow until you saw the victim's chest rise, repeat — but now it was time for the professionals to take over.

"Get the fuck off me!!!" was the first sign of life I heard.

17. I HAVE ALWAYS BEEN HERE BEFORE

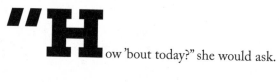ow 'bout today?" she would ask.

"Not today, baby."

Every day started the same. The same question followed by the same answer.

The exchange was our mantra, a promise we made and kept daily. My end of the bargain was that one day I would help her, but not today. If she were on tour she would call from a hotel room — from Chicago, from Toronto, from Cleveland — the vagueness absolving any fear of scrutiny from bandmates, friends, family. After that, we could both rest easy, knowing there would be at least 24 hours of deadly serious pinky-swear assurance that both of us would awake the next day to address the issue all over again.

"How 'bout today?"

"Not today, kitten."

She didn't really need my permission, of course. It helped her feel less alone, less insane, to have me set the guidelines. She called me M or Master, like Jeannie used to call Major Nelson, but in reality I was the child and she was in charge. She trusted me to know when it would finally be too much for her to take, and I pretended to not know how unfair this was. If the circumstances of her life were fine but the distortion was bad, my answer was "Not today," because I knew the distortion would pass. If the circumstances were bad, my answer would still be "Not today," because no "thing" could claim her life and not be an insult to her. Was I going to say today was the day because the label was being a dick? Because the voices in her head voted unanimously that the time was now? Because some frat boy had besmirched her choice of outfit? Was I finally going to nod in agreement with her because...I didn't know the answer, but I did know how to buy time, how to hopelessly hold out and hold on, waiting for a breakthrough: a new pill, a new therapist, a revelation.

It was not a morosely approached daily chore. It was our little secret. Sometimes words weren't even necessary, she would nod her head yes, yes, yes and I would shake my head no, no, no. We hadn't done it yesterday. She'd just woken up and asked me what I was doing and I'd said, "Cooking breakfast." She hadn't yet asked me about the day's possibility and I hadn't considered and rejected the day and called her sugar.

"How 'bout today?"

"You can't do that, sir."

I was dabbing her lips with a moist washcloth I had found in the tiny bathroom her room shared with the patients next door. There was no water on the table next to her bed, just a small, dusty vase with a faded plastic flower in it.

"Sorry, her lips are dry and cracked, I didn't think it would be a problem," I said to the large lady in the white uniform.

"No, that." She pointed to the restraints I had undone a few minutes before.

"I really don't think that's necessary, ma'am. I don't want her to wake up like that."

My words fell on deaf ears and she went about the business of strapping her back to the bed.

"She was a real handful, fella. We had to move poor Miss Gosnell down the hall till we could calm her down," she said, pointing to the empty, unmade bed across the room. "She doesn't wanna set foot in this room again, which means *I* gotta gather her personal belongings."

If by "calm her down" she meant "render her unconscious," then job well done. Carrie hadn't moved a muscle since I'd gotten there.

"She'll have a roommate soon enough, though. You don't get your own room just because you're a problem." She waddled out the door with a brown paper bag full of Miss Gosnell's stuff.

It was at this point I realized just how deep my issues with authority went. I suppose I'd had them all along, but you don't really consider something an "issue" if you don't give a fuck about the consequences. But here I was in the unfamiliar situation of trying to keep my snide remarks in check. I never use the word bitch; it's just too easy. I'd like to think I could always come up with something a little more clever and hurtful. Using a go-to word like bitch just makes you lazy, but in this situation I found myself struggling for something better. I was in enough trouble with Carrie that I didn't need to make anything worse. I knew the poor and uninsured didn't get a lot of compassion in any hospital setting, and the poor and uninsured in the middle of a psychotic episode get even less. Replace the excuse of "psychotic" with "really, *really* pissed at her boyfriend," and she wouldn't get any compassion at all.

I sat on the foot of her bed, "in trouble" in a way I couldn't remember being. Soon she would awaken and I would have to explain myself. If I told her the truth — that I had been selfish and scared — it would break her heart. The deal was that I was supposed to be strong when she was crumbling. When the distortion gripped her so hard that all she yearned for was a sharp object to take away the pain, I was supposed to be the one person she could count on to turn my back and let her go. The day would come when my love, my arms and Roky's voice would never be enough, and all I had to do was not pick up the phone.

I had told many lies to her before, but I had never broken a promise. Now I had set her free only to have her brought back by the adrenalin needle of an emergency medical technician. I had failed her. And though I could rationalize what I did in many ways, the truth was I wasn't ready for her to go yet.

"I've narrowed it down to three different options," she announced.

"Oh yeah?" I was watching television, not really listening.

She stood in front of the screen to get my attention. She had a yellow legal pad and a pencil in her hands. She was only wearing red panties and her reading glasses. She had my attention.

"First off, jumping off the Space Needle would be a logistical nightmare, and besides, it's too corny." She scratched it off her list.

I nodded my head in agreement.

"And slashing your wrists is so…unladylike."

"Loser move," I agreed. Maybe I didn't quite understand the logic, but I didn't tell her that.

"Jumping off a bridge is sexy, but what if some poor kid finds my body a few miles away in the lake? That could be traumatizing."

"Aren't you sweet."

"Two out of the three I like would require me to lose weight."

"Lose weight? You barely weigh a hundred pounds," I laughed.

"No, since I grew boobs and hips this year I'm up to 110, 112 pounds," she protested.

"They are a nice addition."

She looked at me and raised an eyebrow.

"Anyway," she said in the elongated way that indicated she was ignoring the last thing I said, "I'm gonna have to lose 20 if I'm going to hang myself from any of these lighting fixtures or that pipe running across the ceiling of the bathroom." As she spoke she pointed out the questionable gallows with her pencil and put the legal pad to her side. I really had no choice but to admire the new additions we had spoken of only seconds before.

"Listen to me!" she shouted, covering her tits with her notes.

"All right, all right, I'm listenin'."

"The trick to overdosing on pills is the body-weight-to-alcohol-to-food-to-pill ratio, so the skinnier the better."

"I read here," she pointed at a magazine on the floor with her big toe, "that eating saltine crackers makes it less likely that you would throw up."

"And I read here," she flipped though her notepad and pulled out a cut-out newspaper article, "that a successful sleeping-pill overdose was done by drinking a bottle of rubbing alcohol last week. That's nasty, I'm drinkin' scotch."

"And the third option?" I inquired.

"How much does a gun cost?" she asked.

"With bullets?"

"Yes, with bullets!"

"$5,000 dollars. With bullets, $5,100," I lied.

"Well, that's out then."

It was 6 o'clock; visiting hours were over. Being careful not to disturb her IV bag, I lay my head on her chest and listened to her heart beat for a minute. She smelled like disinfectant and unfamiliar soap. I kissed her and brushed her hair from the bandage on her forehead, a little souvenir from head-butting the EMT.

"Good night, princess."

There was a different woman at the front desk when I was leaving.

"Hey there, I'm packing a bag to bring back tomorrow for the patient in room 334, and I was wondering what I could bring besides PJs, cigarettes and lipstick?"

"No smoking," she said, handing me a pamphlet without looking up from her paperwork.

"Thank you, dear." Be nice, be nice, be nice, I thought to myself as I turned to leave. I wanted to add, "This will be very helpful," but I knew I could never pull it off without sounding sarcastic, even if I didn't desperately need to get a couple hours of sleep before work.

"Hold up." She waved me back, looking at her clipboard over her glasses. "Miss Finch won't be here tomorrow. As soon as she wakes up, she'll be transferred to the psychiatric ward over at Harborview."

"Psych ward? Why?"

"Says here, 'Attempted Suicide.' She's one of Dr. Bhaskaran's, so off to Harborview."

"No ma'am, it was an accidental overdose."

"Says here, 'Attempted Suicide.'" She showed me the clipboard and tapped each syllable of the words with her pen as she repeated them back to me.

Keeping in mind that something about my very presence, perhaps my voice itself, seemed to disturb normal people, I cleared my throat and gathered my most civil baritone.

"May I call here in the morning and see where she is?" I asked in the most honey-soaked cadence I could muster.

"The number is on the pamphlet," she fired back.

"If you have any room left in your little black book, I want you to write my father's number in there," she once told me, handing me a scrap of paper with his phone number and address on it. "When it happens, I want you to call him. He's an old man and it's going to be hard on him. I know you can be sweet, Charlie.

125

"And, Charlie," she said, her eyes suddenly holding tears, "You are to burn my journals before he sees them, before *anyone* sees them. Promise me."

"I swear to God, pumpkin," I said, putting my hand over my heart.

"I'm serious," she said, poking her finger in my chest.

I held her look. "I know you are," I said.

He had done everything he could think of. She had been analyzed, tested, probed and prayed over. Time that should have been spent skipping rope and taking swimming lessons was spent on psychiatrists' couches and inside MRI machines. When her mother found turpentine and a can of Roach Prufe in her Partridge Family lunch box, Carrie was sent off to Bible camp, where she learned how to make rope in lanyard class and how to tie it into a noose in rock climbing class. They sent her to a place in Houston for troubled teens. They sent her to a guy in New Mexico who waved giant magnets around her head. They tried Western medicine, they tried Eastern medicine, they tried everything short of exorcism. All he knew for sure, sitting in his La-Z-Boy recliner flipping though her baby pictures in the family photo album, was that as long as he heard her practicing in her room, everything would be fine.

I wasn't on a first-name basis with the word *grateful* then, so I walked the three blocks home from the hospital naming the things in my life that were not totally and completely fucked. I didn't have to make that phone call. That was not totally and completely fucked. I wasn't in jail. That was not totally and completely fucked. I was glad to have another chance, an opportunity to right all the havoc I had been causing. That was not totally and completely fucked. Carrie was still alive. I could say that without reservation.

18. CREATURE WITH THE ATOM BRAIN

Wayne Newton was, at that time, the closest thing to a "best friend" I had. You know it's a dark time in your life when the person you need to spill your considerably heavy-duty guts to is muttering the word "nice" every time he flips another glossy page of a lactation and pregnancy fetish periodical titled *Knocked Up & Milky*. When you live at night and spend your free time hunting drugs, your circle of friends can shrink quickly. On the one hand, Wayne was the one person around who would not immediately have me arrested. On the other hand, he had just grabbed a personal lubricant from behind the counter and strolled off to the employee restroom with a magazine under his arm. I was, as they say, truly alone.

I thought about praying. Then I laughed out loud. I stepped outside to smoke a cigarette instead. Carrie once told me that Native Americans believe that when they exhale smoke from the peace pipe their prayers float up to God. I thought about what it felt like to kiss her unconscious lips before I left the hospital and attempted a smoke ring. I got three pretty good ones out when I heard a loud pop over my head. The S of the store's flashing red neon sign had burned out. Ordinarily the nine letters would come up one at a time in sequence until the words were complete, then all together they would flash three times, like a beacon to the lonely, before beginning the whole process over again. I don't know how many thousands of times I had looked at that sign since I'd worked there without ever thinking about it. That night it just read "LIVE GIRL -." I laughed again, said thank you out loud to somebody or something, crushed my cigarette out on the sidewalk and walked back inside.

When I put my Lucky Strikes back in my jacket pocket, I found a cassette I had meant to leave at the hospital for Carrie. It was a compilation tape of her favorite Roky Erickson songs she had made for me on my birthday years ago. I carried it with me always, in case of an emergency. Whenever she was frantically running around the apartment before leaving on tour I would stick it in her purse, in case of an emergency. Side A had the word "Rokers" scrawled across it in blue ink. It contained psychedelic gems from the early days of his career and insanity-soaked monster anthems. Side B read "Not so Rokin'" and was a mix of spooky acoustic numbers and mid-tempo love songs. Ordinarily, a tape that traveled around the country on punk rock tours, living in my leather jacket's pocket at all other times, would have been destroyed several times over. But we both knew how important this one was to us, and I took care of it like a baby.

Carrie's father had a very eclectic record collection. Although he had very strong feelings about the hierarchy of music, with symphonic composers at the top, he also understood the storytelling value of folk and country music. As a college student at the University of Texas in Austin, he immersed himself in the acid-rock sounds of the day. And later in life, as a responsible, yet still mischievous, father of two, one of his favorite things to do in order to fracture his wife's delicate nerves was to innocently put on "The Psychedelic Sounds of the 13th Floor Elevators" just before bedtime. He knew darn well it would send his son careening wildly through the rumpus room on his Big Wheel and more importantly cause his 3-year-old daughter to immediately shed herself of the constraining armor of her pajamas and dance in the living room like she had seen the big kids do on those black-and-white beach party movies.

"Turn it up, Daddy, turn it up!"

The young, LSD-drenched Roky Erickson was the frantic, cartoonish voice of this crazed, draft-dodgin' rock 'n' roll band that Mr. Finch spent way too many nights seeing at the New Orleans Club on Red River Street instead of attending to his studies. For him, putting on the record was just a way to fondly recall a temporary lapse of judgment, a rebellious phase that would come to an abrupt end upon receiving the first piss-poor marks of his once-perfect scholastic career. But when his daughter plopped her butt down on the burnt-orange shag carpet to examine the album's artwork, it would change her life. When she ran her little fingers across the picture of the scruffy, yet cherubic face of the band's leader, she experienced an altogether new feeling: love.

Later, while her peers were cooing over Leif Garrett and Shaun Cassidy pictures in *Tiger Beat* magazine, Carrie and her best and only friend Liz would pore over the pages of *Goldmine* looking for any Roky news they could find. They agreed that each of them would marry him but only for ten years, so the other one then could have a turn. Roky himself would choose which one he would marry first, and there would be absolutely no hard feelings between them. They wrote "Mrs. Elizabeth Erickson" or "Mrs. Carina Erickson" on their respective Pee Chee folders and went about the business of 4th grade. Carrie was pretty sure she would be chosen first because she most resembled his current wife, who was a lovely woman but would certainly be too old for him by the time it was Carrie's turn.

Liz came running up the stairs and into Carrie's room.

"Lookit, lookit. I found this in my brother's room. It's got mostly gross boys in it but there's an article on Roky!" she said, waving around the latest issue of *Creem* magazine.

The girls jumped onto a giant, cozy beanbag chair and took turns reading the article aloud to each other between sips of Dr. Pepper. It was the same-old, born-in-Dallas, child-of-an-architect and would-be-opera-singer, piano-lessons-at-five/first-guitar-at-eight stuff they had read dozens of times before, but there were a couple of pictures they hadn't seen and he was looking as dreamy as ever.

They didn't know or care what terms like "garage-bred psychedelia" or "hallucinogenic-induced madness" meant. They were just two kittens curled up next to each other reading about their secret boyfriend. Carrie snatched the magazine so she could have a turn reading.

"His arrest in Texas for possession of a single marijuana cigarette led to his being committed for three years to Rusk State Hospital for the Criminally Insane, where he was reportedly subjected to Thorazine, electroshock therapy, and other experimental treatments..."

"Marijuana?!" gasped Liz.

"Oh my god, oh my god. Liz, they're hurting him."

Carrie dropped the magazine and they threw their arms around each other and wept. Something had to be done.

That evening Carrie skipped *Happy Days* and *Laverne & Shirley*, hid away in her room with markers, paper and cellophane tape and transformed a boxful of old Jimmy Carter for President buttons she found in a desk drawer into Free Roky buttons.

The next day the girls spent their morning recess in the arts and crafts class with cardboard and paint, planning their siege upon the school cafeteria. They threw away the first prototypes they made after agreeing that, in order to be taken seriously as opponents of injustice, they couldn't have red hearts on their protest signs.

It didn't go well. The crowds they had hoped to rally in support of their wrongly imprisoned hero were only interested in sloppy joes and french fries. The sit-in they staged at the entrance of the cafeteria was only a tad bit of an inconvenience to most of the student body, who chose instead to use the other door that was 20 feet down the hall. Some of the older, mean kids just stepped over them and laughed. Still, when the 5th period bell rang, the two remained there, waiting for the police officers to come and drag them away to the paddy wagon.

"Remember, just go limp," Carrie reminded Liz as they nervously looked toward the ends of the hallway for baton-wielding pigs in tear gas masks.

Instead, their social studies teacher, Miss Thurmond, came walking up in her billowy hippie skirt and sat down between them.

"You ladies are missin' class, you know," she said, examining their signs.

"Yeah, we're going to be arrested," sighed Liz.

"I'll tell you what," Miss Thurmond laughed, "I'm so pleased with your interest in civil disobedience that today's class is gonna be about Martin Luther King, Jr. I bet if we pack up right now, we can get outta here before 'The Man' shows up."

As the girls walked hand-in-hand with their teacher through the common area to the social studies building, Carrie was a little disappointed not to hear the sounds of wailing sirens and police dogs barking. To help cheer up her new favorite students, Miss Thurmond offered to get the address for the Rusk State Hospital for the Criminally Insane and to help them craft thoughtful yet strong letters demanding Erickson's immediate release.

Their fervor for social justice would come to a screeching halt, however, when they would both receive letters back from Rusk thanking them for their interest in Mr. Erickson's case, but informing them that the patient had been released several years earlier and was said to be doing fine.

The comforting familiarity of his voice always soothed her trembling hands and sobbing heart. In a way, I was jealous. I did the hand-holding, the late-night talking and the reassuring. I went to the store for the Diet Cokes, the cigarettes and the videos. I lay in bed and stared at the ceiling while she stared at the wall. I held her close, but he flew in like Superman and saved the day every time. Yeah, I was definitely jealous.

"What is it about those songs?" I once asked, grasping for something I could emulate, or maybe a hint of some characteristic I could adopt as my own.

"He has the kindest eyes I've ever seen," was all she said.

She did meet him once. Kind of. In the fall of 1980, her whole family drove out to Austin so her father and his brother could go to an important football game at the college. They were all having breakfast at a diner and the grown-ups were talking about people from the olden days. Carrie was sitting at the end of the table with her cousin Jason, who was a year younger and just sat there staring at her. It would have been terribly boring, but she ordered coffee from the waiter and no one stopped her. With enough sugar, it was downright delicious, and every time it got half empty, the waiter came around with his bitter-smelling urn.

She saw him sitting in the corner booth by the door. She couldn't believe her luck. He had hardly touched the stack of pancakes in front of him and there was a mean-looking man sitting across from him who smoked cigarettes. Roky was wearing a bright Hawaiian shirt and had a bushy beard, but she was absolutely positive it was him.

When the mean-looking man got up to use the restroom, she made her move, darting across the restaurant and hurling herself into the booth across from him.

"Hi Roky, I really like your music a lot!" she said, maybe a little too loudly, perhaps due to the excessive caffeine she had on board.

"Yeah, OK, that's fine," he said as their eyes locked.

"My name is Carrie." She would have stuck her hand out for him to shake, but her 11-year-old social graces were not that evolved.

"That sounds like a dangerous place," he said.

"Um, I know you like horror movies and I do, too."

"That little girl stabs her with a spade," he said, covering up the plastic bracelet on his wrist with his other hand.

"Ooooh, *Night of the Living Dead*. Yeah, that's one of my favorites."

"The stabbing?" he asked, sticking his finger in his water glass.

"No, the movie…the stabbing is pretty good, though." She laughed as if she had said the funniest thing in the world.

"All right then."

"It was nice talking to you. Take care of yourself," she said, standing up to leave.

"OK, be careful out there."

I was out the door at 8 a.m. exactly. I had shortchanged enough customers that night to buy four or five balloons from Otis when he strolled in, and I told Wayne Newton that I was skipping the traditional after-work beer. I avoided the bus stop. I decided that hoofing it up the hill might be quicker and lessen the odds of being diverted from my mission by Kelly Thompson or anything equally sinister.

I was torn. The selfish side of me wanted to just go to the hospital, pick her up, bring her home and pretend like this whole thing never happened. The other selfish side of me knew that spending some time in a psychiatric hospital setting might be good for her. The most selfish side of me wondered if post-accidental-overdose sex was a possibility and how fantastic it might be.

The pamphlet from the hospital was next to the phone and her overnight bag sat in the giant plastic hand chair by the window. As I dialed the number I pulled a pair of socks out of the bag.

"Good morning, ma'am. I'm checking on the status of a patient there."

I dropped two balloons of dope into the opening of one of the socks.

"Miss Carrie Finch. F-I-N-C-H."

I folded the socks back together in a pair and pushed them deep into the bottom of the bag.

"Oh, do you know what time they moved her?"

I zipped up the bag and threw it over my shoulder.

"Thank you, dear."

I practiced being polite the whole walk there. I would be dealing with day-dwellers. They required smiles and kindness. They were way more delicate than we were. I went to the drugstore for a carton of smokes. I went to Bulldog News and bought some music magazines. Everywhere I went I threw "nice days" and "how are yous" around like confetti. When I spent my last five dollars on a bunch of daisies at a convenience store, the man who rang me up muttered something about the Mariners. I nodded knowingly. Jesus Christ, I was agreeable. I believed I was ready to ingratiate myself to the mental heath system.

The large automatic doors opened and I strolled into the lobby with confidence and poise. Clean shirt, check. Combed hair, check. The finest fake smile this side of the Mississippi, you know it.

"Good morning, ma'am. I'm here to drop off some stuff for a new patient."

"Good morning, sir." So far, so good, I thought.

"Name?" she asked.

"Mine or hers?"

"The patient's name, please."

"Miss Carrie Finch, like the bird," I said, setting the flowers down on her desk.

"And your name is?"

"Charlie Hyatt, how do you do?" I reached out and gave her a firm, but not too firm, handshake.

"Like the hotel?"

"Hyatt Hotels, that's right. No relation, though. What time are visiting hours around here?"

"It says here that I'm not to accept packages, phone calls or messages from you."

I froze as the unseen record scratched, stopping the easy-listening music that had been bubbling along.

"I'm sorry? There's...there's obviously been a mistake here."

"I don't think so, Mr. Hyatt. It's written in bold letters, quite clear and distinct."

"Let me speak to the doctor, please." Shit. That booming voice was mine. I heard it get loud. I knew no good was going to come of it, but it was out of my hands now.

"This is at the request of the patient, sir."

"Look, lady..." A large, pasty man in a gray uniform approached me from the corner. I recognized the pepper-spray canister on his belt.

"Please take your things," she said.

I reached into the inside pocket of my jacket. The security guard quickly unsnapped the holster of his gun.

"No, no...it's fine, it's just a tape," I said, holding the cassette up in plain view of everyone.

"Please, it's very important. Make sure she gets this." I set it on the woman's desk as the guard grabbed me by the back of the neck and forcefully directed me toward the front door.

"Please," I begged.

I assured the monster as he escorted me to the door that I wasn't going to cause him any trouble.

"I'm pretty fuckin' sure you won't," he said under his breath.

Halfway to the sidewalk I managed to turn around just enough to see the lady pick up the cassette tape as though it were a used Kleenex and drop it into the wastebasket next to her desk, followed by the daisies.

19. I'M GONNA FREE HER

The medicine-cabinet mirror lay dead on the bathroom floor. I had turned my reflection into a spiderweb with a right hook. It mocked my left uppercut by smiling unaffectedly. A quick right jab and another uppercut and it rained diamonds and droplets of blood on the tile and sink. The carnage crunched under my boots as I walked over to the answering machine.

I pushed "Play." Certainly she had found a pay phone by now, surely she had formulated an escape plan, and without a doubt it would require me as an accomplice.

"Hey Carrie, it's Jenny, gimme a —" *Fast-forward.*

"Carrie, it's Amanda —" *Fast-forward.*

"Caaaarrrrie —" *Fast-forward.*

"Hello darlin', it's Dad..." *Fast-forward.*

Fuck.

I sat on the couch of our apartment cradling my head in my hands, rubbing my eyes. I felt the blood trickle down from my knuckles to my forearms, then drip on my jeans. I was sure I'd pick the glass out at some point before work, but at that moment it just felt right. I reached for my cigarette pack and found it empty.

I was drinking whiskey at noon. I had just beaten the shit out of an inanimate object in an uncontrollable burst of rage. I hurt inside and out. By all accounts, I should have been feeling pretty fuckin' masculine. It was only when I realized that the mirror would still be destroyed when she returned that the tears began. She would be standing there, lipstick at the ready, and there would be questions, and pretending that nothing had happened would be impossible. When she waltzed in that door in a couple of minutes or a few hours or the next day, everything had to be perfect.

Sure, I could sweep and mop up the wreckage, but replacing it would require some handyman prowess. If I were a real man this whole situation would be remedied with a trip to Ace Hardware and about 15 minutes of semi-skilled labor. Of course, if I were a real man I would have hubristic pride in a job that mattered. I would not be content to stand behind a cash register and supervise as humanity gasped for air before me. My kingdom's walls would not be lined with prurient VHS tapes and filthy magazines. My calling certainly wouldn't be to provide a safe, clean environment for sad outcasts to stroke their pathetic cocks. If I were a real man my priorities would be family, home and financial stability, but none of these things meant shit to me. The only things I cared about in this world were a crazy redhead and getting high. I honestly wish I could say in that order.

The only thing I had in common with real men was their shortcomings. Like real men, I was oblivious to the way simple words or deeds could knock the shit out of an innocent bystander. Like real men, I was selfish, brutish and unkind sometimes. One thing I knew for sure was that when there's something a real man can't fix, he drinks, right?

That notion I picked up from movies and books and not from the man that was supposed to have schooled me in such matters. I had only ever seen my father drunk once. Sure, I'd seen him tip a couple of Coors or Pabst

Blue Ribbons back at barbeques and softball games, but I'd only seen him shit-faced once.

I was sitting home on a Friday night at the tender age of 15 watching *The Midnight Special* or *Don Kirshner's Rock Concert*, I can't remember which. The Canadian rock band Rush were performing in all their kimono-wearing, double-bass-drum-pounding, we-think-we're-smarter-than-everyone-else glory when my dad came in the front door and half-stumbled down the stairs into the sunken living room. He stood there looking at the screen with his head tilted to one side and one eye closed, trying to focus.

"That's the ugliest broad I ever saw," he managed to say.

Howling with laughter, I realized I had never loved the man more.

"Turn that shit off," he said, "let's have a drink."

Having never drunk alcohol before or heard my father cuss, I was all in. This was exciting. We walked up the three stairs to the not-so-sunken part of the living room, and I sat at the table while he went into the kitchen and poured something from a green bottle into two highball glasses and dropped a couple of ice cubes into each.

"You're gonna like this, kid."

I took a healthy drink and decided it best not to move until the burning sulphur-born dragon in my throat quit having its seizure. I stared at him, trying to make my tear-brimmed eyes convey the message, "Yup."

"The first time I drank Jameson's was in Vietnam," he said. "I couldn't have been much older than you."

I didn't bother correcting him; I didn't want to sour one of our few father-son bonding moments.

"We were out on patrol, I was in charge. We were walkin' down some fuckin' dirt road and two Viet Cong kids come walkin' up the road toward us, little kids," he said, taking a long pull off his drink. "Charlie had been sending kids strapped with bombs in and blowin' the shit out of us.

"I had two kids of my own at home, for Christ's sake," he said, his voice suddenly sullen.

I wanted to say something about being one of them, but he wasn't talking to me anymore. He was talking to a stranger in a bar.

"So I give the order to fire," he said, then cleared his throat.

"They just fell over. There were no blood-curdling screams or explosions. They just fell over like dominos."

He got up, walked back over to the kitchen counter and unscrewed the cap on the bottle.

"When we got back to camp I had to see the sergeant and file a report. I remember...he had a framed picture of Jesus and a framed picture of the commandant on his desk, but none of his wife or kids. He pulled a Jameson's and two glasses out of his desk drawer after he heard the story," he said, pouring himself another and topping off mine.

"The sergeant poured about a half of a shot in each glass 'cause booze was like gold out there; we didn't have any ice, of course. Then he made a toast."

He lifted his glass and then gestured for me to lift mine.

"The sins of some men are obvious, reaching the place of judgment ahead of them; the sins of others trail behind them," he said, deliberately and slowly to avoid slurring.

"What's that from?" I asked, finally able to break my silence.

"The Bible, I guess."

His chest began to heave and he hung his head and sobbed. I had never seen my father cry before or since. He was our family's bearer of bad news, but through all the passings of grandpas and great aunts and even his own mother, he remained composed and unemotional. It was his job, I'd supposed.

I was at a loss for what to do. Mr. Cunningham never cried. Mr. Brady never cried. My interpersonal family protocol for sadness didn't run much deeper than the episode when Tiger ran away from home. I was clueless. I got up, walked around the table and put my hand on his shoulder. Words were impossible and worthless. The only comfort I could offer was an awkward touch and the tears that came with the realization that my father was human.

"I'm sorry, I'm sorry, I'm sorry," he whispered.

"S'ok, Dad," I said, knowing again he wasn't talking to me but to a couple of kids he left on a hot, sticky dirt road ten thousand miles and many years away.

The slowest second hand I had ever seen ticked away until a full minute had passed. Then as suddenly as the wave of regret and shame had crushed him, it disappeared.

"How's school, kiddo?" he said, gathering the glasses and pouring the remainder of my whiskey down the kitchen sink.

"It's fucked up, Dad."

"Yeah, I bet."

I clumsily pulled the little shards of mirror from my wounds, right-handed or left-handed, it didn't matter. I stood over the tiny sink in our tiny kitchen with Carrie's tweezers and alternately dug the glass out of my cuts, then passed my fingers under the cool running water to wash away the blood. I stopped occasionally to sanitize the lacerations with whiskey, old Western-film style. A splash on my knuckles and a shot for me. Another splash on my knuckles and another shot for me. It might have hurt for all I know. I was soaked in Jameson's and fentanyl and was in no position to judge.

I watched the clock, I looked out the window, I rummaged through the trash can and smoked every cigarette butt down to the filter as I walked the 14 steps from one end of the room to the other, over and over. I washed both dishes in the sink. I did a pristine job of making the bed until I realized I was leaving little streaks of blood on the sheets. I wrapped each of my fingers in tissue, then secured them with masking tape, each one looking progressively worse until my hands resembled a badly abused bouquet of paper flowers. Mostly I just stared at a phone that didn't ring.

The girl sitting up in bed with the NA Big Book in her lap, praying with her new temporary sponsor, wasn't her. My Carrie was hiding in the closet making a rope from torn hospital sheets, calculating the distance from the third floor to the ground. The girl thanking the nurse for bringing her lunch to her room wasn't her. My Carrie just threw the tray at the door as it closed behind her. The girl slowly walking arm-in-arm with her physical therapist down the hall wasn't her, either. My Carrie was wondering if the emergency exits really have alarms or not. The girl opening the blinds of her room with the big smile as the sun hits her face for what seems like the first time in years, no, she wasn't her. My Carrie was flirting with a janitor in hopes that one of those keys hanging from his belt would give her access to her clothes. The girl discussing her treatment options with Dr. Bhaskaran definitely wasn't her. My Carrie was conning a Xanax script out of that asshole. And I absolutely know the girl who requested that she get no visitors, especially me, wasn't her. My Carrie just tore the IV needle out of her arm and ran for the elevator.

I had finally reached that place I wanted to be: I didn't care anymore. If she wanted to see me I was easy to find. I had stumbled into the bathroom with a broom in one hand and the bottle in the other to put the final touches on my inept, yet thoughtful, attempt at sprucing the place up for her impending return. I was sure it would look great. But then, as violently as I had beaten my own reflection hours before, the sadness and failure of the last 24 hours exploded from my throat and painted the floor with even more insult. In spite of my best efforts, I fell to my hands and knees with an almost religious fervor while the remaining dismay and shame dripped from the corners of my mouth. I was empty, I was free, and I was home. I spat into the expanding puddle of bile and glass as it engulfed the palms of my hands. I laughed hard, knowing that laundry and mopping were as out of the question as time travel and God, and if this is the way she found her prince, then so be it. I rested my head on the cool toilet seat. I just needed to rest my eyes.

The polite tapping on the door turned to pounding, and I tried to ignore it. Only when it occurred to me that of course she wouldn't have her keys did I find myself on my feet. She had likely been left strapped to a gurney, probably screaming combinations of obscenities even I had never heard before, so she sure as fuck wouldn't have been given much thought to such trivial matters as where the fuck her keys were. The absurd notion of making myself presentable was just that; you couldn't just sweep my kind of mess under the rug. I unlocked the deadbolt both excited and horrified.

"Babe, you look terrible. We're calling you in sick."

Kelly Thompson stood in the doorway, her eyes moist with concern for a dear friend. Fuck. Whatever this was, it was not going to be a good thing.

20. REVERBERATION (DOUBT)

"**Y**our tits look spectacular in that dress."

The dress was a low-cut, yellow polka-dotted summer number. She also wore a large straw hat, dark Ray-Bans and a black bra whose straps she now pulled up, creating all the more reason for me to focus on that dress.

"That's kind of the idea, isn't it?" she asked, sliding her sunglasses to the tip of her nose.

"I mean, seriously, you could do Shakespeare off a balcony like that."

"Shut the fuck up."

She bent down to check her teeth for lipstick in the side mirror.

"Wish me luck," she said, lightly pecking me on the lips.

I watched as she walked down the block, not knowing if she was exaggerating the swing in her ass for my benefit or if she was just warming up for what awaited inside. It was a sunny day — an integral component of our strategy — and the light shining through her dress was as wonderful to behold as she no doubt figured it would be. People, especially in Seattle, were much more easily distracted on a pleasant day. The sunshine and that yellow dress would leave anyone — male or female — hard-pressed to describe her face after the fact.

Kelly Thompson was born into violence, baptized in crashing lamps and broken dishes. The parade of men who moved in with her mother were not so much stepfathers as they were adversaries. Kelly could negotiate the living room in the midst of full-blown domestic war without spilling a drop of milk or dropping a single Oreo cookie. She'd sit herself down a couple feet in front of the television, turn it up loud enough to drown out the yelling, and become invisible.

Chaos was her comfort zone, bedlam and disorder her playground. She would size up each new man her mom moved in with and see the day she would be used as a human shield as they escaped with a couple of suitcases and her cat. She taught her babysitters how to smoke. She learned the joys of NyQuil and cherry-flavored codeine cough syrup at an early age. She was the most prolific pre-teen shoplifter eastern Washington had ever seen. She was — in a word — ambitious.

Consequences were nonexistent. The most severe punishment she ever received — for even the most blatant violation of what few rules there were — was a stern look. Mrs. Thompson (or whatever name she was using at the time) didn't get along with other women. Kelly was her lone source of female companionship. The adorable little sociopath she had given birth to, raised and was grooming to be her future best friend had other ideas about this arrangement.

Kelly never thought of herself as evil. She never thought much at all. She plotted, schemed and planned, sure, but not in a way you'd exactly call "thinking." For her, it was nothing but the search to fill her empty chest cavity with harder, faster, more, now. If it weren't for me appealing to the tiniest sliver of reason she possessed, there would be a 9mm pistol inside the pastel pink backpack slung over her shoulder.

When she walked through the front doors she noticed a machine in the corner of the lobby. "Your Weight And Fortune, 25 Cents." She stepped on the scale and stuck a quarter in the slot. There was a clicking sound and a printed slip of paper was dispensed:

145

118 pounds
Your life becomes more and more of an adventure.

Her fortune tucked in her bra strap, she walked over and calmly picked up a deposit slip. *Hmmm, better make it a withdrawal slip,* she thought.

She had composed the note a million times in her mind. Nothing too dramatic or corny; just a simple and clear directive. She took a black ballpoint pen out of her backpack and wrote in large capital letters:

FILL UP THIS BACKPACK WITH MONEY

She got in line, her awareness rising like a jungle cat sensing its prey.

Four customers in front of her. Two trainee tellers behind the counter. One male, one female. Supervisor handling the drive-thru behind them. Bank manager in the office eating soup, engrossed in a romance paperback.

The sun poured in through the window onto Kelly's back. A drop of sweat ran down her spine. Both tellers could see the outline of her body through the light material of her dress, but neither could tell if she was wearing panties or not.

Three people in front of her now. Elderly man with a cane. Young mom with a toddler draped over her shoulder. Dreadlocked kid holding a skateboard. Supervisor baby-talking with a golden retriever puppy in the backseat of a customer's car through the intercom. Manager slurps and turns a page.

TV monitors told Kelly she was on camera now. The screen switched from the line to behind the counter to the parking lot just like I told her it did. I had come into the bank and purchased a money order with cash the day before at the exact same time.

Now there are two. Baby squeals, blows spit bubble. Smile at child to appear human. Bong-water smell emanating from skater's matted locks.

By day, Kelly worked as a hairdresser in a fairly posh downtown salon. This was one time where such a flagrant mistreatment of hair would have to pass without comment from her.

Now there was just one person standing between her and a life of more and more adventure. It was odd that bad hair was the last thing between this moment and the next, because the entire idea for this little caper was born at the salon, a diversion to keep her from thinking about how badly she wanted to pull back her customer's head and pour Barbicide disinfectant down his throat just to watch him convulse on the floor.

He had been an ordinary douchebag, the kind whose tip she could bump up a dollar at a time with each "accidental" brush of a breast. This one, however, unknowingly had a spark of gold hidden in the ad nauseam blather dribbling from his mouth. Embedded in the narration of his grand dreams of becoming a hedge-fund manager was the information that he first had to undergo a grueling two-week training program at the Crown Hill Washington Mutual. Kelly smiled and nodded and snipped away, setting herself to see what goodies she could get from him.

"Yeah, I'm startin' as a teller while I'm still at school so I can really get my claws into the world of high finance, ya know," he said, woefully attempting to impress the wrong woman.

"Oh my, isn't being a bank teller dangerous? Especially in Crown Hill?" Kelly had suddenly acquired a slight Southern twang in her voice — and a nervous flutter in her stomach — at the mention of what she knew damn well was the most completely milquetoast Caucasian neighborhood Seattle had to offer.

"Well, let's just say no shit went down on my watch," he said, the ability to look tough suddenly crossing his lily-white face.

"Goodness," she fanned herself as if she were going to faint.

"The truth is, we're not even allowed to put up any resistance if there's a robbery. Our first concern is always the safety of the customers and our co-workers. We let the perpetrator get out as soon as possible so no one gets hurt."

"Do you use those dye pack thingies?"

"Nope. Bank robbers watch TV too. They're hip to those things. We've got some new hi-tech homing devices we slip in the bundles *if* there's enough time."

"I get goose bumps just thinkin' about it," she said, not actively lying for the first time.

She brushed the stray hairs from his collar and shoulders, then bent over to lightly blow on the back of his neck.

"Since you're so big and brave, I'm going to give you the serviceman's discount," she said, holding up a mirror so he could take a look at her work. She charged him the full amount, of course.

He tipped her $45 for the $55 haircut and strolled out the door beaming with pride.

"Dumbass."

I looked in the rearview, then the side mirrors, then the rearview again. *Thump, thump, thump.* What the fuck is taking so fucking long?

I checked to make sure all the doors were unlocked. Again.

I looked at the gas gauge. Half a tank. Still.

I switched off the radio.

I looked in the visor mirror. My hair was pulled back in a ponytail under a Mariners baseball cap. I looked like an idiot. I lit a cigarette and listened to my heart pound in my throat: *thump, thump, thump.*

"Next customer, please."

He flashed an awkward smile. He's wearing his father's shirt and tie, she thought. She wondered if he, too, was putting in his two weeks on the way to a life of high finance, and if he was, would he buy some clothes that fit him when he got his first juicy paycheck? Had there been an ounce of doubt inside her, one look at his over-gelled fade haircut would have been enough to convince her that people were, in fact, stupid, and deserved to have things taken from them. She unzipped her bag and placed it on the counter with the opening facing him. She slid the folded note in his direction with one finger.

He read the note twice, scratched his nose and looked up at Kelly.

"Keep your eyes on my tits, mister," she said in a calm, sultry voice.

"Yes, ma'am," he mumbled, fumbling for the cash drawer.

She read his name tag: Vincent Pella, Trainee.

"Lovely day, isn't it?"

"Yes, ma'am," he said, shoveling bundles of twenties into her backpack.

"Vince darlin', you wouldn't try and slip one of those homing devices in my bag, would you?"

"No, absolutely not," he stammered, reaching back into the bag and retrieving the last bundle he'd stuck in there.

"Thank you, dear. I'll be going now."

She twirled around and did her best Holly Golightly amble. Traversing the lobby she never missed a beat, never lost her cool, never broke into a full run until she was on the other side of the door.

I threw it in drive as soon as I saw the yellow sunflower blur turn the corner, one hand gripping the backpack, the other securing the hat on her head. She tore open the door and dived onto the backseat. Without squealing tires or reckless abandon, I simply pulled into traffic and disappeared.

She lay hidden on her stomach, frantically tearing open the paper strips that held together each bundle of cash and searching for hi-tech tracking gadgets or ticking blue-dye time bombs. I took a left into the neighborhood. Her mom's blue four-door Chevy Celebrity wasn't going to put up much of a fight in any high-speed chases, but it was as anonymous of a car as you could possibly drive, and the idea was to blend the fuck in. I took a right on

8th Avenue. Kelly discovered two bills taped together with what felt like a credit card inside.

"Vincent! Motherfucker!" she screamed.

"Who?"

"Never mind, just drive," she said, rolling down the window and tossing the offending money into the street.

I watched her in the rearview mirror as she pulled a black T-shirt over her dress and shook out her auburn curls. I took a left onto Market and went up the hill. She crawled over the seat to the passenger side and grabbed her cigarettes. She put her feet on the dashboard and lit up.

"So? How was work, honey?" I asked in my best Ward Cleaver voice.

"That was fucking amazing!" she screamed. It was the first time I'd ever seen a sincere smile on her face.

"How much did ya get?"

"We, baby."

I rephrased the question. "How much did *we* get?"

"I dunno. Who cares? We'll count it when we get back to the room." She was glowing.

She took my right hand off the steering wheel and placed it under her skirt as she stared out the open window and exhaled a giant cloud of smoke. Her panties were soaked. I turned onto Aurora.

"Seriously? That's how you finger a girl?" she groaned.

"That's how I finger a girl and drive a getaway car at the same time, yeah."

21. TRUE LOVE CAST OUT ALL EVIL

Dear Charlie,
    I've tried to write this letter so many times. There must be a hundred balled-up pieces of paper with just the words "Dear Charlie," written on them in the dumpster behind this hospital. I'm not mad at you. You need to understand that.
    It ain't so bad in here. I call it Dr. B's Home for Wayward Suicidal Junkie Chicks, ha ha. I'm either cowering in the corner or I'm taking over the world depending on what time of day it is or how long its been since I've been shocked. There are quiet days too. Sometimes they bring me classical tapes from the library.

There are 12 other girls here. We get along pretty good. We listen to lectures and watch films but mostly we sit in a circle and talk about our feelings, you'd hate it, haha.

We've had to write a bunch of letters lately. We write goodbye letters to drugs and alcohol. We write goodbye letters to the dead fathers who ignored us and we write goodbye letters to the uncles who molested us and then we take them out to a metal trash can in the courtyard and burn them. I can hear you snicker, I can see your eyes roll.

This is one of those letters, Charlie.

How is it that I can hardly remember yesterday but I can remember everything about you too clearly? I'm gonna miss your beautiful cock and your wicked tongue. I'm gonna miss your gravel voice and the way it turned every lie into the relief I felt when I woke up from a bad dream and found myself in your arms. I'm gonna miss the fights. The way you punched that cashier in the nose for accusing me of stealing even though you saw me do it with your own eyes. The way I knew no one could hurt me when you were around. I guess that was my fucked-up idea of security. I know that's an unhealthy way to think now. I need to let the sun in, darlin'.

I hope that you'll keep the promises you made to me. I know that my secrets are safe with you because underneath all that nasty unwashed hair you are a good man. You are a good man.

I stole a stamp from the receptionist's desk to send this to you. Hopefully it'll be the last dishonest thing I do.

I wish I could say I didn't love you anymore, but that would be a lie. Goodbye, Charlie.

XX Carrie

22. SPLASH 1 (NOW I'M HOME)

The Thunderbird was not the shittiest motel in town. It was the motel across the street from the shittiest motel in town. One could argue that the differences between the Marco Polo and the Thunderbird were slight, but I contend they were vast and important. As far as amenities, the establishments were carbon copies of each other. Behind the front desks of each, the defeated owner/operator suspiciously eyeballed new guests through a curry-scorched haze. Not that they really cared. Your room key was promptly handed to you even if you registered as Charles Fictitious from East Fabrication, Utah and suddenly couldn't find your ID, so long as your payment was up front and in cash. Rooms in each offered bedspreads made of fibers not found in nature, tastefully decorated with cigarette burns, hairs and questionable stains; each showcased delightfully moldy shag carpeting; each had handwritten signs on the back of the room doors prohibiting drug use and kindly requesting that there be no parties after 11 p.m.

Their histories were shared as well. In their American-owned, fresh-faced heydays, both had provided clean lodging for value-minded families coming to town to gaze with wonder at the mind-blowing and futuristic vision that was the Space Needle. From those golden days, both properties began their slow march to the present, each becoming completely ravaged by shady characters, outlaws, hookers, pimps and drug addicts seeking shelter. Eventually they were given up on by Mom and Pop, who had dishearteningly watched their investments and dreams become crime-infested warts on the ass of Aurora.

Aurora Avenue runs north from downtown past Queen Anne, through Greenwood and on up to Shoreline, Lynnwood and other suburban areas that might as well be Canada. Once upon a time, as part of Highway 99, it was the primary artery in and out of the city. As Seattle grew, it was bullied into submission by the new and oh-so-glamorous Interstate 5, which ran parallel maybe a mile to the east. Stripped of her identity, resentful of the attention and jealous of the federally funded construction program, Aurora slipped into a depression and let herself go.

The fact that it sat on the west side of the street was the predominant reason I favored the Thunderbird. A cement barrier of considerable girth lay in the middle of the road, separating north and southbound traffic, stopping drunk drivers from swerving into oncoming cars and thwarting foolhardy pedestrians trying to cross the deceptively busy thoroughfare. It also inadvertently protected us from a great deal of law-enforcement scrutiny. Every day around dusk, just like clockwork, two or three police cruisers would roll north into the parking lot of the Marco Polo to harass loitering patrons and question the proprietor about suspicious activity in the area. They would go room to room knocking on doors under the false pretense of showing pictures of recent runaways to guests, but their real agenda was sniffing out pot smokers for an easy bust. Most of the time they would cuff their quota or be distracted by an emergency radio call and peel out of the parking lot onto other pig business, leaving the Marco Polo reeling from her nightly shakedown while her seedier twin sister sat on the other side of the concrete median unmolested.

No one stayed at the Thunderbird Motel. You ended up there. You hid there. But no one stayed there on purpose.

Kelly and I paged Eddie, we paged Tommy, we paged the Miguels, we paged the Josés. We paged every drug dealer we knew as if pagers were going out of style. I would meet them in the parking lot of the Food Giant in Wallingford one at a time and Kelly would stay in the room and monitor the local news on TV. We bought every piece of dope and every gram of coke we could get our hands on. Our plan was simple. Hang the Do Not Disturb sign, pull the shades and fuck and suck and shoot drugs until either the heat was off or the world ended, whichever came first.

I rested my elbow on the towel rack as I patiently waited for my bladder to empty. The rack crashed to the floor as one of the mismatched screws that haphazardly attached it to the rotten wood paneling bounced into the toilet bowl.

"What are you doin' in there?" she yelled from one of the two unmade twin beds.

"Just destroying the bathroom, dear."

Continuing the destruction of the bathroom would have been more apropos. We were getting sloppy. The sink and towels were splattered with black hair dye and the lid of the toilet tank was covered in black smudges from burned bent spoons. We had been insanely lucky so far, but if we had to ditch that room in a hurry it wouldn't have taken a master sleuth to realize they needed to update the description of their person-of-interest and the places she would be likely to frequent.

Due to a technical glitch in its barbaric video system, not to mention the ridiculously large summer hat Kelly had been wearing, the surveillance footage from the first bank was useless. When the footage from the second bank robbery hit the local news, however, it caused quite a stir, temporarily putting a halt to our little reign of terror and fortuitously imploding the career of a very popular news anchor.

Clay Bartel was handsome in a way on which mother and daughter could agree. He had the standard-issue anchorman's head of hair, unmovable and impenetrable, the kind of hair one could imagine would still remain on his skull years after his soul had left this mortal coil. But he also had piercing blue eyes that had what I believe is called a twinkle. He was so beautiful that even the punk rock girls didn't mind his mandatory newscaster's mustache. He had been seen playing pool in Belltown, drinking pitchers of beer with local fans, and it has since been rumored that he was observed smoking pot with members of Pearl Jam backstage at a Neil Young show.

The only one who was more aware of his charm and appeal than the female demographic of the greater Seattle-Tacoma area was Bartel himself. He would sit in front of his mirror while his make-up girl added a little color and contemplate adding a wink to his nightly sign-off. When his perfect skin had attained that unnatural, yet on-air-ready shade of orange, his make-up artist gone, he would stand and square off with his own reflection.

"Are you ready?" he'd ask himself.

"KING 5's News Bad Boy Clay Bartel, let's do this!" Pounding his chest once, he'd then head down the hall to shoot the live tease for that evening's program.

Kelly loved hotels. Less than an hour after the first robbery, she gave me five hundred-dollar bills out of random bundles of cash in her backpack and I dropped her off downtown while I checked into the Four Seasons by myself. We figured that since tempting fate had worked out pretty well so far, we'd live like royalty for a night. If the door hadn't been kicked in by the cops come morning, everything would be fine.

She locked herself in the restroom of the Elliot Bay Bookstore, peeled off her sundress and shoved it deep into the trash can, making sure it was covered in paper towels and debris so as not to be discovered by a janitor or customer. She pulled on some Levi's she had stashed in her bag and wiped off her bright red lipstick. She pulled her hair back in a ponytail and plain-Janed herself up as much as possible to avoid unwanted attention. On her way out of the shop she stopped and purchased a Houdini biography, a *People* magazine and a cute pair of reading glasses. She didn't much care about the book or the magazine and she didn't need the glasses, but she did want to appear a leisurely shopper and not a newly wanted felon. Mostly, she just wanted to break the seal on her first paycheck.

She laughed maniacally as she dumped bundles of cash onto the bed from her backpack, then flopped into the giant comfy chair in the corner of the room.

"Toss me that room service menu, Charlie. I'm so hungry I could eat a rhinoceros dick."

We didn't turn on the TV that night. We ordered rare steaks and one of every dessert they had. We got high and we fucked and we got high again. When night fell we stepped onto the balcony wrapped in sheets and smoked cigarettes while staring at the lights of the city. I could see the "LIVE GIRLS" sign of the Champ Arcade blinking away, and I wondered if I still had a job.

I never counted the money. I honestly didn't care. As long as there were hot and cold running narcotics and my cock ended up in her mouth at least once a day, it didn't occur to me to ask questions.

"This afternoon, for the second time in less than a week, a woman walked into a Washington Mutual bank branch, handed the teller a note demanding money and escaped on foot with an undisclosed amount of cash. KING 5 has received this footage from the bank's security cameras from Seattle Police, who are asking for help identifying the young woman..."

Clay Bartel watched on the monitor as the screen filled with sequential still images of Kelly walking up to the teller and placing a dark-colored backpack on the counter. She was wearing a long blonde wig with bangs she had cut herself that morning in our bathroom, dark wraparound sunglasses and a very low-cut black vintage dress.

Due to the angle of the camera, the most clear and concise images were those of her breasts and her hand passing the note forward. The only good shots of her face were a tad blurry, but not completely unrecognizable. We looked at each other as we watched this all unfold on the fucked-up TV from one of the fucked-up beds in our fucked-up motel room. Fuck. I pretended not to panic. She pretended not to panic.

"More on this story, news, sports and the weekend weather, when we return at 6 and 11 on KING 5 news," finished up the dreamy on-air personality as the music was cued and the screen once again filled with Kelly's best I-mean-fuckin'-business sneer.

Then something that would not be unfair to categorize as a miracle happened.

Clay Bartel leaned over to his new co-anchor, Linda Savage, and said, "Wow, that chick is hot. I would totally bang her." It wasn't just that he was being inappropriate — Bartel was always boisterous and a little crude. The problem was Miss Savage's mic was still live.

Suddenly, the big story was not the news but what happened *after* the news. Bartel had the highest ratings and the biggest paycheck of anyone in local television history, so the competition pounced gleefully. In cutthroat fashion the other stations ran with the story within the story, furiously trying to dethrone their nemesis, and while they may have succeeded in terms of rallying advertisers to pressure him off the air, Seattle wasn't exactly a holier-than-thou hotbed in the mold of Birmingham, Alabama, or Salt Lake City. Instead of shocked faces and finger-wagging, the men of our fair city just laughed and nodded their heads in solidarity while the ladies secretly swooned at Bartel's reckless swagger. Not only was the competing stations' *coup d'état* a net failure, having given Clay Bartel the outlaw persona he so desperately craved, it also inadvertently made the lovely but potentially dangerous hot-chick bank robber the It Girl of the moment.

Lying in bed half-naked in our smoky little room, we had no way of knowing all this, of course. The things we knew for certain were that misdirection and chaos were our friends, and — as became blazingly apparent as I switched from channel to channel — that Kelly had graduated from troublemaker to criminal mastermind to superstar in just a few hours.

"How the fuck do we celebrate this?" I asked.

"Dick's Deluxe, fries and large vanilla shake," she said, pulling a hundred-dollar bill out of her bra and sticking it in the waistband of my boxers.

I knew what to do, and I knew that right away was the time to do it. The truth was that even though I was her conspirator, her facilitator of safe houses, her getaway car driver, mostly I was simply the errand boy. I don't say this as a disclaimer or any attempt to understate my role in these or any other illegal activities. Criminal-empire-wise, this was our relationship. And I can't say that was not for the best. To this day, I am purposefully ignorant of any statute of limitations that might apply to this situation and I hope to remain so. I am still uneasy whenever I walk into a bank. My knees start to twitch nervously when I think of the bedlam that ensued over the course of those next several days. I was the errand boy not because I didn't want to be as guilty as she; I was just the errand boy because she knew that I was.

I parked the car on a side street off Broadway, figuring that should it become necessary, it would be easier to run than to elude capture in a high-speed car chase through the often-crowded parking lot of Dick's Drive-In. It was also just nice to be out walking in the fresh air for a change, enjoying the smell of cigarette smoke and french fries. As I approached, I noticed a congregation forming on the sidewalk. A fast-acting and enterprising young screen printer with two large cardboard boxes had set up shop next to a store that sold stripper heels and trashy lingerie. His girlfriend stood on a milk crate and held the merchandise high over her head so both the crowd and passersby could see. It was a black T-shirt with white lettering:

I'D TOTALLY BANG HER TOO
THE CLAY BARTEL DEFENSE FUND

"You have these in girl sizes?" I asked when it was finally my turn.

"Told ya, dumbass," shot his girlfriend from above the mob.

"Large and extra large," said the entrepreneur.

"Two larges then."

He had no trouble making change for my hundred-dollar bill.

23. THE DAMN THING

In the darkness I saw the burning cherry of a cigarette unencumbered by host. It hovered, swelling occasionally to reveal the sweet, sexless face of a child. I was too lost in thought to notice the strangeness of this. I was paused inside a narcotic bender that had been upgraded to rampage, attempting to collect myself.

I was in the motel parking lot, still sitting in the car, waiting for some feelings to pass. I'd made a couple of mistakes that night. Driving by the hospital was one, talking to strangers the other.

I had walked the perimeter of Harborview, searching each of the hundreds of windows for a sign. The first few floors were administrative offices that had been put to sleep hours before. The grounds were silent except for the hum of generators and my footsteps. My eyes darted from one pane of glass to the next, looking for a familiar mop of hair or the words "Rescue Me, Charlie" written in red lipstick. The rooms were lit by nightstand lamps and televisions. I swallowed each shadow whole as they crossed their ceilings, knowing that any one of them could be hers. I stood still and watched the cement giant as the lights clicked off one at a time. Then I slid behind the steering wheel and blew a kiss toward the building, unaware that at that very moment she was turning off her reading lamp in another hospital eleven hundred miles away.

Both arms filled with provisions, I kicked the car door shut with the heel of my boot.

"Hey, Mister."

"Jesus!" I screamed, dropping everything on the ground and holding my hands up to show I was unarmed.

Instead of the sound of heavy boots and the thumps of police batons on my cranium, I heard giggling.

"I gotta warn ya, I'm a person of color but I mean you no harm," a soft voice said behind me.

Relief turned to embarrassment as I bent down to gather my belongings. A young woman stepped out from the shadows, knelt down beside me and started to help. A shoulder-length explosion of dark ringlets obscured her face from me; a cloud of cocoa butter and menthols enveloped us. She was kind enough to slide the box of condoms and package of Ex-Lax chewing gum toward me without a wise remark. We both stood and brushed the parking lot debris from our knees. I towered over her. She was compact sex appeal, 5-foot-1 of carnal knowledge teetering on the heels of burgundy cowboy boots. Her red paisley Western shirt was tied in a knot at her bosom to reveal her smooth brown midriff and the cut-off jean shorts that barely clung to her hips.

"My name is Baby Satan."

This just kept getting better and better.

I juggled the six-pack, the quart of ice cream and the greasy bag of burgers to free up my right hand. Her grasp was delicate and cold. I was pretty sure I was about to hear a sob story about needing some money for a bus ticket to see her mother in Walla Walla, but I was too intrigued to give her a fake name.

"Charlie," I said. "Nice to make your acquaintance."

"Are you a cop, Charlie?"

"No, ma'am. Hell, no," I replied.

She claimed she was the motel's concierge, unofficial and self-appointed perhaps, but diligent in her duties nonetheless. Of course, she didn't use those exact words. I was so beguiled by her full lips and gold-plated incisor I didn't even hear her exact words as she ran down the myriad of services she would provide to guests if the price was right. Young girls, young men and she-males in a variety of colors and sizes were five minutes away. Weed, coke, speed and smack could be there with a snap of her fingers. And if you needed somebody roughed up, she had people for that, too. If you were new in town, she could be your lifeline to the finer things in life.

"So...what are you into, sweetheart?" she asked.

"Oh, no thank you," I knew better than to add any new characters to my current entanglements. "I'm just here on vacation."

"By yo' self?" she inquired.

"Nah, I'm here with my girl...this girl I know."

Baby Satan was a born hustler. In fact, she was born 19 years earlier not three miles from where we stood and had, quite literally, been raised in the Thunderbird motel. Her daddy had been a pioneer in the deconstruction of that little oasis of the Northwest. Since the mid-'70s, before the paint cracked and the neon broke, with Baby playing at his feet, he had run an escort service out of the very room she occupied that night.

"Oh, Dick's," she said, glancing at the bag. "I love Dick's."

As that last part had nearly gotten by me, I decided to let it go the rest of the way. "Well, I bought a shit-ton of food if you're hungry."

"Nah, I gotta keep this shit tight," she said, raising her arms and slowly spinning around to show off her physical attributes, only taking her eyes off me for the split-second her back was toward me.

I gave her the standard line about how nice it was to meet her and wished her a good night before digging in my pocket for the room key.

"By the way," she said, "the best blowjob you ever got is waitin' for you in No. 12." Her face told me there would be a financial transaction involved, and though I didn't know how much it was, I knew I could not afford it.

I walked into a miracle. I couldn't believe it. Kelly had actually tidied up the place while I was gone. The beds were made, the candles lit, and she sat at the table, dressed and with a fresh coat of lipstick, reading about her criminal activity in the newspaper. It was real Norman Rockwell stuff. I liked to see her get dolled up for something besides a robbery. It was nice to remember she was more than just trouble.

"There's some real unsavory types out there tonight," I remarked.

"Want some?" she asked, pouring some unfamiliar red wine into a plastic keg cup.

"I thought we agreed I'd be the only one going out for a couple of days."

"I know. I got bored. The store's only a couple of blocks away."

The lecture I was about to deliver got caught in my throat when she stood up to hand me the drink. My favorite plaid skirt had returned, and her new hair had been freed from the bondage of its ponytail for the first time since the Clairol Natural Blue Black bathroom massacre. She looked stunning.

"I appreciate you indulging me, you know that, right?" she said, right before kissing me on the lips.

"Oh, I have a surprise for you," I said, remembering the T-shirts I had accidentally left in the car. "You are not going to fuckin' believe this."

Somewhere in the melee of fornication, a curtain had been torn down and the rudest of sunny days shook me awake. The generic landscape painting that hung above the bed now rested comfortably against my skull, and Kelly softly purred next to me, my belt still wrapped around her neck.

Naked, I dragged the cover of the bed over to the window and tossed it over the curtain rod for some temporary relief from the obscene light, not to mention cover from our neighbors' wandering eyes. It was noon. I rinsed my head in the sink, lit a cigarette and switched on the TV. The screen was alive with rapid-fire jump cuts. There were aerial shots of police cruisers, on-the-scene reporters fumbling with microphones and gravitas-drenched anchors in newsrooms.

"Babe, wake up!"

Within ten minutes of each other, two women had entered two different branches of Washington Mutual and handed the tellers notes demanding money. Maria Guillot wore a blonde wig and blue contact lenses. Elizabeth Knight had her 15-year-old son cut her bangs just like the lady she'd seen on TV. He'd done the best he could. One wore a revealing halter and the other a tube-top; each made the rookie mistake of wearing heels. Neither of them made it to her awaiting car in the parking lot.

Seventeen-year-old Cheyenne Deville and her best friend Honey Broussard stood in line at the Seafirst bank in Wallingford. They were holding hands, their fingers tightly intertwined. They wore matching Catholic girls' school uniforms and aviator shades. They both had their hair in pigtails and one too many buttons undone on their school blouses. On the count of three, Miss Broussard held a World-War-II-era hand grenade she had found in her grandfather's basement over her head with one hand and and stuck the index finger of her other hand in the firing ring. Miss Deville slung her duffel bag on the counter and unzipped it.

"Fill this with cash or we're all gonna fuckin' die!"

Fifteen minutes later, Kathryn Boyd pulled a large kitchen knife out of her purse and waved it at a college student working behind the register at the Big Top convenience store on Elliot Way. When the young man calmly put down the *Auto Trader* he was thumbing through and produced a shiny aluminum baseball bat seemingly from nowhere, Miss Boyd yelped, dropped the knife and ran out the door as fast as her tight pencil skirt would allow. The man didn't even call the police until he heard about the other hold-ups on the radio.

An hour later, across the lake in Bellevue, Amelia Kaye and her boyfriend, Jesse Warren, entered the Bank of America. Jesse pointed a shotgun at the elderly security guard as Amelia casually strolled past the line and straight up to the teller wearing a shockingly short minidress, her blonde wig barely hiding her long, dark ringlets.

By the end of the day a half-dozen women and two men had been arrested. It was a full-blown crime spree, and that's not even counting how many others sat in vehicles across from their favorite banking institutions, chickening out.

The police were holding the four women who had claimed responsibility for the first two hold-ups in separate cells downtown until they could sort out the mess. None of them seemed to have much in the way of criminal record. If they had been organized, surely they would have cracked under the pressure of the serious charges they now faced. The cops frantically searched for a connection. A book club, a knitting circle, a cult, anything. All law enforcement personnel, on or off duty, were dispatched to every bank, credit union and savings and loan in the Seattle/Tacoma area. Mayor Norm Rice flew home from the first vacation he'd had in many years to meet with local FBI agents. The city had never seen anything like it before — no city had. No one was prepared to call it a state of emergency, but at the same time, no one knew what the fuck was going on, either. The chief of police, the King County Sheriff, and some person who apparently was the head of Special Ops — a position the chief and the sheriff hadn't even known existed — argued at a large desk as the phones and fax machines went insane. None of it made any sense to them, but they weren't ready to settle for the possibility that they were just dealing with a gaggle of attention-seeking sociopaths.

KOMO news had an exclusive. Footage of Elizabeth Knight's arrest — from a startled tourist with a video camera — was presently showing a facedown and handcuffed Knight screaming in a parking lot, the contents of her purse strewn about. As the officers picked her up by the feet and the scruff of her neck, the news station was kind enough to augment the poor audio with subtitles.

"I love you, Clay! I love you!" read the TV screen.

I had no trouble imagining Seattle's most popular unemployed newscaster sitting in his underwear with a Bud Light in one hand and a fat cigar in the other, his phone's ringer turned off, a yellow notepad next to him filled with the names and number of agents, managers and publicists. Lifting his beer bottle, he toasts the television that gave him his very own criminal phenomenon.

Relieved of it being *our* criminal phenomenon, Kelly and I toasted it, too.

"We love you, too, ladies! We love you, too."

24. ROLLER COASTER

"Does this gun make my butt look big?" she asked.

She laughed as if she'd said the funniest thing ever, and perhaps she had. I did not join her in her laughter, preoccupied as I was by a sense of impending doom and an enormous rush of blood, two things racing each other to be the first to my cock.

She stood with her back toward the mirror in a black bra and tight-fitting jeans. She arched her back and craned her head over her shoulder to take in as much of her reflection as possible. The barrel of a new Browning 9mm pistol was strategically shoved down the crack of her ass. Even with her heaving chest and beautifully exposed jugular, I couldn't help but be concerned.

"Where the fuck did you get that?"

"I met your lady friend in the parking lot. Shame on you for keeping her a secret."

Shit.

"What does she know!?"

"Relax, sweetness," she said, raising her best you're-startin'-to-be a-real-fuckin'-drag eyebrow at me.

"What did you tell her you needed a gun for?" I asked her slowly and methodically.

"To kill you."

"Damn. I thought she liked me."

"She does. She thinks you have sexy hands. She thinks you abuse me," she said as she looked over the other shoulder, checking her profile from the opposite side.

"And whatever gave her that idea?"

"She sleeps on the other side of that wall, dummy," she said, dramatically removing the weapon from her pants and taking aim at the thin sheet of plaster that separated us from Room 12.

Shit.

"You gotta put those bullets," she pointed the gun at a small box on the table, then at a plate-metal object on the chair next to them, "in that cartridge thingy for me, please. It's too hard for me, and Baby Satan just got her nails done."

The only thing stopping me from grabbing my few possessions and walking out the door that very second was everything. Or at least everything I could think of, which was another way of saying drugs. We Seattelites were experiencing a drought. Our once-wondrous pile of drugs had recently dried up, and the tiny cotton balls at the bottom of every spoon had been reanimated with water, reheated and wrung dry in pursuit of each opiated microparticle. Given the choice between not having money to buy drugs and having money but not being able to find drugs, I would choose our current situation, of course. But a duffle bag full of cash doesn't stop your nose from running any more than it stops your skin from crawling or your meal ticket from getting on your last frayed fuckin' nerve.

I stood by the pay phone pretending it didn't smell like piss. I considered my answering strategy. The trick was to pinch the nasty thing between your thumb and middle finger and hold it just close enough to hear and be heard but far enough away to avoid tasting it. I passed the time by repressing dry heaves and smoking cigarettes.

My job was to procure dope. It was a pretty good set of skills to bring to the table, but at that moment even I was questioning my usefulness. I wanted to keep friends out of this. There were certain truths I was hiding from in our cozy rat's nest of a bed, and even junkie friends exchange pleasantries, inquire about your well-being and — worst of all — ask about your significant others. I didn't want to talk about any of it. Explaining my disappearance was one thing, explaining Carrie's was quite another. Far preferable to me was the cold, professional-client relationship of guys who passed cellophane packages of brown sticky heaven out the windows of their primer-gray Camaros. Alas, even they were coming up short.

We Northwest junkies had to put up with a fragile drug economy. Any major busts or beefing-up of security on the Mexican border meant trouble. We were on the losing end of a trickle-up situation. Los Angeles and San Diego got the cream of the crop. The dope was stepped on but still in pretty good shape by the time it got to San Francisco and Sacramento. It was weak but at least still abundant upon its arrival in Portland. By the time we got our hands on it here, it was more costly and far less potent. Even the slightest disruption in the flow left us with nothing at all. We were the red-headed stepchildren of the West Coast narcotic trade.

It had been a fucking hour since I'd paged him. I paced back and forth, choleric and agitated. I was disgusted with myself. I knew damn well I was going to pick up that urine-caked receiver and check to make sure there was a dial tone for the fourth or fifth time, causing yet another split-second when he would get a busy signal. And I did. And then I threw up. I played a game with all the more than enough reasons I had to seek oblivion. Since heroin was my coping mechanism, I pretended that the removal of it was just what all my inner demons, turmoil and bullshit were waiting for to come bubbling up and out any exit they could find. I just kept puking it all up. Hands on my knees, retching in the sunlight as the real world enjoyed a Sunday afternoon, I played my game and waited for the phone to ring.

Kelly was not the whining, sniveling mess I was. She had tapped into that tolerance for pain that women have. The one that allows them to be nobly ripped in half delivering our sons and daughters. The one that allows them to subject themselves to the massive amounts of electricity being pumped into their skulls so their fathers can relax and know they're doing all they can for their little girls. The same tolerance that heals the hearts we stomp on also fends off the crushing aches of wanting.

She sat there in our room plotting, scheming, with grace. Outwardly serene, the only sign of her inner turmoil was her foot tapping. She was not at all content with the clean escape that getting lost in the quagmire of copycat criminals allowed us. No, she was angry about the loss of her newfound celebrity, offended that her crown had been so quickly stolen. She would not have her spotlight diverted by low-rent plastic replicas, cheapening her genius and mocking her artistry. How dare they! She rocked back and forth in her chair, quietly seething.

When I finally walked back in the room with my hair and clothes stinking of failure, I was met, much to my surprise, with arms and lips and an idea that for some reason had never crossed my mind.

"How 'bout that old man you used to buy the white dope from?" she asked sweetly.

The Frontier Room would do nicely. With its dark, shadowy booths, strong drinks and drug-addict-friendly, locking bathroom stalls, it was the ideal place to stash Kelly while I searched out my old janitor/drug-kingpin friend. She had insisted on coming. She was going a little stir-crazy in our crusty little room.

The angry barmaid approached our booth.

"Drink," she said, not a question but a command.

"Whiskey, something Irish," I said, avoiding eye contact and lighting a cigarette.

"Do you have fresh pineapple juice?" Kelly asked, gleefully pushing the woman's already disgruntled buttons.

"Oh, for fuck's sake," she said as she turned and stomped back to the bar.

Kelly counted out $3,000 on the table with no regard to who might be watching. I shook my head quietly and wondered how long it would be before I was wearing an orange jumpsuit and using a stainless steel toilet.

The woman returned, put two shots and two beers on the table and stuck out her hand without saying a word. Kelly took a twenty off the pile and told her to keep the change.

"Gee, thanks," she said, eyeballing the stack of bills.

We formulated our plan. Otis would be getting off work soon but unfortunately, his pockets would be empty of colored balloons. His real money was made early in the morning, before he even attacked the first private booth with his trusty mop. I was hoping that in exchange for the many times I'd had to endure the Ray Charles shoeshine story and the genuine fondness I had for him, not to mention the large amount of cash we were carrying, he might invite me to his place to do business. If he agreed to this, Kelly and I would hop the next bus after his and meet him there.

For whatever reason, $3,000 was a threshold number in Kelly's mind. Though she'd sent me off many times with hundreds of dollars to meet up with all kinds of ne'er-do-wells, she apparently thought $3,000 was the figure that was just tempting enough to make me abscond with the cash and never return. She was probably right.

"Try not to cause any trouble," I said, finishing my beer. I kissed her on the forehead and walked out onto 1ˢᵗ Avenue.

"Hello, Otis."

"Damn son, you look like hell," he said, looking up from his newspaper.

Otis was sitting at his usual bus stop, Mariners cap slightly tilted back on his head, Thermos sitting on the sidewalk at his feet.

I looked at my reflection in the storefront window, the ghost of a god-damned wreck. I hardly recognized me. Gone was the badass rock 'n' roller with his perfectly unkempt hair and ever-present leather jacket. Even if it wasn't true, I'd always at least looked the part. Flannel shirt, sweatpants and cowboy boots. A fucking flannel shirt, fucking sweatpants and a mother-fucking pair of cowboy boots? What the fuck? Carrie wouldn't have let me leave the house like that.

"How you doin', sir?"

"Now, don't take this the wrong way, but I can't be seen socializing with the likes of you," he said, holding the newspaper back up in front of his face. "Have a seat so we can talk."

I sat down on the bench and stared at the concrete.

"Where you been, kid?" he asked out of the side of his mouth.

With Otis as cleric and the sports section between us his confessional, I leaned in and whispered a succession of seemingly stunning and heart-felt lies. I told him I couldn't take it anymore. I told him the ugliness of that place had gotten to me, that my humanity, no, *our* humanity, had been scorched. I declared a very real concern that both of our souls were being cannibalized. I wept. I stammered.

He slid a handkerchief on the bench toward me.

"Settle down, son. It's just tits and ass," he laughed. "Unless you've found Jesus or some shit, you need to get your head on straight and get your ass back to work."

Against his better judgment, and only after the sincerest of promises to get my shit together, Otis said he was all right with me and my lady friend coming by the house just this one time.

I flooded the Frontier Room with light when the door opened.

"Over here," beckoned an unfamiliar voice above the laughter and the crunching guitar chords of the jukebox.

Kelly and the once-sourpuss bartender sat on stools while Baby Satan stood on an ice chest on the working side of the bar, dealing blackjack and pouring shots. They had stacks of 24-hour sobriety AA chips they were using to wager with. The house had acquired many of these in its popular 24-hour chip/free drink exchange program.

"Charlie, this is Tawnie," Kelly said, introducing her new friend.

"Hello there."

"What would you do?" Tawnie asked, gesturing toward her cards. It was not a traditional greeting but I was fine with it. I didn't plan on knowing her long anyway.

"Always hit on 16," I said, shaking off the shot of whiskey that burned its way down my throat.

She tapped her cards twice with the tip of her finger. Baby flipped over a king. The three-girl riot broke out into jeers and cursing. Baby Satan leaned over the bar and kissed me on the cheek. I pulled up a stool.

"Whose is this?" I asked, pointing at the unattended beer, stack of chips and smoldering cigarette in the ashtray before me.

As soon as the question left my lips Wayne Newton's giant paw draped over my shoulder.

"Where the fuck you been, man?" he bellowed in my ear over the Aerosmith song.

Baby Satan leaned over the bar and kissed him on the lips, deeply, very deeply, before going back to her card-dealing duties.

"Ain't she somethin'?" he asked as we both admired the way she jiggled when she jumped up on the ice chest.

"Yeah, she's something, all right. When did you meet her?"

"Couple days ago, man. She just walked into the store, came right up to me and introduced herself," he slurred.

Just as I was getting ready to mumble something about things that were too good to be true, I stopped. He never took his eyes off her. She met his stare with a cartoonish wink before tossing down another bust card, this time for Kelly. Again the place erupted into howls and cheers and obscenities.

25. GONNA DIE MORE

"**O**h fuck, turn that shit up!"

Baby Satan lunged over the front seat and cranked the volume knob on Wayne Newton's crappy car radio. The two of them and Kelly were crooked and loud. I, being the responsible one, was driving. She stopped at the nape of my neck and inhaled deeply, followed by a long, protracted sigh.

Hey, did you happen to see the most beautiful girl in the world?

She fell into the back seat singing along at the top of her lungs.

And if you did, was she cryin'?

The puzzlement on my face as she bellowed Charlie Rich's biggest hit must've been obvious, the question it brought to my mind transparent. I adjusted the rearview mirror looking for the answer.

"What? My Daddy used to sing this song to me."

She brushed away a chocolate ringlet that had stuck to her lipstick.

"I got my blue eyes from him."

Her mouth was so otherworldly it was the first time I actually looked in her eyes.

"I'll be damned," I mumbled to myself.

"Ya know what?" she said, "You kinda look like dear ol' dad."

He was small-time but charming. His Southern accent, his halfway-decent vocabulary and his impeccable manners were all very novel in the taverns along Aurora. He specialized in the rookies who were afraid to talk to the scary Negro pimps or the timid types who came over from the University District to lose that pesky virginity that had followed them from Boise or Spokane. The seasoned sharks couldn't be bothered explaining the rudimentary ins and outs of the world's oldest profession to newbies; they had a small army of volatile women, a city of greedy policemen and their own vulnerable backs to consider, so they allowed him.

They weren't the least bit threatened by this odd creature. They had seen his type before. Many an overly enthusiastic, fast-talking clown who thought he could parlay his talent for talking his way into high-school girls' panties into an occupation had crossed their path. Theirs was a calling steeped in tradition. There were regulations that had been in place since the very first trick had been turned. There were rules that he either refused to follow or was completely unaware of. Manner of dress and skin color aside, he was just strange.

He referred to himself as the ladies' agent. He opened doors for them. He never called them whores or lifted a hand to them. He didn't have to. They worked for him, or "with him," as he always corrected them, not because of intimidation or violence but because they loved him. They genuinely loved him.

The old guard knew these were not the building blocks on which a long-term, successful pimp-hooker relationship was built. Besides appearing weak, this sort of behavior could set unrealistic standards for the way this type of business was conducted. These were certainly future headaches for the career-orientated hustler, but this new guy had a pretty good eye for talent and didn't seem to mind acting as buffer between them and nosy patrolmen who would drop in from time to time. A Caucasian face seemed to help in those matters.

They indulged him in conversation occasionally, hoping to learn the secret of his baritone drawl and how it soothed unhinged female minds and made even the most outrageous requests seem perfectly reasonable. Try as they might, they were cavemen who only understood the slap and the growl. They felt confident that, if they wished, and if his body didn't end up in a random dumpster some morning, they could simply take his clientele, his women and his money and kick his ass back to Dixie any time they wanted.

One evening, with one swift and vicious act, he changed their minds forever and cemented his legend in Seattle's filthy underbelly. A loudmouth motherfucker feeling the swagger that comes with a night of whiskey and a wallet full of salmon-fishing money is always dangerous. Their desire for pussy and booze is accelerated from being caged on a boat on the frozen sea between Canada and Alaska for six months, and the pride they somehow feel from having performed such a task is expounded upon at boastful and insufferable volumes. They are reluctantly welcomed, but only long enough for the bartenders and pimps to fleece them of their paychecks. When one of these out-of-town thugs, a 300-pound unlikeable monster who was practicing insanely poor judgment, put a knife to the breast of a troubled princess with the already peanut-sized Baby Satan in her womb, he was probably just showing off.

"I'm gonna cut this nigger's titty off," he announced to the bar.

The last thing he saw before the blood from the open wound on his forehead filled his eyes was Baby Satan's father standing there with a half-grin and a straight razor.

Daddy pushed the giant to the front door of the barroom, held him there with his forearm, disarmed him and endured brutal, hairy-knuckled blows to the head and kicks to the shins as he calmly and methodically dismantled the stranger's abdomen with his own knife. The Neanderthal's brown leather belt was the only thing stopping his intestines from spilling out onto the floor. He felt the heavy warmth of his blood as it first soaked his long johns and socks and then filled the new work boots he had purchased that morning. By the time he gained the wherewithal to scream, Daddy held his head back by a handful of hair and performed open-throat surgery before letting the ravaged man fall to the floor. The bartender reached for the phone to dial 911, only to hang up again when Daddy waved a blood-soaked finger at him. Witnesses to the horror say they saw the devil cut a man in half that night. They watched in silence as he slowly wiped his blood-splattered face with his sleeve, spit out a tooth and limped out of the Lion's Lair with his arm around a young lady's waist.

If the man's filleted larynx had still been in working order, one might have heard his last words: "I was just kiddin', I was just kiddin.'" Instead, they bubbled out onto the barroom floor.

Broadway starts out well enough in the north, but by the time we went far enough south to angle off on Boren, espresso stands and cafes became less frequent, being replaced by 7-Elevens and fast-food dumps. The skin tones of pedestrians became darker and darker. My hands were at 10 and 2 instead of being wrapped around my cramping guts. Expired or suspended, I wasn't sure what condition my driver's license was in, but I wasn't about to give some random pig an excuse to pull us over. The cure for my current physical plight was just a mile away, but the fact that I was hydroplaning through the streets of the city's least-desirable neighborhood with three wild cards was not my foremost concern. I had bigger-picture issues.

I was pretty sure I didn't have a place to live anymore. Sure, I could grovel and get my job back, no problem. But then what? To maintain the anesthetized lifestyle I had recently grown accustomed to would require the kind of funds I couldn't make slingin' porn. Plan B was a mystery. I had not given one single thought to the future, nor to my inevitable exit.

Otis's place was nice. I didn't know what I expected, but it hadn't been this cozy bungalow with multiple Big Wheels in the yard and a well-tended hedge that I assumed would burst with tuberose when spring rolled around.

I didn't expect something so grandfatherly, I suppose. I checked the address again before I put the Oldsmobile in park.

"All right, you guys sit tight. I'll be right back," I said, gesturing toward Kelly for the cash.

"Oh no, I'm goin' in too," she insisted, grabbing her purse and checking her bangs in the visor mirror.

I waited for her on the sidewalk. My foot tapped uncontrollably. I suppressed throwing up the beer I drank an hour before. She got out, shut her door and then leaned into the back window of the car talking to Baby and Wayne. Fuck, enough chitchat. My only solace was a brief moment to admire Kelly's flawless ass. I imagined Otis was doing the same from his dining room window, but I didn't turn around to check.

We rang the doorbell twice, then — addicts have no patience — pounded on the screen door. Finally, we heard footsteps and the door finally opened.

"Hello, welcome," Otis said, while adjusting his hearing aid with his left hand and removing his apron with his right, "I was just tidying up."

"Hello sir," Kelly was the first to enter with her hand extended in Otis's direction, "my name is Trixie, so lovely to meet you."

"Yes, yes," he said, "I gotta turn my ears down when I do the dishes. It makes an awful racket. This way." He turned around and we followed him into his living room.

"Trixie?" I whispered.

"Shut it, I like the name."

The room was heavy with the smell of a thousand old books and three thousand old records and rice cooking in the kitchen. McCoy Tyner's "The Real McCoy" played quietly on a stylish Zenith wooden console, the words "stereophonic high fidelity" proudly displayed under the brand name. African artwork, abstract kindergarten crayon masterpieces and vintage baseball memorabilia littered the walls. I looked around for something to make small talk about. Nothing too involved, nothing too lengthy, nothing that would delay narcotics from entering my bloodstream, but maybe something that would resemble normal social interaction. The awkward silence was made even more cumbersome by our cultural and generational differences. The things we had in common — our work, the illegal activity we were currently involved in, the odd circumstances that brought us together — weren't subject matter for casual conversation. I was painfully unskilled at sports talk, and the topics of grandchildren and dead wives were too emotionally risky. There were too many things we just couldn't discuss in the short period of time that I hoped our lives would intersect.

My eyes were drawn to the framed black-and-white photos above his kitchen table. In the first one were four menacing-looking black men standing with shotguns on the stairs of what appeared to be a government building. I moved in closer for a better look. I touched their faces, removing the slightest layer of dust from the glass with my fingertip as I named each one of them.

"Huey P. Newton."

"Bobby Seale."

"Little Bobby Hutton."

Under the giant 'fro and significant sideburns of the next man gleamed the once-fierce eyes of our now-humble host.

"Otis Dixon," I said, turning toward him, suddenly realizing the esteemed company we were in. "I'll be damned."

"Yeah, well, that was quite a ways back," he said, a sly grin coming to his lips.

"Honey, we are in the presence of an American treasure," I announced.

Kelly came up behind me and removed the photo from the wall for closer examination.

"Were you in a band?" she asked.

I tried to sound as stern and earnest as I could, considering my retainer and the onslaught of puberty. I hoped for fire and brimstone, but knew the odds of profuse sweating and a poorly timed erection were much higher. Still, show any fear during a 7th grade oral book report and you are dead meat. My mission was more important than a grade, or the valuable experience of public speaking, or even the opportunity to impress Jenny, the light of my 13-year-old life. I was spreading the gospel on my newly acquired worldview, starting with Mrs. Wilson's American History class. I cleared my throat.

"*Seize The Time*, by Bobby Seale," I began.

I spun a righteous tale of how, at that very moment, even as we sat in class, a war was being fought on the streets of Oakland, California, between police officers and a small but mighty band of Afro-American superheroes called the Black Panthers. I rhapsodized of white bourgeois monsters and imprisoned ebony saints. I told tales of free love and revolution, of battles in courts of law and the commandeering of public parks in Chicago. And all the while my voice fluctuated between its recently developed Barry White register and that of an excitable little girl.

The pigs had pretty much won the war at that juncture, but I didn't know that then; I was just a kid who had read half a book and was hysterically encouraging my peers to take up arms.

Kids squirmed in their seats and Mrs. Wilson sat at her desk massaging her forehead as if she had a migraine. The one black kid in our class shrugged his shoulders as my fellow students looked to him for confirmation. Jenny smiled big as I began reciting the Black Panther Ten-Point Program from memory.

"1. We want freedom. We want power to determine the destiny of our black and oppressed community.

"2. We want full employment for our people.

"3. We want an end to the robbery by the capitalists of our black and oppressed community.

"4. We want decent housing, fit for the shelter of human beings.

"5. We want decent education for our people that exposes the true nature of this decadent American society.

"6. We want completely free health care for all black and oppressed people.

"7. We want an immediate end to police brutality and murder of black people…"

"OK, that's enough, Charlie!" Our teacher slammed her fists on the desk top.

"We want land, bread, housing, education, CLOTHING, JUSTICE, PEACE AND PEOPLE'S…" I continued, shouting the last over my shoulder as I was escorted out of class by Mrs. Wilson and was walked, finally in silence, to the principal's office.

Otis unlocked a filing cabinet next to his small, cluttered desk and went about the business of weighing and bagging the most drugs I had ever seen at a single time in my life. He poured a huge pile of the white synthetic painkiller onto a tray. I made a conscious effort not to drool.

I was overwhelmed with reverence for the old man who sat at the same kitchen table as I did. Cooler than Keith Richards, he hummed a bass line as he shoveled powder into several sandwich bags. He was no less important than Martin Luther King, Jr. or J.F.K. to me. He was a real agent of social change in America. He was a goddamn unsung superhero hiding in plain sight. I wanted to ask him what it felt like to point a loaded shotgun at a police officer while defending your neighborhood. I wanted to ask him if he'd fucked Angela Davis. I wanted him to be my father.

"I gotta say, Otis, I admire what you guys did back then," I said, returning the photo to its proper place on his wall.

"We were just a bunch of crazy kids, no different than y'all, really."

I laughed out loud as I watched Kelly wave out the front window to Wayne and Baby in the car. I assumed they were halfway to coitus in the moldy back seat by now.

"No sir, I don't believe that for a second."

Otis placed three sandwich bags in front of me and cleared his throat as subtle request for payment.

"Honey, come over here and pay the man."

Kelly produced a wad of bills from her jacket and waited patiently for him to count it before pocketing the dope.

Otis groaned softly with pain as he stood; his 71 years made his body ache after a night with the mop, but his impeccable manners still compelled him to escort us to the door.

Then Kelly did something inconceivably rude.

"I don't want to impose, but would you mind if we used your bathroom?" Kelly asked, batting her eyes.

Manners be damned. As uncouth as I considered such a move, I wanted to throw my arms around her. Otis sighed and pointed down the hall.

"Make it quick before the little ones get home," I heard him call out as the bathroom door closed behind us.

Casting all chivalrous behavior aside, I tore off my jacket and rolled up my sleeve quickly to claim my place in line.

"Sit," she said.

I followed orders and sat on the edge of the tub, a shivering mess.

"I just need a little, enough to get me back to the motel."

"Fuck that, we're getting high, baby."

With a few drops of water from the sink, a pinch of dope and the passing of her lighter under a spoon that seemingly appeared from nowhere, she knelt in front of me to administer the medicine. My veins jumped out to meet her. The puncture was glorious. A red rose of blood obscured the clear liquid in the syringe. My heart pounded, my cells fell immediately into place and I was happily lost in the darkness of my eyelids.

"Shit, someone else is gonna have to drive, babe," I said.

I opened my eyes to find Kelly standing with her back to the door and holding her shiny new Browning in both hands, the barrel toward my face.

Suddenly, breaking glass and splintering wood erupted in the living room.

"Get on the ground!" shouted a male voice. I could barely recognize it through the locked bathroom door, Kelly's 120 pounds of betrayal and the ringing in my ears that resulted from having a real pistol pointed at my head for the first time.

The second was Baby Satan's.

"Don't make me hurt you, old man!"

I stood quickly. Instinctually, my hands balled into fists.

"Don't you fuckin' dare!" I screamed at the wall, as if I had a say in the matter.

"You don't wanna stop this, Charlie," Kelly hissed at me as she cocked the hammer of her weapon.

26. WHITE FACES

It was the witching hour once again. I bent over my paperwork on the counter, hoping to get it finished before the madness began, before the unruly ones appeared. Before the beaten and bruised, the vampires and the sick clamored for my attention. Sometimes they were wild and out of control, stinking of whiskey and vomit. Sometimes they had to be wrestled to the ground. But mostly they just wanted someone to talk to, the latter being the most taxing on me, to tell you the truth.

I didn't dream of carrying pepper spray anymore; I obviously couldn't be trusted.

When the phone rings at 2 a.m., it can only be trouble.

"Yeah, I'll meet you out front." I sighed.

I stepped out the front door, lit a cigarette and waited.

They brought me the worst of them, the most wounded of soldiers. These people were dragged out from under the bushes in city parks, some from between unwashed sheets in fraternity houses. They were dogs backed into corners. Their lives had been downsized to a dirty spoon or a sip from a paper bag. They had become resigned to the fact that the floor would always have her way. Each of them would always meet her there, face to face, a broken tooth and a crushed nose, a tiny pool of blood as a substitute for a welcome-home kiss.

They had been pleaded with, threatened, bargained with and cajoled. They had suffered humiliation, heartbreak and sickness. They had been arrested, divorced, disowned and degraded. They had tried prayer, psychiatry, self-control and clinging to their own sorry resolve. They had even stood at the observation decks of skyscrapers and the safety railings of freeway overpasses only to step back in total defeat once again. When all these measures failed, they were dragged to the last place on earth that would have them: my place.

A pair of headlights pulled off the foggy street and into the parking lot. You couldn't judge them by their vehicles. No one arrived unescorted. No one drove themselves. If you were lucky, you had a loving husband or wife who dutifully brought you there; if you were less so, you arrived in handcuffs.

I approached the passenger door and opened it. I tried to keep in mind that it was the worst day of their lives, really I did, but to me it was just Tuesday.

"Welcome, Mr. Turner. Let's get you out of this cold."

Gin and cigar smoke surrounded Robert T. Turner like an aura, like an atmosphere or his own weather system hovering three inches above his skin. A thousand showers and changes of clothes and it would still hang there. His face appeared soft and pink and looked fragile, as though a tiny spiderweb of veins might burst from beneath the surface if you touched him. He was the frail shell of a once-proud, tough-guy newspaperman from Tacoma whose life was collapsing around him.

Mrs. Turner needed to be comforted. They would all like to hand off their loved ones to a physician, maybe a handsome older gentleman with graying temples and kind eyes, but at 2:30 in the morning they got me.

"You're lucky I'm working tonight, my dear. I specialize in grumpy old men," I told her with a wink. She cracked what may have been the last smile left inside her.

She was exhausted and heartbroken. She may have been planning this night for years. She wore his favorite color and her best wig and made sure to slip photos of the grandkids into the bag she had carefully packed for him with the advice of one of the daytime counselors: no mouthwash, no instant coffee, no outside reading material, no clock radios, no cellular telephones, just clean clothes and no more than $10 in cash.

The poor thing had to believe that I and my nicotine-stained smile and my pre-fabricated speech about what good hands her husband was in were the genesis of something grand and new and divine. She had to trust this monster. If she and I were to have approached each other on a city street before that night, she would have clutched her purse closely to her breast and her eyes would have darted nervously in search of other pedestrians. But last hopes make knights in shining armor out of unlikely candidates, and I was all she had left.

They followed me through the front door and into the waiting room, hand-in-shaking-hand.

Civilians always made me nervous. I rolled the sleeves of my work shirt down to conceal my tattoos. I said "ma'am" and "please" and refrained from swearing as much as I could. I truly did want to ease her mind, smooth her furrowed brow and give her a reason to sleep well, but I was ill-equipped when dealing with human beings. All I could do was hand her a coffee-stained pamphlet and try to sound convincing when I promised her I would return her husband to her as good as new.

The clients were easier — they were out of their minds. I could tell them to give me 20 push-ups and they would. I could tell them to sit down so I could shave their heads and they would. I could tell them it was required of them to sing "Happy Birthday" to me at the top of their lungs, regardless of the date, and they would sing. But I didn't do any of that. I had learned something about sympathy and kindness.

If you decided on The Milton Lake House, the first choice for effective, affordable treatment, or if your loved ones or a court of law decided it for you, there was paperwork to be done upon your arrival, plenty of it. If you checked in at a respectable hour, you were greeted by Mrs. Hanson, with her sunny disposition and her smart pantsuits and firm, but fair, loving ways. She would hug you and tell you everything was going to be all right. You fucking believed her and you held on to that complete stranger and you cried like you didn't think you could. At least that's what had happened to me.

If you were a good sleeper or some kind of chronic rule follower, you'd never even meet me. I arrived after lights-out and was driving home just before morning meditations. I was the creepy man who listened to classical music at the dimly lit desk and filed papers. The one who licked the tip of his finger as he sorted through your secrets and made you shudder on the way to the restroom in the middle of the night. The one who made you think twice about what you confessed to your counselor earlier that day. The one the teenage girls with their crystal meth dependencies and their eating disorders called "the icky vampire."

This was not merely the life I was used to, but the one I had chosen out of fear. It was the place I could live out this unnatural act, this life that had turned so upside-down. Something grave was the matter with me, absolutely, but this place and this time were safe.

First things first. We had to establish that this obviously Caucasian male in his mid-to-late-50s was indeed a Caucasian male in his mid-to-late-50s. That would require the filling out of forms.

I asked Mrs. Turner to have a seat in the waiting room. Robert may have to tell me things he was not ready to confess to his sweet wife just yet, and it was best done out of earshot.

Mr. Turner's pace slowed the farther we got from the sightlines of the missus. His demeanor and physical appearance seemed to age in the hundred feet we walked from the foyer to my desk. As we passed the nurse's office, I knocked on the door.

"Incoming," I warned. All I got in response was a grunt.

By the time I pulled out a chair for him, he was using me as a crutch. By the time I sat down, found a working pen and pulled a crisp, new file out of the top drawer, he was totally and utterly defeated. Totally and utterly defeated was a good place to start this process.

From where I sat I could see directly down one hallway and, with a slight tilt of my head and a strategically placed convex mirror, I could monitor the other direction. Whenever the patients sensed unusual activity, most of the doors came ajar just enough for a single eye to peek out from each to do reconnaissance.

Detecting tomfoolery had become one of my many fields of expertise. For the first couple hours of my shift I would work in silence, my ears finetuned to whispers and mysterious bumps in the darkness. The latter part of my work night was spent bathed in the low-volume strings and piano of Chopin or Brahms, organizing the day's harvest of notes, assessment forms and surveys alphabetically and chronologically.

New patients always felt the need to test boundaries. Not on the first night, of course, but once the initial shock of their situation left their systems they became insufferable. They demanded I let them use the phone. No. They demanded I call them a cab. Absolutely not. They demanded to see the nurse. Show me where you're bleeding. They demanded I let them smoke. Say "please," and I'd consider it. I understood the need for nicotine. I understood the part of them that delighted in doing something against the rules. We strive for progress, not perfection, our book told them. I had been progressing for eight years, eleven months but was still a little shy of perfect.

My own protocol for patients' nocturnal behavior was already in place. It was generally passed on from established patient to newbie in whispers on the night of their arrival. Not to worry, there was nothing sinister or malfeasant going on, but it was a clear subversion of policy. For example, I had a higher tolerance for inappropriate clothing. We are not saints. I had no problem with a quiet Yahtzee tournament between two addicts in the throws of an oxycontin withdrawal. There was no sleep in the near future for them anyway. Gum and candy were not an actual endangerment to one's sobriety, in my eyes at least, and late-night smoking was an absolute necessity for maintaining one's sanity. Still, all of these were privileges, not rights.

I was neither unfriendly nor warm and fuzzy. I was a cordial listener with a long list of sage reasons for you not to leave, if that was your intent, or a hawk at distinguishing your bullshit, if you chose that route.

Above all, I insisted on order. I didn't want to see any faces until 2 a.m. Most of them would lapse into slumber before that, leaving me with the hardest of hardcore and the sickest of sick. They were to approach me two at a time — no more, no less. They were to be of the same sex, and preferably roommates. I wasn't going to be caught sneaking a single lady out the side door for an unsanctioned cigarette. Certainly, my $11 an hour before taxes would have been in jeopardy. They were to engage me in some kind of conversation relating to addiction, and after the proper amount of time I would suggest we continue our discussion on the stairs — the fresh air would do us good. This action would repeat itself until all interested parties had an opportunity to seek counsel with me or until I tired of the whole farce. This song and dance was not for my benefit; there were checks and balances in place. It would have been foolish to leave only one person in charge of this potentially volatile situation. Fortunately, the truly adult component of graveyard supervision was the downtrodden nurse who hadn't poked his head out of the office once since he joined us six months ago.

Decorum dictated that those with seniority were first. This week, the position belonged to a couple of manipulative she-monsters who were about to be released on the unsuspecting greater Kirkland/Bellevue area.

April was an almost comical homage to babies-first fetishes. Her bleached-blonde hair was tied into toddler-like pigtails, her huge breasts and perpetually hard nipples were crammed into a tight wifebeater, her satin gym shorts were snug and an ever-present Tootsie Pop was stuck in her preposterously red mouth. Molly was her erotic opposite. Girl next door, with thick-rimmed reading glasses sitting on the tip of her petite nose, well-worn men's pajamas camouflaging any hint of a woman's curves, brown hair firmly pulled into a ponytail and a face free of make-up that made her seem impossibly innocent. She carried her treatment-center-issued Big Book with her at all times, but the bookmark never moved. Molly did all the talking while April did the stretching and jiggling.

Last night, after working themselves into a frenzy, they had stormed the counter waving their notebooks at two seconds after 2 a.m. The last week of your stay with us, you are given the assignment of turning in a fourth step; presumably its completion is a prerequisite for your graduation. If not the widowmaker of steps, it is considered an intimidating stumbling block on the road to recovery. For those of you not in the know, this particular step of a 12-step program is a handwritten "searching, fearless moral inventory" to be shared with another person and the god of your choice. If this seems like a daunting task for a freshly converted drug fiend, you are correct.

For our clients it is merely an exercise; practice, if you will, for the real world. Treatment centers as a general rule are there to prepare you to discuss your feelings in future church basements with other drug addicts. When all is said and done, you will embrace the discomfort of a folding chair. The smell of dust and terrible coffee will stir your heart. The trembling voice of a newcomer will make you smile in sympathetic reflection. You will put your hand on his or her shoulder in support. You will have moments of unselfishness. You may act like a human being for the first time in your life.

At least that's what happened to me.

April rotated a pack of Marlboros in her hands while she pretended to listen to me explain the benefits of purging the dastardly deeds of one's past and the joys of AA meetings.

Tonight the two stared anxiously from the four-inch opening in the third door on the left. Molly was on her knees peeking, the light reflecting off her glasses. April leaned over her clumsily, the white cardboard stem of her Tootsie Pop clearly visible even in the shadows. I looked at them and shook my head.

Our intake paperwork was about 12 pages long. I would ask a series of questions, you would spill your guts on my desk, and I would check off the appropriate boxes. At this juncture, most clients were generally beyond lying. Some surely felt relief at finally unburdening themselves.

The first few pages were dull, unimportant factoids. We determined the language you preferred to speak, your ethnicity, your age and the god you were inclined to worship. The middle part was the more meaty fare: all the details concerning how and for how long you abused whatever substance you chose to abuse. The last several pages dealt with the results of such behavior and were, as a rule, the more emotional portion of the admission process. I pulled a box of Kleenex from the desk drawer.

Robert Turner was 10 years older than I suspected. Say what you want about narcotics but they do preserve some of us quite nicely. He developed a taste for morphine after being injured as a young correspondent in the Vietnam War, but then opted for the more socially acceptable pharmaceuticals of the '70s before settling on a daily bottle of Beefeaters for the last two and a half decades. This man had been hanging on for dear life since I was an infant, but then again, so had I.

We talked DWIs, arrest records and pink slips, all of which he had somehow managed to avoid. In fact, near as I could tell, he had refrained from all seven of the deadly sins with the exception of gluttony, of course.

"You'll have a roommate," I mentioned to him as I went to the office to make a copy of his license for his file and grab a large manila envelope for his freshly confiscated wallet and keys. "He's a quiet kid, shouldn't be a bother."

Contact numbers and addresses were kept on separate index cards and stored on a Rolodex for easy access in case of emergency. I filled it out as I waited for our prehistoric copy machine to warm up.

"Address?" I inquired through the open door.

"4114 Aurora Avenue North #22," he said, methodically and rehearsed, as if it had only recently been committed to memory.

Fuck. I knew that address well. My heart started to race. That was the Marco Polo motel. I had driven past it many times in the last few years, always staring intensely at its sign to avoid making eye contact with its wicked sister across the street. I glanced down at Mr. Turner's license, then looked through the open door. His head hung low and his shoulders slowly shook as he sobbed.

Shit.

I excused myself and darted quickly down the hallway toward the waiting room. Vivian Turner was gone. I cracked the front door just enough to see that her parking space was empty.

27. GOODBYE SWEET DREAMS

Nurse Paul sat at his desk and glanced up at the clock. Shit. Only 2:30 a.m.? There were still hours to kill. He ran his finger around the circumference of his one-year sobriety coin. He had picked it up that day, at the downtown noon meeting at the Claremont Hotel. He liked it there, because he could take a seat and blend in with all the old men. At least that seemed somewhat normal. But he was certain that he was the only man there who had first celebrated his 365 days of sobriety with a stop at the Champ Arcade and a handful of tokens that morning. Sigh.

He remembered sipping coffee from his Styrofoam cup at the meeting, but he hadn't been able to focus on the message. He couldn't even hear the words over the white noise of shame rushing in his head; he just watched other people's mouths moving. The only thing he could feel was the moist spot on the front of his underwear. He shifted in his seat. He wondered what it was that pulled him back over and over again. Not to the meetings, that was easy — he was told to "keep coming back" more times than he could count — but to the porn store. In honest moments, he knew he had lost everything to that place: his wife, his home, his financial security, his sanity. Everything.

He pulled a leftover token out of his pocket and placed it next to the coin on his desktop. He had even lost hope of ever finding another good woman after an unpleasantness that occurred one night after he'd gotten a little too reckless at the Champ. He pinched the material of his slacks and found the scar tissue on the tip of his dick. It was the result of a botched self-treatment of a chemical burn he'd been too embarrassed about to go to the ER many years ago. It was also a recurring reminder of the end of his marriage every fucking time he took a piss.

In his darkest moments, he even blamed his attraction to men on the Champ Arcade. Not that he was attracted to men; he just couldn't stop thinking about them.

He heard footsteps go by in the hallway, sending his inner rant down a new path: How could he be subjected to working in such an environment? With such fucking idiots? He was a goddamned trained mental health professional, for Christ's sake. Things came so fucking easy to them. He just couldn't understand. He scratched his forehead so hard it almost drew blood. He tried hard to determine if God had failed him or if he had failed God. And what the fuck difference did it make anyway? He drifted from disconnected thoughts to incensed mumbling.

"Oh, so *funny*, so *popular* with the staff and *patients*, such an *inspiring* story, blah, blah, blah. Why can't everyone just shut the fuck up?"

Sometimes the apparently sainted co-worker was just a passing thought, an annoyance. Other times he was the bane of Nurse Paul's existence. A curse. A tormentor. And a man he hadn't even made eye contact with in more than a decade. Me.

He nearly jumped out of his skin when he heard two quick thumps on his door.

"Incoming," I warned.

I had only the length of the hallway to come up with a really convincing lie. I wasn't worried, but I took my time. I was a master craftsman, an artist, and deception was my canvas. I was Michael Jordan and Mr. Turner was a 4th-grade white kid with polio. I had this one. I smirked at how easy it would be. I was a howitzer tank. He was a tricycle. Lying was my most finely honed skill. It was what I was born to do. I was unstoppable. Boxing had Ali. Prose had Nabokov. Drinking had Hemingway. This was my game.

I was excited. Would I water down her absence, or rose-color it? The possibilities were endless, and the result would be more pleasant than the truth, because the truth would simply not do, not tonight. I made the approach with confidence. I sized him up. His slumped shoulders and caved-in chest would make this child's play. I licked my lips and cleared my throat.

"Umm, Robert…"

I stood there with my mouth agape and choked…on nothing.

"I know she wasn't there, kid," he said, mercifully breaking the silence.

I smelled smoke. Now I had lost control of everything. Cigarette smoke meant mutiny. I didn't doubt for a second where it was coming from. I excused myself, stomped down the corridor and barged into their room. Molly and April stood there in T-shirts and panties with their backs to the open window, each concealing something behind her back.

"We're sorry, Daddy," they said in unison.

"I will deal with you two later," I barked.

I didn't give them the satisfaction of slamming the door, nor did I wait around long enough to hear whatever wisecrack they had chambered for me.

I had expected to catch Justin reading the dog-eared copy of *The Bell Jar* he had hidden in his pillowcase, but instead found him lost in thought sitting on the edge of his bed in his boxer shorts. He was startled when I walked in with Robert.

Justin was an oxycontin addict, a sensitive little teenage intellectual with a lopsided jet-black haircut that hung over one eye. I liked him anyway. He was another sparkly clean suburban kid who had gotten caught up in his grandparents' medicine cabinet. The place was rotten with them. Doctors practically had these high-powered synthetic painkillers in candy dishes in their waiting rooms, enticing hapless youngsters with just the right genetic predisposition to gobble them up. This level of narcotics was like a newfangled junkie land mine. The withdrawals were brutal. The number of people under the age of 30 who were currently lying in creaking treatment-center beds in disbelief as their joints seized like unoiled pistons and their flesh crawled with hot-and-cold-running misery could quite fairly have been called an epidemic.

When I first told Justin his story would end up being the same as mine if he didn't get his shit together, he believed me. When I underlined the parts of the book that he should pay attention to, he took note. He was quite pleased to find out that he had a spiritual malady, a mental obsession and an allergy of the body. He smiled as if his whole life were making sense to him now. There was no sleep to be found in his not-too-distant future, so we had talked late into the last few nights about movies, music, books and how to maintain your sobriety despite the fact you don't now, nor ever will, believe in God.

Yes, I had been playing favorites. But there was only one empty bed in the place, and Justin's turbulent nights would have to be made a little bit worse with the addition of an old drunk from Tacoma's snores.

I introduced them. They nodded at each other.

I sat Robert's suitcase on the edge of his bed. He unzipped it, he fumbled with his shaving kit, he dropped toiletries, a Chapstick, his loose change. He stood there red-faced, partly angered, partly embarrassed, looking down at his useless, shaking hands.

"Sorry Mr. Turner, it's house policy that I unpack your bag for you, you know, in case of contraband."

I had already checked his bag at my desk, but in the last 30 minutes his life had been fucked and rolled in dog shit and this seemed like the least I could do to help. His trembling fingers, untrustworthy bladder and broken heart would heal with time, but a little bit of his dignity needed rescuing at the moment.

"Charlie, can I talk to you in the hall?" Justin asked sheepishly.

"First things first, buddy. You and I are gonna be of service.

"One of the things you'll learn around here, Justin, is that the best way to get out of your own fucked-up head is to help another person out," I said, while removing Robert's neatly packed, dry-cleaned dress shirts from his suitcase and laying them on the bed.

"And our new friend here has had a rough night...hang those up, would you?" I asked, pointing to the shirts as I gathered Robert's socks and underwear.

Justin didn't move. He stared straight ahead. I was surprised and a little disappointed. He knew he was going to get a roommate sooner or later. This was just plain childish. I picked up the shirts myself.

The noose hung eye-level to me when I opened the closet door. Crisp, white, perfectly knotted. The strong smell of the bleach used on institutional bedding stung my eyes. The noose had been fashioned from Justin's torn bed sheet. I looked up. The pole that had served as the clothing rod was wedged up high between the top shelf of the closet and the apex of the door molding. I pulled on it to test its strength. On the floor was a stack of AA Big Books for him to stand. I held the noose in my hand and admired the kid's resourcefulness, his craftsmanship. I looked over my shoulder at him. He was frozen, pale, knees pulled up and tucked under his chin.

I knew what they did to kids like him. I remembered the distant look in her eyes. I remembered the half-smiles she would manage just for my sake. I remembered the pills and the bruises on her back from the electrically induced seizures. I wasn't going to let that happen again.

I stood on the pile of Big Books and disassembled the gallows quickly. I threw the knotted bed sheet over my shoulder. Robert's mind was somewhere else. He was unaware of the fact that my hands were now shaking as bad as his, unaware of the chaos. I took a deep breath and exhaled slowly.

"You, follow me," I said, pointing at Justin.

He could barely keep up with me as I bolted down the hallway and out the back door. I wrestled with the knots of the noose until they came apart and then buried the fabric as deep in the dumpster as I could without falling into the wretched thing. He stood there with his arms crossed over his bare chest, shivering.

"Do you know what we are now?" I asked.

"What?"

"Co-conspirators. If I don't report this, I'll be shit-canned."

He nodded his head and wiped the tears from his face with a forearm.

"This way," I said, heading back to the building and striding toward the rooms.

"Molly, April, get your coats." I said, tapping on the door of their room.

They came out, zipped up and stood at attention. They were puzzled, of course. Were they going to be taken out back and executed? Why was there a boy in his underwear following me around in the middle of the night? They were leery of me, smelling of garbage and all. I must have looked crazed, even to these lunatics. I put an arm around each of their shoulders and pulled them in close for a huddle.

"There's an old man sitting in room 26. It's his first night," I whispered. "I want you to take him out the side door to smoke. I want you to be nice to him. I want you to tell him everything's gonna be all right. Do you understand?"

They nodded.

"Get to work," I hissed.

They scampered off in the opposite direction.

We all live with the possibility of death every day. To most people, it's a stranger you run into occasionally. Your grandmother's delicate grip on your hand releases for the last time in her hospital bed, or you pass a smoking, twisted metal mess on the side of the freeway. You don't grow comfortable in its presence.

Some of us, however, have a more personal relationship with it. I hadn't for some time held it in my arms and slow-danced with it, smoothed back its hair or whispered in its ear that everything would be OK. I hadn't looked at the world like that in a while. Back when I kept tabs on the plastic bags and rubbing alcohol and razor blades, and when the new set of knives Mom sent for Christmas that year were just too sexy, too inviting, I dropped one in the trash every day until they were gone so my girlfriend wouldn't notice. You get used to it. I scrubbed that dark, rust-colored stain out of the bathtub the first time she tried it. She said she had just wanted to see what the water would look like, and I believed her because I had to. She was too young and wild and staggeringly perfect for me, so I took all of our change to the drug store and bought bandages and cigarettes and pretended everything was fine. Some mornings I quietly and slowly moved my lips close to hers, not to pirate a kiss during her slumber but instead to confirm that she was still breathing. And to be prepared for the very real possibility that she wasn't. These are the things that people who have grown accustomed to death's proximity do.

"Charlie, what do you do? You know, when it gets bad?"

What do I tell the kid? Smoke cigarettes till your throat is sore and jerk off till your cock is raw?

"You know what? Just fake it, man."

He looked disappointed.

"It's true," I continued. "Guys like you and me, we don't know how this life shit works."

Through the two-inch opening of the office window I could hear the girl's hushed giggles outside as they listened to Robert spin a tall tale in a low register.

"Fake-smile," I said. "Nod your head. Say 'yes' to kickball games and the picnics and the bullshit you'd never do in a million years. Say 'good' to the barrage of how-are-you's that are gonna come your way. Just fucking do it."

Almost 9 years earlier, I stood in the exact same place Justin did now, also in the middle of the night. I had been considering grabbing the old man behind the counter around the throat and demanding the keys, not realizing the doors were unlocked and I was free to leave at anytime. He smiled at me and gave me a carton of milk and suggested I take a hot bath. It was at that moment I knew that the miserable impersonation of a human being I had been doing needed work.

When they told me to pray, I acted like I was praying. When they said the obsession to use drugs would be lifted, I pretended like I didn't think about shooting dope every minute of every day. When they told me I would know a new freedom and a new happiness, it was all I could do to suppress my laughter, but I managed. When they said I would suddenly realize that God was doing for me what I could not do for myself, I fake-smiled and nodded.

And then at some point it struck me: It wasn't *what* they told me, it was simply the fact they were telling me *anything*. They were helping me, for no reason at all. They were strangers, our afflictions similar, our backgrounds different, but our lives dependent on one another. If there was ever any evidence of anything divine in this world, that was it.

"Here's the truth, Justin: it's just us," I said. "And pushing aside all of the steps and traditions and bumper stickers and the book thumpin', we are just a great mass of scared, insecure and seemingly unable fuck-ups who huddle together in our storm of sickness and take care of each other. It defies reason. But we do it and it works and you just have to fuckin' believe me.

"I'll help you out when you're insane, and you help me out when I am. Deal?"

I stuck my hand out in the customary way people do when they've made a pact. He yawned. It wasn't exactly the reaction I was looking for. But then he walked past my hand, put his arms around my torso and gently squeezed.

"I think I'm gonna try and lie down for a while," he said to my chest, and then turned around and headed toward his room.

"I need you to be here when I come to work tomorrow night," I said.

"I'll be here."

We all got what we needed that night. If it weren't for the containment of our skulls, the endorphins would have ricocheted off the ceiling like fireworks accidentally discharged indoors. Molly's desire to misbehave and April's need for approval were both met. They had unintentionally used the charms the devil had given them to do a good deed, make an old man smile. Pretty girls, as we all know, will make life's poison go down smoother, and Mr. Turner was very grateful for the brief suspension of his heartache. Justin just wanted a reason to stay, and I got to make slight recompense on the sum of my sins. Sleep eventually took them all, leaving me to my filing.

When the phone rings at 5 a.m. it could be anything.

"Hello, Milton Lake House."

"Hello, is Charlie Hyatt there?"

"Speaking."

"It's David Finch, Carrie's father. She told me it would be OK to call you there."

I knew what it was right away. My brain raced to compose small talk or pleasantries or anything to stop the next words from coming out of his mouth.

"Carrie is gone. I'm so sorry."

28. IF YOU HAVE GHOSTS

There's a brief pause. You hear him inhale. Or maybe it's just the windshield wipers. Then he goes for the throat.

Ain't no sunshine when she's gone

Bill Withers isn't fucking around. And he isn't singing the blues. The blues is something you'll get through. This is despair. The blues is something that happens to you. This is something you brought on yourself. It's much worse.

Only darkness everyday

He's holding a mirror up to your disgraceful nature, your willful arrogance, your sloth-like neglect. Whatever it was that made her walk out the door. When the strings kick in, it gets personal. He fights dirty. He reaches into your sockets and pulls out tears by the fistful.

Wonder this time where she's gone

It's too short. It's a mugging, an emotional hit-and-run. He takes everything from you in two minutes and three seconds. He beat the shit out of me and left me for dead at a Chevron station in Medford, Oregon. I sat there with my head against the steering wheel and pitifully wished that song were longer. I wished I could wallow in it a little bit more. You could feel the collective chills of all the men currently tuned into KLDZ. They were being reminded of her, and I don't care how long it's been, or how many kids you're driving home from soccer practice in your fairly new minivan, there is a her.

Mine was lying on a steel table in a hospital somewhere in Los Angeles. A nervous intern removed the color from her lips with disinfectant, her skin much colder to the touch than he imagined. She had consciously applied more Chanel No. 5 than usual. She would not allow the idea of revolting whomever it was that would find her. She put on her best black slip and combed her hair for the first time in a week. The policeman who kicked in her door thought she looked like a silent-movie actress.

I doubt they needed to run too many tests. There really wouldn't be a lot of questions. A quick look at her medical history and a phone call placed by her father that he had rehearsed in his head for many, many years would clear up any mysteries. She may have been prepped for cremation before I crossed the state line and that was OK; seeing her body was not the purpose of my trip. I was driving to keep a promise.

There was an address on a scrap of paper sitting on the dashboard of the 14-year-old piece of shit I was driving. It was my handwriting, but I honestly did not remember jotting it down. I couldn't remember most of the conversation I had had with Mr. Finch. I'm not even sure if I spoke. The hows, whats and whys were questions whose answers I had long given up hope on ever making peace with. The end result was inevitable. The one thing I knew for sure was that I had to get there first.

As if on cue, the clouds disappeared outside Yreka, California. It was clear and cold and I was underdressed. After the phone call, I don't even remember hanging up. I didn't grab my jacket or my hat or my cigarettes; I just walked out the door and started my car. I didn't say a word to anyone. By the time the kitchen staff arrived to do what they could with oatmeal and powdered eggs, I was on the 520 bridge. By the time Nurse Paul made his uncomfortable morning pilgrimage past my desk to the restroom, I was southbound on Interstate 5.

The full moon hung like a bare bulb. It was stunning. I guess I should maybe say here that I never spent too much time camping. Maybe it always looked like that. I studied it at two-second intervals. First its ghostly glow, then the road in front of me; its impossible beauty, then the solid white line to my right, the broken one to my left and the art of staying between them. My world had become so condensed — work, television, meeting, bed — that it was hard to believe that the giant illuminating that mountain and lighting the way for me was the same one that peeked through our clouds occasionally. Here, a hundred miles from any truck stop or supermarket, he was king, unquestioned, and perhaps the most amazing thing I had ever seen.

An alabaster arm reached across my line of vision and pointed at it. She left the tip of her finger on the cold glass just long enough to leave a phantom outline of a print.

"I made that for you," she said. My heart skipped a beat.

She sat in the passenger seat and made that "tsk tsk" sound as she kicked aside the empty coffee cups and cigarette packs to make room for her clunky witch shoes. Her pale skin was bathed in that ridiculous moon, her hair long, soft and beautiful. She smiled. Gone was her reckless, frantic energy, replaced instead by a tranquil ease. A ball of yarn fell between her knees and onto the floorboards.

"When did you start knitting?" I asked.

Well, that was stupid. Regardless of the fact that I was caught quite understandably off-guard, surely I had something at least a little better to be the first thing to come out of my mouth since injecting just a little too much heroin into her tiny body all those years ago. I wanted to kick myself, but then again, that's what she had always been good for.

"When did you get a gut?"

She stuck her knitting needles in the slight paunch protruding over my seatbelt.

I stared at the road. I didn't want to look back over and find her gone. I listened to her humming along with a country tune on the radio and to the clicking of hard plastic as she worked away. All the anger and sadness I had lugged around with me for the last decade dripped down the back of my neck and ran down my spine, soaking my T-shirt. Was this peace? As near as I could tell, it was something like it.

"I loved you so much," I finally blurted out.

"No, you *love* me so much, dummy."

"You're wearing the same dress," I said.

"Same dress?" she smoothed out the skirt on her lap as she looked for clarification.

"The one you wore to Dad's funeral."

"Oh," she paused for a moment, "you saw me."

A high-volume foghorn momentarily shook the car, then disappeared. The steering wheel rattled as if I were manning a Gatling gun or barreling into the epicenter of an earthquake.

"What the fuck was that?"

Carrie just looked at me and shrugged. Knit, purl, knit, purl, knit, purl.

My father had been devoured by cancer five years earlier, forcing me to make the journey to the most distasteful of destinations, Phoenix, Arizona. It was absurdly hot and I was numb with disbelief at his passing. I had to borrow a suit from my uncle and see my mother cry for the first time in my life. I also had to endure the pitiful looks of friends and relatives, not only for my grieving-son status but also as the newly ordained black sheep of the family.

My sister, who had written for the Phoenix newspaper her entire adult life, was delivering a beautiful eulogy. I was to speak next, and I was surveying the crowd, looking to have a word with whomever was in charge of the line-up, when I saw Carrie. Sitting alone in the very last pew, her face nearly concealed under the wide brim of her black sun hat, I saw her unmistakable scarlet lips as she dabbed the perspiration from her neck with a patterned handkerchief. Heedless of the itinerary, I made my move toward the back of the church. Having no other siblings to run interference, I was accosted with consoling embraces and outreached, concerned hands. By the time I got to the last pew it was empty. By the time I burst out the front door, all I saw were the taillights of her rented Town Car entering the furnace that is Phoenix afternoon traffic. I lit a cigarette, sat on the curb.

"You looked nice, dressed up like a grown-up and all," she smiled.

Again, a nerve-shattering blast of a foghorn, followed this time by the rat-a-tat-tat of what sounded like machine-gun fire.

"Did you fucking hear that?' I screamed.

BRRRRRAAAAAA, RAT-A-TAT-TAT! The car vibrated till it shook my teeth.

"Of course I hear it, darlin'," she said, as calm as can be, "but the message is not for me; it's for you."

The rumble strips on the side of the road screamed at me one last time.

BRRRRRRRAAAAAA, RAT-A-TAT-TAT thump.

I woke when my head fell to the left and thumped on the pane of glass. I sat up straight, just coherent enough not to slam on the brakes. I pulled onto the shoulder of the highway to regain my composure while the engine sputtered and died. The moon flooded my car with soft light. The static on the radio defused my panic. *Shhhh*, it whispered. I rolled down the window, took deep breaths through my nostrils and exhaled them slowly though my mouth. There were no oncoming headlights or fading taillights or howling coyotes in the distance, just silence. Without looking, I reached over and placed my hand on the empty passenger seat.

"Coffee," I said out loud to no one.

I started the car and eased back onto the road.

29. BURN THE FLAMES

Ｉt was like a fuckin' movie.

I took off my shirt, wrapped it around my fist and punched through the glass. I stood in her kitchen, perfectly still. I didn't even breathe. I listened for dogs or neighbors or law-enforcement types who might not understand. I wasn't sure if my hands were shaking from the perpetual IV of caffeine and nicotine or the foul cheeseburger I ate in Sacramento or the sudden realization that I was standing in *her* place.

Thy canopy is dust and stones

I'd parked my car a block away. I tried, without success, to estimate the hours I had been awake while I sat on the bus stop bench across the street from her apartment and smoked a cigarette. She had lived on the first floor of a tiny building, maybe four units total, on Silverlake Boulevard. It was four o'clock in the morning. There were many bouquets of daisies littering the steps that led to the temporary particleboard door the cops had installed to replace the one they'd kicked in. There were cards and notes and cut-out red paper hearts and flickering candles, all coming to an abrupt stop where the crime-scene tape began.

I imagined the parade of handsome actors and musicians and writers pulling up in their new cars and solemnly walking to her door with their ribbon-and-crepe-paper-wrapped tributes to a remarkable yet peculiar girl they had once loved, only to find a half-dozen others had done the same. I smiled.

I had always taken her daisies after her shock treatments. I told her they were her favorite, and with her crippled memory she was in no position to argue. The truth was it was all I could afford. When I got out of my court-appointed treatment center, there were two-dozen daisies waiting in the room at the halfway house I was assigned to, a card with two X's typed on it, no return address.

I had heard about her boyfriends, of course. People talked and I pretended not to care or be hurt or give a shit or a rat's ass or a flyin' fuck. I was protecting myself. Whether she looked great or she looked like hell, I didn't want to know. I wanted her to be fine but not necessarily happy, not ecstatically so anyway. I wanted her to be like me, a little empty.

I had gambled today on the theory that her closest neighbors might be staying elsewhere for a couple of days. The morbidity of their living situation would have driven them to the Comfort Inn or a well-to-do relative's place for a spell. If your building is old enough, the odds are pretty good that you are separated from suicides and murders by just a few inches of plaster. Her landlord would be put out, of course, but clean-up would be minimal. Eventually someone would rent the place, and the shivers or goose bumps you'd get living next door would fade with time. Maybe she would attain local legend status, and neighborhood kids might dare one another to peek into her window or consider any cat or crow spotted near the property to be her supernatural familiar. She would've liked that.

I lit a match. I couldn't risk switching on the lights. My mouth tasted like a cat box. The refrigerator was covered with cave etchings, stick figures with orange hair and magic wands. There were dozens of photographs held in place with magnetic letters, her smile impossibly big as if her face would tear in half. In each picture she was with a child with an equally preposterous grin, usually with her arm draped over the child's shoulder. The children could have been four or five or ten years old for all I knew, mostly girls, and each moppet more adorable than the next. I touched her face in each one until the match expired.

And death's pale flag is not advanced there

I cracked the door and reached in for water only to find juice boxes and pudding cups. There was a ceramic mug on the counter. It boasted that the owner was in fact the greatest violin teacher in the world. It was officially presented to her in the guise of a birthday or Christmas gift, I imagined, and once in her possession I knew she would never drink coffee or tea from anything else, ever. She would beam with pride and think of Emma or Alison or Jason or whomever bestowed her with that honor every morning. I filled that cup from the sink and drained it three times and lit another match.

I knew there would be no food in the refrigerator. I knew the contents of her stomach would be saltine crackers, pills and alcohol. I knew she would weigh next to nothing. I knew it had been just a matter of time. We — well, she — had talked about it often. The only thing I didn't know was why now.

At the end of any road trip nature calls, but after consuming a dizzying amount of truck-stop, high-octane piss-coffee, nature insists, practically begs. I felt my way through the darkness to her bathroom.

There were two or three inches of water in the bathtub. Submerged in that water was an object that I couldn't quite make out from my vantage point in front of the toilet. Was it moving? Did I see tiny fins or was the flickering light and my lack of sleep fucking with me? I held a St. Jude Sacred Heart candle in one hand and my cock in the other. I shook off the tardy drops of pee and buttoned up before approaching the tub with caution.

It fluctuated between inanimate and aquatic. It was black. It grew a tail and snout and then collapsed in on itself, becoming ridged and flat. I rubbed my eyes with my thumb and forefinger. I got down on my hands and knees and placed the candle on the ledge of the tub. I rested my chin on the cool porcelain and fixed my gaze on it. I was prepared for a hasty retreat in case it lunged at my face, but it remained motionless. As my eyes adjusted to the scant light I realized there was a word printed on it, four white letters. I quickly reached in and grabbed it.

DELL

I set her waterlogged laptop on the tile floor and fished out her cell phone. She had cut off all communication, eliminating the possibility of return or remorse or change of heart. No knights in shining armor, please. She was ensuring there would be no cries for help. That this time would be the last time.

I used her toothbrush. The words "it's ok" were written in the corner of the mirror in red lipstick. I'd changed my policy about opening strange medicine cabinets. They are full of secrets and precipice, like going through someone's wallet or reading their mail. I will admit that I looked at this one longingly, though. It's a strange phenomenon, that of staring past your own face and coveting a pharmaceutical mystery on the other side of the glass. I watched myself mouth the words "Take one tablet by mouth as needed." I was taken aback by my reflection. I knew I would look tired, but I was surprised by how old I had become. The lines that used to reveal themselves only in the harshest of broad daylight were now clearly visible by candle.

I put the palm of my hand on the mirror and leaned on it as I spit into the sink. I knew that pulling open that magnetized latch could, at best, divulge a decade of secrets she had accumulated or, at worst, be the first step to me becoming a danger to myself and others. We all have things about us that are better left unknown, and it was nice to have at least one pure, sweet memory. I spit again and put the toothbrush in my back pocket as a souvenir.

She had lived in stark contradiction, her face and her guts. The kitchen was awash in turquoise and bright red curtains. There were music stands and brightly colored notebooks and crayons and a life where *Clementine* and *Do Re Mi* were played over and over and over again. This was her smile and clear bright eyes. The bedroom was dark and musty, with the kind of thick curtains that the daylight cracks through like a laser, making sea monkeys dance in its brash golden beams. These particles that darted back and forth, dust, spores, lint, chaos, bad thoughts, muted screams, these were what rattled between her hip bones, barely contained by a thin layer of waxen skin.

When I pushed open the door I was relieved to find she had made it easy for me. She knew I would gravitate toward her bed. But I was wrong. What appeared to be stacks and stacks of journals was in fact sheet music, covering her mattress, huge piles of it, neither alphabetized nor organized by genre, coated in a thin layer of dust. I grabbed a few sheets off the top of the pile and blew. Chopin. The next pile, *Bye Bye Birdie*, the next, something by Frank Zappa. The pages spilled off the foot of the bed. I could tell it hadn't been slept in in months.

In the corner were a sewing machine and a filing cabinet bursting with patterns. Unlike the sheet music, the patterns were uniformly organized, all doll clothes, mostly Halloween costumes. Each outfit was stored in a large Ziploc bag and placed neatly into the top drawer of her dresser. The lucky recipient of all this work stood atop the desk in a shimmering, black witch outfit. She had shoulder-length red hair and gorgeous green eyes. Just like her mother, I thought.

There was an Edward Gorey print hanging on the wall next to the figurine. She'd always said if she ever had money she'd buy one. Her desk reflected the potency and frequency of her shock treatments. It served as her nerve center, her base of operations, her frontal lobe and a testimonial to the length a human would go to keep a secret.

There were two boxes of index cards, one marked professional, one marked personal. At the top of her students' cards were the words "Tuesdays and Thursdays at 4 p.m." or "Mondays at 3 p.m." etc., etc. Then came a name, age, birthday, address, pet's name, favorite food, favorite song and a note about the child's progress. At the bottom of each card was the sentence: _____ is a very special kid.

The cards referring to the adults in her life were less organized, more cautionary. As a general rule they seemed to serve as a warning system. They contained the usual contact information, but at the bottom of each was a note about the subject's behavior. These were personal insights she couldn't risk disappearing from her conscious.

I continued to rummage though the cards even though I didn't want the gory details, I didn't want to know who made her heart sing or her panties wet besides me, but I couldn't avert my eyes. The addresses and phone numbers were unimportant. I picked out random cards and read the comments at the bottom.

> Lucy is crazy. Avoid conversations about men.
> Sean is cute but he only wants sex - he is not
> really a big-time record producer.
> Dr. Jennison will give you better sleeping pills
> if you flirt with him.

You owe Sarah $50 - don't forget to pay her.
Vito ~~is a lovely man~~ watched you sort your
undies at the Laundromat.
Tim C. might be in love with you.
Don't go to the store with Sherry,
she's a shoplifter.
Rick is a son of a Ditch. Do NOT go back.

I couldn't help but look myself up. I figured it was a bad idea, but I watched as my fingers flipped through the cards until we got to the Hs. There were four phone numbers and a half dozen addresses written down for me.

Charlie Hyatt
~~The Thunderbird Motel~~ ~~The King County Jail~~
~~The Milton Lake House (patient)~~
~~1224 Roosevelt Way~~ ~~321 Boylston #201~~
1,809 15th Avenue #204 (home)
The Milton Lake House (work)
Charlie made you happy for a long time.

Everything was written in pencil and dismissed with a single line through the middle of each location after I'd moved on. I had eluded police and bill collectors, but I did not live below Carrie Finch's radar.

Above the tattered copy of the Physicians' Desk Reference, I noticed three envelopes taped to the wall. The first was addressed to her father, the next one to me and the last simply said, "Roky Erickson, Austin TX." I peeled my envelope off and stumbled into the living room.

The out-of-place coffee table told me where they found her. It was several feet farther from the couch than what one would consider the usual distance, more than likely moved to make space for the stretcher. The couch was a large, well-worn but stylish, orange monstrosity from the '60s. I could picture her eyeing it through the window of a hip vintage store in her neighborhood, nervously calculating the amount of paychecks it would take her to save up, knowing that no one on earth could possibly think it was as pretty as she did.

Thou womb of death, gorged with the dearest morsel of the earth.

The medicine bottles on the coffee table were amber and empty. The liquid in the glass was amber, too. Scotch, just like she always said. When given the option of picking her poison she would always reply, "The Glenlivet, please."

I held the rim of the glass to my lips and inhaled its once-familiar sting. I tasted her lipstick with the tip of my tongue.

Come, bitter conduct, come, unsavoury guide!

And what difference could I have made? Could I have stopped her? Would I have stopped her, or would I have lain down next to her and held her till she was cold?

Here's to my love! O true apothecary!
Thy drugs are quick. Thus with a kiss I die.

I tilted the glass quickly before I could change my mind. It burned just right. I held her last sip of whiskey in my mouth for as long as I could, then swallowed. I was so tired. I carefully peeled back the seal of the envelope and took out the letter. A stack of hundred-dollar bills fell out and onto the hardwood floor. I unfolded the letter, but my eyes couldn't focus. I lay back on the couch. I stretched out. I placed her letter over my face and sunk into her last stand. I breathed in the ink of a ballpoint pen and the relief of the words she finally got to say. Her arms reached up through the earth, the floor, the upholstery and wrapped themselves around my chest. She kissed me on the back of the neck and we closed our eyes.

30. BE AND BRING ME HOME

Dear Charlie,

Well, here we are. It's been way too long. What I miss most is your voice. The way it ripped me out of bed each morning like a rag doll and poured me back in at night. The way you always said the perfect thing at the perfect time. Of course, I may be remembering just the good parts because I am a tad bit drunk and I haven't been in many, many years. Sometimes I'd be sitting at dinner on a date with a boy and I'd close my eyes and think, Please say the perfect thing like Charlie would. Of course, they didn't.

Is it presumptuous of me even to think that you are reading this letter right now? I don't think so. It comforts me now to know you'll be

here to take care of things - there is something truly beautiful about not fighting this
anymore. There have been some good things.
I got to play music to people who listened
and I got to teach a lot of really badass
kids and I got to know you I think like
nobody else did. It isn't that I couldn't dig
my nails into my thighs and hold on for
another day - I could - but I am weary. I am
weary and I am ready.

Please, let me say that I'm sorry. Not
for what I'm about to do but for what I didn't
do. I knew you were just as sick as me but
I left you behind. Please don't think
poorly of me. I can't remember a day
I didn't miss you and I lost count of the
times when I was at a record store or
going to a movie or just walking down the
street and I put out my hand to hold
yours before I realized you weren't next
to me.

When Charlie Hyatt is the best boyfriend
you ever had, you are one sad-luck dame,
haha.

But when all is said and done, my love,
when whatever is in store for us when we
leave this place is upon us, I will find you.
I will meet you in Jackson Square and we
will drink wine at 9 in the morning and we
will laugh at tourists and I will sit in the sun
and you'll sit in the shade and say perfect
things to me.
                    See you there.
                    I love you no matter what.
                    X

31. BLOODY HAMMER

It should have been a simple assault. Things just got, um…out of hand, I guess.

He was choking. His face was beet red; his hands were turning purple. I placed the head of the hammer to his temple and warned him not to make any noise or I would use it. Recent experience had taught him I wasn't bluffing. I pulled the duct tape off his mouth quickly, like a Band-Aid. There was a tooth stuck to it, and lots of blood, plenty of blood. I cupped my hands under his chin and let the warm liquid flow into them.

Jesus, there was blood everywhere.

More ran down his forearms from the lacerations on his wrists caused by the fishing line I had used to hold him in place against the wall, his arms outstretched like a frog ready for dissecting, or Christ in his most provocative pose. It had soaked through his once-perfect beige-colored vintage Western shirt with the pearl snaps. He had it all, the shirt, the boots, the long but not too long feathered hair; it was the uniform of the new California singer-songwriter, those who worship at the altar of Gram Parsons as if he invented country music. You know one of these assholes, don't you?

I returned to the wall with a fresh handful of blood to finish the job at hand.

RICK MCCULLEN BEATS WOMEN

I smeared the words in two-foot letters. I suppose I could have used marker or spray print, but there wasn't time to run to the store. If he managed to get himself down later he would probably feel compelled to clean it up himself. But if the police found him first, the message would help speed up that whole establish-motive thing.

Somewhere in my prefrontal cortex I knew this was real lunatic-type stuff, but it had to be done. There were ribs to break, black eyes to conjure, a throat to bruise and seemingly endless amounts of kicking and punching to be done, none of which the little prick seemed to be willing to stand still for.

I would have thought I had become more evolved by this time. I had been sure that the fundamental changes I had made in my life made me better prepared to interact with real people in the real world. I wanted him to know that, although I was angry with him, this wasn't personal. I was giving him an opportunity, which unfortunately he declined.

"You would think," I explained as I finished my lettering, "that committing acts of violence when you're sober would be a totally different animal."

I stepped back to admire my work.

"You know, being aware of my character defects, knowing I should've called my sponsor and talked this through before I drove over here…all that knowledge should have slowed me down."

He attempted to turn his head to see what I was doing, to no avail. He spit a mouthful of blood on the carpet.

"My hands…I got no feeling in my hands," he coughed.

I brought the hammer down on his left hand. His scream told me he got some of that feeling back. I shoved the palm of my hand into his mouth and pushed his head against the wall as he worked through his pain. "Shhhh…I understand you weren't much of a guitar player anyway."

You don't wake up in the morning and plan for something like this to happen, of course. What really happens is you bolt up fear-stricken, you remember where you are, you wish it were just a nightmare. You make coffee in a strange kitchen, you smell the half-and-half to make sure it's not sour, you arm yourself with lighter fluid and matches, kiss your favorite picture of her on the refrigerator, take a deep breath and go to work.

The garage door required a little bit of muscle to roll up. When the dust settled and the gasoline fumes dissipated, what was left were the floor-to-ceiling remains of one who did not choose to live in the past, but instead let it rot in cardboard boxes. There were slabs of vinyl without covers piled waist-high, a record collector's nightmare, covered in cigarette ash and candle wax and grime. There were boxes and boxes of photographs and magazine clippings and faulty wiring hanging here and there, and how that place didn't burst into flames on its own accord is a mystery to me still.

Against the back wall there were three six-foot stacks of notebooks, nearly all of them the black-and-white Mead composition ones that she favored. I stood close and breathed in vanilla, clove, shady boyfriends, catty girlfriends, true love, confusion and loneliness, triumph, laughter, bitterness and longing, cinnamon and hair spray. In the corner, a shorter stack of the most recent journals sat in the palm of that goddamned black plastic hand chair. She had dug it out from under the rubble of her life and dusted it off to show me she still had it.

In the last 48 hours, I had punched steering wheels, cursed fate, trespassed and behaved generally recklessly. But this was the first time I cried.

At the top of the stack on the chair was a lone manila folder; written on the tab were the words LEGAL SHIT.

I pushed the button on the intercom.

"Yeah," the rude little box said.

"Rick?"

"Yeah, who's that?"

"Hey man, it's Kevin," I lied.

There was a long pause.

"I talked to you last week about a tour of the studio." More lies.

Another pause.

"I'm a friend of Eddie's." Technically, I did have a friend named Eddie once, so this was not a lie.

"Yeah, yeah, gimme five minutes. I'll be right there." I had obviously woken him up.

When he answered the door I was disappointed. He was much shorter than I'd imagined and appeared to be hungover and disheveled. This would hardly be fair.

We shook hands the way regular people shake hands. He welcomed me in and I excused his mess and I declined the customary offer of a beverage. He explained to me that they were building out a such-and-such booth and that I shouldn't worry because it would be totally ready by the time I got in there and that I should check out this reverb and that delay and this totally killer compressor, and I stood there and nodded my head like I knew exactly what the fuck he was talking about.

I'm sure the sales pitch on his goods and services was usually quite good, but the fact that I had no questions and contributed very little to the conversation was probably off-putting. After a half-hearted attempt to push his skills as a producer/arranger on my next project, we stood there in silence.

I picked a hammer out of the toolbox lying at the foot of an exposed beam.

"This is nice," I said, cradling it in my palm, feeling its weight.

228

"Um, yeah. Like I said, all this construction will be cleared up after the weekend."

"What I'm really interested in discussing is this," I said, pulling several folded pieces of paper out of the inside pocket of my jacket. "Have you seen these before?"

He squinted his eyes.

I noticed a pushpin in the bulletin board over his coffeemaker.

"May I borrow this?" I asked, pulling it out without waiting for an answer. A business card of some guitar player fell to the floor.

"This is a domestic violence report filed by Carrie Finch last year," I said, pinning the document to the wall.

"I don't know what you're talking about," he stuttered.

"Really? How about this one she filed seven months ago?" I stuck it on the wall next to the first.

He looked around nervously. I reached behind me and dead-bolted the door shut.

"Now, I know you remember this restraining order, because your mommy and daddy had to hire some expensive lawyer pigs to make it disappear."

His eyes darted around until they stopped on the mixing console, where his phone sat next to an ashtray. I read from the restraining order while I crossed the room and picked up his phone.

"Because of the respondent's increasingly violent and erratic behavior…"

I dropped it on the floor.

"…I am afraid that the Respondent will hurt me again."

I crushed his phone with the heel of my boot.

"Look, dude," his voice cracked.

"Listen, unless you're standing on the goddamn beach with a motherfucking surfboard in your arm? DO NOT use the word dude! It's kinda douchey. Sorry. Pet peeve."

"OK, what I'm tryin' to say…"

"Oh yeah, shut up," I suggested, as I grabbed a fistful of hair on the back of his head and escorted him over to the wall. I held him so his face was a couple of inches from the documents.

"I would like you to read aloud from the section entitled 'History of Abuse,' please."

He jabbed an elbow backward into my ribs, which struck me as kind of stupid. I smashed his nose into the wall and held him there while twisting the offending elbow up behind his back between his shoulder blades.

"What do you want from me, man?"

"I don't want anything from you. I am giving you the opportunity to make penance."

"What the fuck are you talkin' about?" A single drop of blood trickled from his nostril.

"Penance? It means atonement, amends."

"It sounds to me like you're talkin' about revenge." His voice went up an octave and cracked.

"Tomato, tofuckinmahto. Now please, read aloud. And you can skip that first bit about the verbal abuse; name-calling never really interested me."

I leaned in close.

"That seems like something you only do if you're a little bitch," I whispered in his ear.

"If I read this, will you let me go?"

I spoke the next words slowly and clearly so as not to be misunderstood.

"I think it's only fair that I replicate the injuries she sustained by your hand...on you."

"Are you serious?"

"Quite."

Things got ugly after that. He had the temerity to be...uncooperative, let's say.

Sometimes I get lucky. I'd like to say it was a thoroughly well-thought-out plan. I'd like to pat myself on the back for being the genius that picked a relatively soundproof recording studio at a musician-unfriendly hour to ambush his new adversary. But that's not true. I'd like to say it was a fair fight. I'd like to say I didn't enjoy myself and that I was merely an agent of recompense and that no good ever comes out of a violent act. But none of that is true, either.

My hand clutched his throat. I squeezed so hard I felt something pop deep inside. His frenzy of flailing arms and feet slowed, and he fell to the floor with a thud. I didn't want him dead, necessarily. I felt his wrist for a pulse like in the movies. I wasn't finished with him yet.

HISTORY OF ABUSE

While we were dating, Respondent was physically violent with me. On or about the 7th of November, he became angry and threw a bottle of beer at me. He then started pouring the beer on me. During this time, the Respondent lived with me.

Shortly thereafter, Respondent beat, kicked and choked me. The neighbors overheard the commotion and they called the police. Because of his increasingly violent behavior towards me I told the respondent to move out of my home. I received treatment for cracked ribs, multiple contusions and a bruised larynx.

"Where did you punch her, Rick?"

He slowly shook his head.

"I'm gonna point at a part of your body and when I guess correctly, you're gonna nod your head, got it?"

I pointed to his forehead. He stared at me blankly. I pointed to his nose. Same stare. I ran my finger down the tip of his nose and stopped at his duct-

231

taped mouth. He blinked.

"What was that? Was that a nod?"

He shook his head frantically but I hit him in the mouth three or four times anyway.

"You punched her in her sweet mouth, really?" I asked, as I paced back and forth in front of him rubbing my sore knuckles.

I hauled back and I punched him square in the nose.

"Oh, shit. I'm sorry. That was gratuitous. Totally unnecessary."

I resumed my reading.

"Let's move on to kicking, shall we?"

RECENT ABUSE

On or about May 6, the respondent began to call me numerous times over and over again. I received over 14 calls in a half-hour period. At approximately 12:15 a.m. the respondent showed up at my home. The respondent tried to get into my home as I ran to the phone and called 911. I was trying to hold the door with one hand as I was on the phone. The respondent forced his way in and grabbed me. I began to scream for help. The respondent covered my mouth with his hand. I managed to bite the respondent's hand and started to run away. The respondent chased me outside and grabbed me again as I was screaming for help. The respondent attempted to kidnap me by trying to force me into his car. The respondent kicked and punched me in the front yard of my home. Neighbors heard me screaming and came out of their homes until the police arrived. The respondent was arrested (see attached Sheriff's booking report).

I needed a break and the pot of coffee smelled pretty good. He only had Sweet'N Low and powdered creamer, which I considered a fucking-dick move of uncalled-for proportions.

I sipped as I watched him shift his weight from one foot to the other in an effort to not apply any more pressure to the wire that bound his wrists to the beams that would someday be that such-and-such booth he spoke so fondly of. As long as he stood upright, the wire wouldn't cut any deeper into his flesh. His feet were crudely duct-taped to either side of a stool I'd set between his legs. I was pretty proud of the job I had done, considering the time and the tools I had to work with and the improvisational nature of our situation.

Dear Ms. Finch,

I hope all is well. If an attorney represents you, kindly forward this letter to his or her attention. Our office represents Mr. Rick McCullen stemming from the false allegations you have made against him. It is my intent to fully advocate his interests, including seeking attorney's fees from you for the falsification of claims in the restraining order. While I understand your condition and need for continued medical treatment, those factors in no way justify harming my client. A judge and/or jury may of course feel differently, and a detailed review of your shock treatments, erratic behavior and questionable past may be of interest...

I set down the letter and I beat him until my knuckles were bruised and swollen. I lifted his head up by his hair.

"You still with us, buddy?"

I picked his missing tooth off the duct tape and slipped it into the front pocket of his shirt. I snapped the pearl button shut.

I wasn't sure if he was still cognizant, but I continued to talk to him as I stapled each sheet of official paper next to the giant bloody letters on the wall as the finishing touches to my masterpiece.

"You may have lawyers and rich fuckin' parents and big-shot musician friends lookin' out for you, but I don't give a fuck and I'll tell the whole goddamn world exactly what you are."

I tore off a fresh piece of duct tape and covered his mouth again, and then I punched him in the face one more time for the road.

"I would say good luck, Rick…but I *really* don't give a shit."

Now what? I drove down Cerro Gordo toward Alvarado Street. I rinsed the blood out of my black T-shirt in the restroom of a Shell station and bought a pair of shades, a carton of cigarettes, a Diet Coke and a full tank of gas. On the passenger seat were two envelopes. I left the one addressed to your father on your desk. He'll be there soon. Except for the broken window panel on your back door, I left your place pretty much the way I found it.

I am enlightened enough to know that revenge is a mortal pleasure and far too trivial a matter to be of interest to you now, but I think you knew what would happen when I found that folder. I'd be willing to bet you had that cute little sneer on your face when you placed it there and clapped the dust off your hands. So, you wink and I'll nod and we'll both agree that I was merely accelerating karma. Still, that's not the kind of behavior that goes unanswered in this world. I have essentially evoked a scorched-earth policy on every bridge I've crossed. Somewhere, soon, a police officer or a Samoan guy with a crowbar is going to get a description of me.

I pulled the cash out of the envelope addressed to me. The bills were so crisp and new that they appeared counterfeit. I held one up to the light like they do in retail stores, but I had no idea what I was looking for. I counted it out on my lap: $7,500, minus the $50 or $60 I had just spent on provisions. This, the carton of cigarettes, and the trunk and back seat filled with Mead composition notebooks, I considered my assets.

I picked up the last envelope, addressed just to "Roky Erickson, Austin TX." It seemed as good a place as any. I started the car.

I caught myself dealing with death the same corny ways other people do. I used the fairytale of heaven and the promise of reconciliation in paradise like morphine. Like when I finally got there too, we would have a big laugh at the ten years we wasted being scared of each other. I numbed my guilt and cowardly negligence with the assumption that you are happier now. That you are looking down and smiling at the horrific thing I did. I doubt it.

I hope we are better than that after this life. I hope you will forgive me. I hope the distortion has been silenced and your pain is gone. I hope the voices in your head are sweet ones. I hope you are dancing with your grandfather as Duke Ellington's big band plays in the background. I hope your absurd laugh is drowning out the music. I do hope you're in a better place.

Fuck that. I wish that you were here right now.

I am beholden to a great many people for inspiring, helping, editing, proofreading, putting grandiose notions in my head and lending their voices to this project.

Dave Alvin, Mark Arm, Lou Beach, Jenny Bendel, Karina Bland, Marilyn Bland, Mark Boone Jr., Kelly Canary, Michelle Cernuto, Blag Dahlia, Lorri Davis, Jesse Dayton, Rob Delaney, John Doe, Greg Dulli, Steve Earle, Damien Echols, Eustace, Exene, Tony Fitzpatrick, Rachel Flotard, Dana Gould, Tom Hansen, Kerri Harrop, Darren Hill, Zach Hitner, Randall Jamail, Nicolle Jeffries, Brian Kasnyik, Wayne and Margaret Kramer, Mark Lanegan, Donal Logue, Liana Maeby, Aimee Mann, Marc Maron, Duff McKagan, Lance Mercer, Carrie Montgomery, Kim Murphy, Amy Nelson, Scott Parker, Craig Parker Adams, Jacob Pitts, Diane Porter, Karen Raymond, Norman Reedus, Michael Reynero, Johnny Sangster, Chris Schneider, John Sinclair, Eddie Spaghetti, Lew Temple, Isabel Trujillo, Cressa Turner and Nicole Vandenberg.

I love each and every one of you motherfuckers.